Thomas Gray

Poems and Letters

SALZWASSER
VERLAG

Thomas Gray

Poems and Letters

Reprint of the original, first published in 1863.

1st Edition 2022 | ISBN: 978-3-37500-151-3

Verlag (Publisher): Salzwasser Verlag GmbH, Zeilweg 44, 60439 Frankfurt, Deutschland
Vertretungsberechtigt (Authorized to represent): E. Roepke, Zeilweg 44, 60439 Frankfurt, Deutschland
Druck (Print): Books on Demand GmbH, In de Tarpen 42, 22848 Norderstedt, Deutschland

POEMS AND LETTERS

BY THOMAS GRAY.

POEMS

AND

LETTERS

BY

THOMAS GRAY

LONDON

1863

CONTENTS.

POEMS.

EXTRACTS.

POEMATA.

EXTRACTS.

LETTERS.

" MR. THOMAS GRAY.

(BY THE HON. HORACE WALPOLE.)

HE was the ſon of a money ſcrivener, by Mary Antrobus, a milliner in Cornhill, and ſiſter to two Antrobus's, who were uſhers of Eton School. He was born in 1716, and educated at Eton College, chiefly under the direction of one of his uncles, who took prodigious pains with him, which anſwered exceedingly. He particularly inſtructed him in the virtues of *ſimples*. He had a great genius for muſic and poetry. From Eton he went to Peter Houſe at Cambridge, and in 1739 accompanied Mr. H. W. in travelling to France and Italy. He returned in 1741, and returned to Cambridge again. His letters are the beſt I ever ſaw, and had more novelty and wit. One of his firſt pieces of poetry was an anſwer in Engliſh verſe to an epiſtle from H. W. At Naples he wrote a fragment, deſcribing an earthquake, and the origin of Monte Nuovo, in the ſtyle of Virgil; at Rome an Alcaic ode, in imitation of Horace, to R. Weſt, Eſq. After his return he wrote the inimitable ode, On a Diſtant Proſpect of Eton College; another moral ode; and that beautiful one on a cat of Mr. Walpole's drowned in a tub of gold fiſhes. Theſe three laſt have been publiſhed in Dodſley's Miſcellanies. He began a poem on the reformation of learning, but ſoon dropped it, on finding his plan too much reſembling the Dunciad. It had this admirable line in it:

'And goſpel-light firſt *flaſhed* from Bullen's eyes.'

He began, too, a philoſophical poem in Latin, and an Engliſh tragedy of Agrippina, and ſome other odes, one of which, a very beautiful one, entitled, 'Stanzas written in a Country Churchyard,' he finiſhed in 1750. He was a very ſlow, but very correct writer. Being at Stoke in the ſummer of 1750, he wrote a kind of tale, addreſſed to Lady Schaub and Miſs Speed, who had made him a viſit at Lady Cobham's. The Elegy written in the Churchyard was publiſhed by Dodſley, Feb. 16, 1751, with a ſhort advertiſement by Mr. H. W., and immediately went through four editions. He had ſome thoughts of taking his Doctor's degree, but would not, for fear of being confounded with Dr. Grey, who publiſhed the fooliſh edition of Hudibras.

" In March, 1753, was publiſhed a fine edition of his poems, with frontiſpieces, head and tail pieces, and initial letters, engraved by Grignion and Müller, after drawings of Richard Bentley, Eſq. He loſt his mother a little before this, and at the ſame time finiſhed an extreme fine poem, in imitation of Pindar, On the Power of Muſical Poetry, which he began two or three years before. In the winter of 1755, George Hervey, Earl of Briſtol, who was ſoon afterwards ſent Envoy to Turin, was deſigned for Miniſter to Liſbon: he offered to carry Mr. Gray as his ſecretary, but he declined it. In Auguſt, 1757, was publiſhed two odes of Mr. Gray; one, On the Power and Progreſs of Poeſy, the other, On the Deſtruction of the Welſh Bards by Edward I. They were printed at the new preſs at Strawberry Hill, being the firſt production of that printing-houſe. In October, 1761, he made words for an old tune of Geminiani, at the requeſt of Mrs. Speed. It begins,

'Thyrſis, when we parted, ſwore.'

Two ſtanzas . . . . . the thought from the French."

* * * * *

POEMS.

ODE

ON THE SPRING.[1]

LO! where the roſy-boſom'd Hours,
Fair Venus' train, appear,
Diſcloſe the long-expecting flowers,
And wake the purple year!
The Attic warbler pours her throat,
Reſponſive to the cuckoo's note,
The untaught harmony of ſpring:
While, whiſp'ring pleaſure as they fly,
Cool Zephyrs through the clear blue ſky
Their gather'd fragrance fling.

Where'er the oak's thick branches ſtretch
   A broader browner ſhade,
Where'er the rude and moſs-grown beech
   O'er-canopies the glade,[2]
Beſide ſome water's ruſhy brink
With me the Muſe ſhall ſit, and think
   (At eaſe reclined in ruſtic ſtate)
How vain the ardour of the crowd,
How low, how little are the proud,
   How indigent the great![3]

Still is the toiling hand of Care;
   The panting herds repoſe:
Yet hark, how through the peopled air
   The buſy murmur glows!
The inſect-youth are on the wing,
Eager to taſte the honied ſpring,
   And float amid the liquid noon:
Some lightly o'er the current ſkim,
Some ſhow their gayly-gilded trim
   Quick-glancing to the ſun.[4]

To Contemplation's ſober eye
   Such is the race of Man:
And they that creep, and they that fly,
   Shall end where they began.
Alike the Buſy and the Gay
But flutter through life's little day,
   In Fortune's varying colours dreſt:
Bruſh'd by the hand of rough Miſchance,
Or chill'd by Age, their airy dance
   They leave, in duſt to reſt.

Methinks I hear, in accents low,
   The ſportive kind reply:
Poor moraliſt! and what art thou?
   A ſolitary fly!
Thy joys no glittering female meets,
No hive haſt thou of hoarded ſweets,
   No painted plumage to diſplay:
On haſty wings thy youth is flown;
Thy ſun is ſet, thy ſpring is gone—
   We frolic while 'tis May.

ODE

ON THE DEATH OF A FAVOURITE CAT,

DROWNED IN A TUB OF GOLD FISHES.[1]

'TWAS on a lofty vaſe's ſide,
Where China's gayeſt art had dyed
The azure flowers, that blow;
Demureſt of the tabby kind,
The penſive Selima, reclined,[2]
Gazed on the lake below.

Her conſcious tail her joy declared;
The fair round face, the ſnowy beard,
The velvet of her paws,
Her coat, that with the tortoiſe vies,
Her ears of jet, and emerald eyes,
She ſaw; and purr'd applauſe.

Still had ſhe gazed; but 'midſt the tide
Two angel forms[3] were ſeen to glide,
  The Genii of the ſtream:
Their ſcaly armour's Tyrian hue
Through richeſt purple to the view
  Betray'd a golden gleam.

The hapleſs nymph with wonder ſaw:
A whiſker firſt, and then a claw,
  With many an ardent wiſh,
She ſtretch'd, in vain, to reach the prize.
What female heart can gold deſpiſe?
  What Cat's averſe to fiſh?[4]

Preſumptuous maid! with looks[5] intent
Again ſhe ſtretch'd, again ſhe bent,
  Nor knew the gulf between.
(Malignant Fate ſat by, and ſmiled)
The ſlipp'ry verge her feet beguiled,
  She tumbled headlong in.

Eight times emerging from the flood
She mew'd to ev'ry wat'ry God,
  Some ſpeedy aid to ſend.
No Dolphin came, no Nereid ſtirr'd:
Nor cruel Tom, nor Suſan heard.
  A fav'rite has no friend![6]

From hence, ye beauties, undeceived,
Know, one falſe ſtep is ne'er retrieved,
  And be with caution bold.
Not all that tempts[7] your wand'ring eyes
And heedleſs hearts is lawful prize,
  Nor all, that gliſters, gold.

ODE

ON A DISTANT PROSPECT OF ETON COLLEGE.[1]

Ἄνθρωπος, ἱκανὴ πρόφασις εἰς τὸ δυστυχεῖν.

MENANDER. *Incert. Fragm.* ver. 382, ed. Cler. p. 245.

YE diſtant ſpires, ye antique towers,
That crown the wat'ry glade,
Where grateful Science ſtill adores
Her Henry's[2] holy ſhade ;
And ye, that from the ſtately brow
Of Windſor's heights th' expanſe below
Of grove, of lawn, of mead ſurvey,
Whoſe turf, whoſe ſhade, whoſe flowers among
Wanders the hoary Thames along
His ſilver-winding way :

Ah, happy hills! ah, pleaſing ſhade!
  Ah, fields beloved in vain!
Where once my careleſs childhood ſtray'd,
  A ſtranger yet to pain!
I feel the gales that from ye blow
A momentary bliſs beſtow,
  As waving freſh their gladſome wing,
My weary ſoul they ſeem to ſoothe,
And, redolent of joy and youth,[3]
  To breathe a ſecond ſpring.

Say, father Thames, for thou haſt ſeen
  Full many a ſprightly race
Diſporting on thy margent green,
  The paths of pleaſure trace;
Who foremoſt now delight to cleave,
With pliant arm, thy glaſſy wave?
  The captive linnet which enthral?
What idle progeny ſucceed
To chaſe the rolling circle's ſpeed,[4]
  Or urge the flying ball?

While ſome on earneſt buſineſs bent
   Their murm'ring labours ply
'Gainſt graver hours that bring conſtraint
   To ſweeten liberty:
Some bold adventurers diſdain
The limits of their little reign,
   And unknown regions dare deſcry:
Still as they run they look behind,
They hear a voice in every wind,
   And ſnatch a fearful joy.

Gay hope is theirs by fancy fed,
   Leſs pleaſing when poſſeſt;
The tear forgot as ſoon as ſhed,
   The ſunſhine of the breaſt:
Theirs buxom health, of roſy hue,
Wild wit, invention ever new,
   And lively cheer, of vigour born;
The thoughtleſs day, the eaſy night,
The ſpirits pure, the ſlumbers light,
   That fly th' approach of morn.

Alas! regardleſs of their doom
  The little victims play;
No ſenſe have they of ills to come,
  Nor care beyond to-day:
Yet ſee, how all around 'em wait
The miniſters of human fate,
  And black Misfortune's baleful train!
Ah, ſhow them where in ambuſh ſtand,
To ſeize their prey, the murth'rous band!
  Ah, tell them, they are men!

These ſhall the fury Paſſions tear,
  The vultures of the mind,
Diſdainful Anger, pallid Fear,
  And Shame that ſculks behind;
Or pining Love ſhall waſte their youth,
Or Jealouſy, with rankling tooth,
  That inly gnaws the ſecret heart;
And Envy wan, and faded Care,
Grim-viſaged comfortleſs Deſpair,
  And Sorrow's piercing dart.

Ambition this ſhall tempt to riſe,
  Then whirl the wretch from high,
To bitter Scorn a ſacrifice,
  And grinning Infamy.
The ſtings of Falſehood thoſe ſhall try,
And hard Unkindneſs' alter'd eye,
  That mocks the tear it forced to flow;
And keen Remorſe with blood defiled,
And moody Madneſs laughing wild
  Amid ſevereſt woe.

Lo! in the vale of years beneath
  A grieſly troop are ſeen,
The painful family of Death,
  More hideous than their queen:
This racks the joints, this fires the veins,
That every labouring ſinew ſtrains,
  Thoſe in the deeper vitals rage:
Lo! Poverty, to fill the band,
That numbs the ſoul with icy hand,
  And ſlow-conſuming Age.

To each his ſuff'rings: all are men,
   Condemn'd alike to groan;
The tender for another's pain,
   Th' unfeeling for his own.
Yet, ah! why ſhould they know their fate,
Since ſorrow never comes too late,
   And happineſs too ſwiftly flies?
Thought would deſtroy their paradiſe.
No more;—where ignorance is bliſs,
   'Tis folly to be wiſe.

HYMN TO ADVERSITY.[1]

—Ζῆνα—

. . . .

Τὸν φρονεῖν βροτοὺς ὁδώ-
σαντα, τὸν πάθει μάθος
Θέντα κυρίως ἔχειν.

ÆSCH. *Agam.* ver. 181.

DAUGHTER of Jove, relentleſs power,
Thou tamer of the human breaſt,
Whoſe iron ſcourge and tort'ring hour
The bad affright, afflict the beſt!
Bound in thy adamantine chain,
The proud are taught to taſte of pain,
And purple tyrants vainly groan
With pangs unfelt before, unpitied and alone.

When firſt thy fire to ſend on earth
  Virtue, his darling child, deſign'd,
To thee he gave the heav'nly birth,
  And bade to form her infant mind.
Stern rugged nurſe ! thy rigid lore
With patience many a year ſhe bore :
What ſorrow was, thou bad'ſt her know,
And from her own ſhe learn'd to melt at others' woe.

Scared at thy frown terrific, fly
  Self-pleaſing Folly's idle brood,
Wild Laughter, Noiſe, and thoughtleſs Joy,
  And leave us leiſure to be good.
Light they diſperſe, and with them go
The ſummer friend, the flatt'ring foe ;
By vain Proſperity received,
To her they vow their truth, and are again believed.

Wiſdom in ſable garb array'd,
  Immerſed in rapt'rous thought profound,
And Melancholy, ſilent maid,
  With leaden eye that loves the ground,
Still on thy ſolemn ſteps attend:
Warm Charity, the gen'ral friend,
With Juſtice, to herſelf ſevere,
And Pity, dropping ſoft the ſadly-pleaſing tear.

Oh! gently on thy ſuppliant's head,
  Dread goddeſs, lay thy chaſt'ning hand!
Not in thy Gorgon terrors clad,
  Not circled with the vengeful band
(As by the impious thou art ſeen)
With thund'ring voice, and threat'ning mien,
With ſcreaming Horror's fun'ral cry,
Deſpair, and fell Diſeaſe, and ghaſtly Poverty:

Thy form benign, oh goddeſs, wear,
  Thy milder influence impart,
Thy philoſophic train be there
  To ſoften, not to wound, my heart.
The gen'rous ſpark extinct revive,
Teach me to love, and to forgive,
Exact my own defects to ſcan,
What others are to feel, and know myſelf a Man.

THE PROGRESS OF POESY.[1]

A PINDARIC ODE.

Φωνᾶντα συνετοῖσιν· ἐς
Δὲ τὸ πᾶν ἑρμηνέων
Χατίζει. PINDAR. *Ol.* ii. v. 152.

I. I.

AWAKE, Æolian lyre, awake,[2]
And give to rapture all thy trembling ſtrings.
From Helicon's harmonious ſprings
A thouſand rills their mazy progreſs take:
The laughing flowers that round them blow,
Drink life and fragrance as they flow.
Now the rich ſtream of muſic winds along,
Deep, majeſtic, ſmooth, and ſtrong,
Through verdant vales, and Ceres' golden reign:
Now rolling down the ſteep amain,
Headlong, impetuous, ſee it pour;
The rocks and nodding groves rebellow to the roar.

I. 2.

Oh! Sov'reign of the willing ſoul,[3]
Parent of ſweet and ſolemn-breathing airs,
Enchanting ſhell! the ſullen Cares
And frantic Paſſions hear thy ſoft controul.
On Thracia's hills the Lord of War
Has curb'd the fury of his car,
And dropt his thirſty lance at thy command.
Perching on the ſceptred hand[4]
Of Jove, thy magic lulls the feather'd king
With ruffled plumes and flagging wing:
Quench'd in dark clouds of ſlumber lie
The terror of his beak, and lightnings of his eye.

I. 3.

Thee the voice, the dance, obey,[5]
Temper'd to thy warbled lay.
O'er Idalia's velvet-green
The roſy-crowned Loves are ſeen
On Cytherea's day;

With antic Sport, and blue-eyed Pleaſures,
Friſking light in frolic meaſures;
Now purſuing, now retreating,
Now in circling troops they meet:
To briſk notes in cadence beating,
Glance their many-twinkling feet.[6]
Slow melting ſtrains their Queen's approach declare:
Where'er ſhe turns, the Graces homage pay.
With arms ſublime, that float upon the air,
In gliding ſtate ſhe wins her eaſy way:
O'er her warm cheek, and riſing boſom, move
The bloom of young Deſire and purple light of Love.[7]

II. I.

Man's feeble race what ills await![8]
Labour, and Penury, the racks of Pain,
Diſeaſe, and Sorrow's weeping train,
And Death, ſad refuge from the ſtorms of fate!
The fond complaint, my ſong, diſprove,
And juſtify the laws of Jove.

Say, has he giv'n in vain the heav'nly Muſe?
Night and all her ſickly dews,
Her ſpectres wan, and birds of boding cry,
He gives to range the dreary ſky;
Till down the eaſtern cliffs afar[9]
Hyperion's march they ſpy, and glitt'ring ſhafts of war.

II. 2.

In climes beyond the ſolar road,[10]
Where ſhaggy forms o'er ice-built mountains roam,
The Muſe has broke the twilight gloom
To cheer the ſhivering native's dull abode.
And oft, beneath the od'rous ſhade
Of Chili's boundleſs foreſts laid,
She deigns to hear the ſavage youth repeat,
In looſe numbers wildly ſweet,
Their feather-cinctured chiefs, and duſky loves.
Her track, where'er the goddeſs roves,
Glory purſue, and gen'rous Shame,
Th' unconquerable Mind, and freedom's holy flame.

II. 3.

Woods, that wave o'er Delphi's ſteep,[11]
Iſles, that crown th' Ægean deep,
Fields, that cool Iliſſus laves,
Or where Mæander's amber waves
In lingering lab'rinths creep,
How do your tuneful echoes languiſh,
Mute, but to the voice of anguiſh!
Where each old poetic mountain
Inſpiration breathed around;
Ev'ry ſhade and hallow'd fountain
Murmur'd deep a ſolemn ſound:
Till the ſad Nine, in Greece's evil hour,
Left their Parnaſſus for the Latian plains.
Alike they ſcorn the pomp of tyrant Power,
And coward Vice, that revels in her chains.
When Latium had her lofty ſpirit loſt,
They ſought, oh Albion! next thy ſea-encircled coaſt.

III. I.

Far from the ſun and ſummer-gale,
In thy green lap was Nature's Darling[12] laid,
What time, where lucid Avon ſtray'd,
To him the mighty mother did unveil
Her awful face: the dauntleſs child
Stretch'd forth his little arms and ſmiled.
"This pencil take (ſhe ſaid), whoſe colours clear
Richly paint the vernal year:
Thine too theſe golden keys, immortal Boy!
This can unlock the gates of joy;
Of horror that, and thrilling fears,
Or ope the ſacred ſource of ſympathetic tears."

III. 2.

Nor ſecond He,[13] that rode ſublime
Upon the ſeraph-wings of Extaſy,
The ſecrets of th' abyſs to ſpy.
He paſs'd the flaming[14] bounds of place and time:

The living throne, the ſapphire blaze,
Where angels tremble while they gaze,
He ſaw; but, blaſted with exceſs of light,
Cloſed his eyes in endleſs night.[15]
Behold, where Dryden's leſs preſumptuous car,
Wide o'er the fields of glory bear
Two courſers of ethereal race,
With necks in thunder clothed,[16] and long-reſounding pace.

III. 3.

Hark, his hands the lyre explore!
Bright-eyed Fancy, hov'ring o'er,
  Scatters from her pictured urn
  Thoughts that breathe, and words that burn.[17]
But ah! 'tis heard no more—
  Oh! lyre divine, what daring ſpirit
  Wakes thee now? Though he inherit
Nor the pride, nor ample pinion,
  That the Theban eagle [18] bear,
Sailing with ſupreme dominion

Through the azure deep of air:
Yet oft before his infant eyes would run
Such forms as glitter in the Muſe's ray,
With orient hues, unborrow'd of the ſun:
Yet ſhall he mount, and keep his diſtant way
Beyond the limits of a vulgar fate,
Beneath the Good how far—but far above the Great.

THE BARD.[1]

A PINDARIC ODE.

I. I.

RUIN ſeize thee, ruthleſs King!
Confuſion on thy banners wait;
Though fann'd by Conqueſt's crimſon wing,
They mock the air with idle ſtate.[2]
Helm, nor hauberk's[3] twiſted mail,
Nor e'en thy virtues, Tyrant, ſhall avail
To ſave thy ſecret ſoul from nightly fears,
From Cambria's curſe, from Cambria's tears!"
Such were the ſounds that o'er the creſted pride[4]
Of the firſt Edward ſcatter'd wild diſmay,
As down the ſteep of Snowdon's[5] ſhaggy ſide
He wound with toilſome march his long array.

Stout Glo'ſter[6] ſtood aghaſt in ſpeechleſs trance:
"To arms!" cried Mortimer, and couch'd his quiv'ring lance.

I. 2.

On a rock, whoſe haughty brow
Frowns o'er cold Conway's foaming flood,
Robed in the ſable garb of woe,
With haggard eyes the poet ſtood;
(Looſe his beard, and hoary hair
Stream'd, like a meteor, to the troubled air)[7]
And with a maſter's hand, and prophet's fire,
Struck the deep ſorrows of his lyre.
"Hark, how each giant-oak, and deſert-cave,
Sighs to the torrent's awful voice beneath!
O'er thee, oh King! their hundred arms they wave,
Revenge on thee in hoarſer murmurs breathe;
Vocal no more, ſince Cambria's fatal day,
To high-born Hoel's harp, or ſoft Llewellyn's lay.

I. 3.

" Cold is Cadwallo's tongue,
That huſh'd the ſtormy main:
Brave Urien ſleeps upon his craggy bed:
Mountains, ye mourn in vain
Modred, whoſe magic ſong
Made huge Plinlimmon bow his cloud-topt head.
On dreary Arvon's[8] ſhore they lie,
Smear'd with gore, and ghaſtly pale:
Far, far aloof th' affrighted ravens ſail;
The famiſh'd eagle[9] ſcreams, and paſſes by.
Dear loſt companions of my tuneful art,
Dear as the light that viſits theſe ſad eyes,[10]
Dear as the ruddy drops that warm my heart,
Ye died amidſt your dying country's cries—
No more I weep. They do not ſleep.
On yonder cliffs, a grieſly band,
I ſee them ſit, they linger yet,
Avengers of their native land:

With me in dreadful harmony they join,
And weave with bloody hands the tiſſue of thy line.

II. I.

" Weave the warp, and weave the woof,
The winding-ſheet of Edward's race.
  Give ample room, and verge enough
The characters of hell to trace.
Mark the year, and mark the night,
When Severn ſhall re-echo with affright
The ſhrieks of death, through Berkley's roof that ring,[11]
Shrieks of an agonizing king!
  She-wolf of France,[12] with unrelenting fangs,
That tear'ſt the bowels of thy mangled mate,
  From thee be born, who o'er thy country hangs
The ſcourge of heav'n.[13] What terrors round him wait!
Amazement in his van, with flight combined,
And ſorrow's faded form, and ſolitude behind.

II. 2.

" Mighty victor, mighty lord!
Low on his funeral couch he lies![14]
No pitying heart, no eye, afford
A tear to grace his obsequies.
Is the sable warrior fled?[15]
Thy son is gone. He rests among the dead.
The swarm, that in thy noontide beam were born?
Gone to salute the rising morn.
Fair laughs the morn, and soft the zephyr blows,
While proudly riding o'er the azure realm
In gallant trim the gilded vessel goes;[16]
Youth on the prow, and Pleasure at the helm;
Regardless of the sweeping whirlwind's sway,
That, hush'd in grim repose, expects his ev'ning prey.

II. 3.

" Fill high the sparkling bowl,
The rich repast prepare,

Reft of a crown, he yet may ſhare the feaſt:
Cloſe by the regal chair
Fell Thirſt and Famine ſcowl
A baleful ſmile upon their baffled gueſt.[17]
Heard ye the din of battle bray,
Lance to lance, and horſe to horſe?[18]
Long years of havock urge their deſtined courſe,
And through the kindred ſquadrons mow their way.
Ye towers of Julius,[19] London's laſting ſhame,
With many a foul and midnight murder fed,
Revere his conſort's[20] faith, his father's fame,
And ſpare the meek uſurper's[21] holy head.
Above, below, the roſe of ſnow,[22]
Twined with her bluſhing foe, we ſpread:
The briſtled boar[23] in infant-gore
Wallows beneath the thorny ſhade.
Now, brothers, bending o'er the accurſed loom,
Stamp we our vengeance deep, and ratify his doom.

III. I.

" Edward, lo! to ſudden fate
(Weave we the woof. The thread is ſpun.)
Half of thy heart we conſecrate.[24]
(The web is wove. The work is done.)
Stay, oh ſtay! nor thus forlorn
Leave me unbleſs'd, unpitied, here to mourn:
In yon bright track, that fires the weſtern ſkies,
They melt, they vaniſh from my eyes.
But oh! what ſolemn ſcenes on Snowdon's height
Deſcending ſlow their glittering ſkirts unroll?
Viſions of glory, ſpare my aching ſight!
Ye unborn ages, crowd not on my ſoul!
No more our long-loſt Arthur[25] we bewail.
All hail, ye genuine kings, Britannia's iſſue, hail!

III. 2.

" Girt with many a baron bold
Sublime their ſtarry fronts they rear;
And gorgeous dames, and ſtateſmen old

In bearded majeſty, appear.
In the midſt a form divine!
Her eye proclaims her of the Briton-line;
Her lion-port,[26] her awe-commanding face,
Attemper'd ſweet to virgin-grace.
What ſtrings ſymphonious tremble in the air,
  What ſtrains of vocal tranſport round her play.
Hear from the grave, great Talieſſin,[27] hear;
  They breathe a ſoul to animate thy clay.
Bright Rapture calls, and ſoaring as ſhe ſings,
Waves in the eye of heav'n her many-colour'd wings.

III. 3.

" The verſe adorn again
  Fierce war, and faithful love,[28]
And truth ſevere, by fairy fiction dreſt.
  In buſkin'd[29] meaſures move
Pale grief, and pleaſing pain,
With horror, tyrant of the throbbing breaſt.
  A voice, as of the cherub-choir,

Gales from blooming Eden bear;
And diſtant warblings leſſen on my ear,[30]
That loſt in long futurity expire.
Fond impious man, think'ſt thou yon ſanguine cloud,
Raiſed by thy breath, has quench'd the orb of day?
To-morrow he repairs the golden flood,
And warms the nations with redoubled ray.
Enough for me; with joy I ſee
The diff'rent doom our fates aſſign.
Be thine deſpair, and ſcept'red care,
To triumph, and to die, are mine."
He ſpoke, and headlong from the mountain's height
Deep in the roaring tide he plunged to endleſs night.[31]

ODE FOR MUSIC.[1]

(IRREGULAR.)

I. AIR.

"HENCE, avaunt, ('tis holy ground)
Comus, and his midnight-crew,
And Ignorance with looks profound,
And dreaming Sloth of pallid hue,
Mad Sedition's cry profane,
Servitude that hugs her chain,
Nor in theſe conſecrated bowers,
Let painted Flatt'ry hide her ſerpent-train in flowers.

CHORUS.

Nor Envy baſe, nor creeping Gain,
Dare the Muſe's walk to ſtain,
While bright-eyed Science watches round:
Hence, away, 'tis holy ground!"

II. RECITATIVE.

From yonder realms of empyrean day
  Burſts on my ear th' indignant lay:
There ſit the ſainted ſage, the bard divine,
  The few, whom genius gave to ſhine
Through every unborn age, and undiſcover'd clime.
  Rapt in celeſtial tranſport they:
  Yet hither oft a glance from high
  They ſend of tender ſympathy
To bleſs the place, where on their opening ſoul
  Firſt the genuine ardour ſtole.
'Twas Milton ſtruck the deep-toned ſhell,
And, as the choral warblings round him ſwell,
Meek Newton's ſelf bends from his ſtate ſublime,
And nods his hoary head, and liſtens to the rhyme.

III. AIR.

"Ye brown o'er-arching groves,
  That contemplation loves,
Where willowy Camus lingers with delight!

Oft at the bluſh of dawn
I trod your level lawn,
Oft woo'd the gleam of Cynthia ſilver-bright
In cloiſters dim, far from the haunts of Folly,
With Freedom by my ſide, and ſoft-eyed Melancholy."

IV. RECITATIVE.

But hark! the portals ſound, and pacing forth
With ſolemn ſteps and ſlow,
High potentates, and dames of royal birth,
And mitred fathers in long order go:
Great Edward, with the lilies on his brow
From haughty Gallia torn,
And ſad Chatillon,[2] on her bridal morn
That wept her bleeding Love, and princely Clare,
And Anjou's heroine, and the paler roſe,[3]
The rival of her crown and of her woes,
And either Henry[4] there,
The murder'd ſaint, and the majeſtic lord,
That broke the bonds of Rome.

(Their tears, their little triumphs o'er,
Their human paſſions now no more,
Save Charity, that glows beyond the tomb.)

ACCOMPANIED.

All that on Granta's fruitful plain
Rich ſtreams of regal bounty pour'd,
And bad theſe awful fanes and turrets riſe,
To hail their Fitzroy's feſtal morning come;
And thus they ſpeak in ſoft accord
The liquid language of the ſkies:

V. QUARTETTO.

“ What is grandeur, what is power?
Heavier toil, ſuperior pain.
What the bright reward we gain?
The grateful memory of the good.
Sweet is the breath of vernal ſhower,
The bee's collected treaſures ſweet,
Sweet muſic's melting fall, but ſweeter yet
The ſtill ſmall voice of gratitude.”

VI. RECITATIVE.

Foremoſt and leaning from her golden cloud
The venerable Marg'ret[5] ſee!
" Welcome, my noble ſon, (ſhe cries aloud)
To this, thy kindred train, and me:
Pleaſed in thy lineaments we trace
A Tudor's fire, a Beaufort's grace.[6]

AIR.

Thy liberal heart, thy judging eye,
The flow'r unheeded ſhall deſcry,
And bid it round heav'n's altars ſhed
The fragrance of its bluſhing head:
Shall raiſe from earth the latent gem,
To glitter on the diadem.

VII. RECITATIVE.

" Lo! Granta waits to lead her blooming band,
Not obvious, not obtruſive, ſhe
No vulgar praiſe, no venal incenſe flings;
Nor dares with courtly tongue refined

Profane thy inborn royalty of mind:
  She reveres herſelf and thee.
With modeſt pride to grace thy youthful brow,
The laureate wreath, that Cecil[7] wore, ſhe brings,
  And to thy juſt, thy gentle hand,
  Submits the faſces of her ſway,
While ſpirits bleſt above and men below
Join with glad voice the loud ſymphonious lay.

VIII. GRAND CHORUS.

"Through the wild waves as they roar,
  With watchful eye and dauntleſs mien,
    Thy ſteady courſe of honour keep,
Nor fear the rocks, nor ſeek the ſhore:
  The ſtar of Brunſwick ſmiles ſerene,
    And gilds the horrors of the deep."

THE FATAL SISTERS.[1]

AN ODE. FROM THE NORSE TONGUE.

NOW the ſtorm begins to lower,
(Haſte, the loom of hell prepare,)
Iron ſleet of arrowy ſhower[2]
Hurtles in the darken'd air.

Glitt'ring lances are the loom,
Where the duſky warp we ſtrain,
Weaving many a ſoldier's doom,
Orkney's woe, and Randver's bane.

See the grieſly texture grow!
('Tis of human entrails made)
And the weights, that play below,
Each a gaſping warrior's head.

Shafts for ſhuttles, dipt in gore,
  Shoot the trembling cords along.
Sword, that once a monarch bore,
  Keep the tiſſue cloſe and ſtrong.

Miſta, black terrific maid,
  Sangrida, and Hilda, ſee,
Join the wayward work to aid:
  'Tis the woof of victory.

Ere the ruddy ſun be ſet,
  Pikes muſt ſhiver, javelins ſing,
Blade with clattering buckler meet,
  Hauberk craſh, and helmet ring.

(Weave the crimſon web of war)
  Let us go, and let us fly,
Where our friends the conflict ſhare,
  Where they triumph, where they die.

As the paths of fate we tread,
  Wading through th' enſanguined field,
Gondula, and Geira, ſpread
  O'er the youthful king your ſhield.

We the reins to ſlaughter give,
  Ours to kill, and ours to ſpare:
Spite of danger he ſhall live.
  (Weave the crimſon web of war.)

They, whom once the deſert-beach
  Pent within its bleak domain,
Soon their ample ſway ſhall ſtretch
  O'er the plenty of the plain.

Low the dauntleſs earl is laid,
  Gored with many a gaping wound:
Fate demands a nobler head;
  Soon a king ſhall bite the ground.

Long his loſs ſhall Erin weep,
  Ne'er again his likeneſs ſee;
Long her ſtrains in ſorrow ſteep:
  Strains of immortality!

Horror covers all the heath,
  Clouds of carnage blot the ſun.
Siſters, weave the web of death;
  Siſters, ceaſe; the work is done.

Hail the taſk, and hail the hands!
  Songs of joy and triumph ſing!
Joy to the victorious bands;
  Triumph to the younger king.

Mortal, thou that hear'ſt the tale,
  Learn the tenour of our ſong.
Scotland, through each winding vale
  Far and wide the notes prolong.

Siſters, hence with ſpurs of ſpeed:
  Each her thundering faulchion wield;
Each beſtride her ſable ſteed.
  Hurry, hurry to the field!

THE VEGTAM'S KIVITHA;[1]

OR THE DESCENT OF ODIN. AN ODE. FROM THE NORSE TONGUE.

Upreis Odinn allda gautr, &c.

UPROSE the king of men with ſpeed,
And ſaddled ſtraight his coal-black ſteed;
Down the yawning ſteep he rode,
That leads to Hela's[2] drear abode.
Him the dog of darkneſs ſpied;
His ſhaggy throat he open'd wide,
(While from his jaws, with carnage fill'd,
Foam and human gore diſtill'd:)
Hoarſe he bays with hideous din,
Eyes that glow, and fangs that grin;
And long purſues with fruitleſs yell,
The father of the powerful ſpell.

Onward ſtill his way he takes,
(The groaning earth beneath him ſhakes,)
Till full before his fearleſs eyes
The portals nine of hell ariſe.

Right againſt the eaſtern gate,
By the moſs-grown pile he ſate;
Where long of yore to ſleep was laid
The duſt of the prophetic maid.
Facing to the northern clime,
Thrice he traced the Runic rhyme;
Thrice pronounced, in accents dread,
The thrilling verſe that wakes the dead:[3]
Till from out the hollow ground
Slowly breathed a ſullen ſound.

PROPHETESS.

What call unknown, what charms preſume
To break the quiet of the tomb?
Who thus afflicts my troubled ſprite,
And drags me from the realms of night?

Long on theſe mould'ring bones have beat
The winter's ſnow, the ſummer's heat,
The drenching dews, and driving rain!
Let me, let me ſleep again.
Who is he, with voice unbleſt,
That calls me from the bed of reſt?

ODIN.

A traveller, to thee unknown,
Is he that calls, a warrior's ſon.
Thou the deeds of light ſhalt know;
Tell me what is done below,
For whom yon glitt'ring board is ſpread,
Dreſs'd for whom yon golden bed?

PROPHETESS.

Mantling in the goblet ſee
The pure bev'rage of the bee:
O'er it hangs the ſhield of gold;
'Tis the drink of Balder bold:

Balder's head to death is giv'n.
Pain can reach the ſons of heav'n!
Unwilling I my lips uncloſe:
Leave me, leave me to repoſe.

ODIN.

Once again my call obey,[4]
Propheteſs, ariſe, and ſay,
What dangers Odin's child await,
Who the author of his fate?

PROPHETESS.

In Hoder's hand the hero's doom;
His brother ſends him to the tomb.
Now my weary lips I cloſe:
Leave me, leave me to repoſe.

ODIN.

Propheteſs, my ſpell obey,
Once again ariſe, and ſay,

Who th' avenger of his guilt,
By whom ſhall Hoder's blood be ſpilt?

PROPHETESS.

In the caverns of the weſt,
By Odin's fierce embrace compreſt,
A wond'rous boy ſhall Rinda bear,
Who ne'er ſhall comb his raven-hair,
Nor waſh his viſage in the ſtream,
Nor ſee the ſun's departing beam,
Till he on Hoder's corſe ſhall ſmile
Flaming on the fun'ral pile.
Now my weary lips I cloſe:
Leave me, leave me to repoſe.

ODIN.

Yet awhile my call obey;
Propheteſs, awake, and ſay,
What virgins theſe, in ſpeechleſs woe,
That bend to earth their ſolemn brow,

That their flaxen treſſes tear,
And ſnowy veils that float in air?
Tell me whence their ſorrows roſe:
Then I leave thee to repoſe.

PROPHETESS.

Ha! no traveller art thou,
King of men, I know thee now;
Mightieſt of a mighty line—

ODIN.

No boding maid of ſkill divine
Art thou, nor propheteſs of good;
But mother of the giant brood!

PROPHETESS.

Hie thee hence, and boaſt at home,
That never ſhall enquirer come
To break my iron-ſleep again;
Till Lok has burſt his tenfold chain;

Never, till ſubſtantial night
Has reaſſumed her ancient right ;
Till wrapt in flames, in ruin hurl'd,
Sinks the fabric of the world.

THE TRIUMPHS OF OWEN.[1]

A FRAGMENT. FROM THE WELSH.

OWEN'S praiſe demands my ſong,
Owen ſwift, and Owen ſtrong;
Faireſt flower of Roderic's ſtem,
Gwyneth's ſhield, and Britain's gem.
He nor heaps his brooded ſtores,
Nor on all profuſely pours;
Lord of every regal art,
Liberal hand, and open heart.

Big with hoſts of mighty name,
Squadrons three againſt him came;
This the force of Eirin hiding,
Side by ſide as proudly riding,

On her ſhadow long and gay
Lochlin plows the wat'ry way;
There the Norman ſails afar
Catch the winds and join the war:
Black and huge along they ſweep,
Burdens of the angry deep.

Dauntleſs on his native ſands
The dragon-ſon of Mona ſtands;
In glitt'ring arms and glory dreſt,
High he rears his ruby creſt.
There the thund'ring ſtrokes begin,
There the preſs, and there the din;
Talymalfra's rocky ſhore
Echoing to the battle's roar.
Check'd by the torrent-tide of blood,
Backward Meinai rolls his flood;
While, heap'd his maſter's feet around,
Proſtrate warriors gnaw the ground.
Where his glowing eye-balls turn,

Thouſand banners round him burn:
Where he points his purple ſpear,
Haſty, haſty rout is there,
Marking with indignant eye
Fear to ſtop, and ſhame to fly.
There confuſion, terror's child,
Conflict fierce, and ruin wild,
Agony, that pants for breath,
Deſpair and honourable death.

* * * *

THE DEATH OF HOEL.[1]

AN ODE. SELECTED FROM THE GODODIN.

HAD I but the torrent's might,
With headlong rage and wild affright
Upon Deïra's ſquadrons hurl'd
To ruſh, and ſweep them from the world!

Too, too ſecure in youthful pride,
By them, my friend, my Hoel, died,
Great Cian's ſon: of Madoc old
He aſk'd no heaps of hoarded gold;
Alone in nature's wealth array'd,
He aſk'd and had the lovely maid.

To Cattraeth's vale in glitt'ring row
Thrice two hundred warriors go:

Every warrior's manly neck
Chains of regal honour deck,
Wreathed in many a golden link :
From the golden cup they drink
Nectar that the bees produce,
Or the grape's extatic juice.
Fluſh'd with mirth and hope they burn :
But none from Cattraeth's vale return,
Save Aëron brave, and Conan ſtrong,
(Burſting through the bloody throng)
And I, the meaneſt of them all,
That live to weep and ſing their fall.

HAVE ye ſeen the tuſky boar,[2]
Or the bull, with ſullen roar,
On ſurrounding foes advance ?
So Caràdoc bore his lance.

CONAN'S name, my lay, rehearſe,
Build to him the lofty verſe,
Sacred tribute of the bard,
Verſe, the hero's ſole reward.
As the flame's devouring force;
As the whirlwind in its courſe;
As the thunder's fiery ſtroke,
Glancing on the ſhiver'd oak;
Did the ſword of Conan mow
The crimſon harveſt of the foe.

SONNET

ON THE DEATH OF MR. RICHARD WEST.

IN vain to me the ſmiling mornings ſhine,
And redd'ning Phœbus lifts his golden fire:
The birds in vain their amorous deſcant join;
Or cheerful fields reſume their green attire:
Theſe ears, alas! for other notes repine;
A different object do theſe eyes require:
My lonely anguiſh melts no heart but mine;
And in my breaſt the imperfect joys expire.
Yet morning ſmiles the buſy race to cheer,
And new-born pleaſure brings to happier men:
The fields to all their wonted tribute bear:
To warm their little loves the birds complain:
I fruitleſs mourn to him that cannot hear,
And weep the more, becauſe I weep in vain.

EPITAPH ON MRS. JANE CLERKE.[1]

LO! where this ſilent marble weeps,
A friend, a wife, a mother ſleeps:
A heart, within whoſe ſacred cell
The peaceful virtues loved to dwell.
Affection warm, and faith ſincere,
And ſoft humanity were there.
In agony, in death reſign'd,[2]
She felt the wound ſhe left behind,
Her infant image here below,
Sits ſmiling on a father's woe:
Whom what awaits, while yet he ſtrays
Along the lonely vale of days?
A pang, to ſecret ſorrow dear;
A ſigh; an unavailing tear;
Till time ſhall every grief remove,
With life, with memory, and with love.

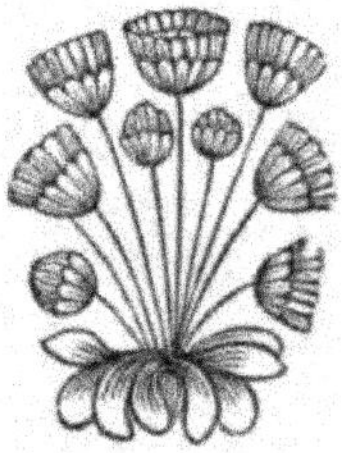

EPITAPH ON SIR WILLIAM WILLIAMS.[1]

" Valiant in arms, courteous and gay in peace,
See *Williams* ſnatch'd to an untimely tomb."
HALL STEVENSON'S *Poems*, ii. p. 49.

HERE, foremoſt in the dangerous paths of fame,
Young Williams fought for England's fair renown;
His mind each Muſe, each Grace adorn'd his frame,
Nor envy dared to view him with a frown.

At Aix, his voluntary ſword he drew,
There firſt in blood his infant honour ſeal'd;
From fortune, pleaſure, ſcience, love, he flew,
And ſcorn'd repoſe when Britain took the field.

With eyes of flame, and cool undaunted breaſt,
  Victor he ſtood on Belliſle's rocky ſteeps—
Ah, gallant youth ! this marble tells the reſt,
  Where melancholy friendſhip bends, and weeps.

ELEGY WRITTEN IN A COUNTRY CHURCH-YARD.[1]

THE curfew tolls the knell of parting day,[2]
The lowing herd winds ſlowly o'er the lea,
The ploughman homeward plods his weary way,
And leaves the world to darkneſs and to me.

Now fades the glimmering landſcape on the ſight,
And all the air a ſolemn ſtillneſs holds,
Save where the beetle wheels his droning flight,
And drowſy tinklings lull the diſtant folds:

Save that from yonder ivy-mantled tow'r,
The moping owl does to the moon complain
Of ſuch as, wand'ring near her ſecret bow'r,
Moleſt her ancient ſolitary reign.

Beneath thoſe rugged elms, that yew-tree's ſhade,
Where heaves the turf in many a mould'ring heap,
Each in his narrow cell for ever laid,
The rude forefathers of the hamlet ſleep.

The breezy call of incenſe-breathing morn,
The ſwallow twitt'ring from the ſtraw-built ſhed,
The cock's ſhrill clarion, or the echoing horn,
No more ſhall rouſe them from their lowly bed.

For them no more the blazing hearth ſhall burn,
Or buſy houſewife ply her evening care;
No children run to liſp their ſire's return,
Or climb his knees the envied kiſs to ſhare.

Oft did the harveſt to their ſickle yield,
Their furrow oft the ſtubborn glebe has broke:
How jocund did they drive their team afield!
How bow'd the woods beneath their ſturdy ſtroke.

Let not ambition mock their uſeful toil,
  Their homely joys, and deſtiny obſcure;
Nor grandeur hear with a diſdainful ſmile
  The ſhort and ſimple annals of the poor.

The boaſt of heraldry, the pomp of pow'r,
  And all that beauty, all that wealth e'er gave,
Await alike th' inevitable hour.
  The paths of glory lead but to the grave.

Nor you, ye proud, impute to theſe the fault,
  If memory o'er their tomb no trophies raiſe,
Where through the long-drawn iſle and fretted vault
  The pealing anthem ſwells the note of praiſe.

Can ſtoried urn, or animated buſt,
  Back to its manſion call the fleeting breath?
Can honour's voice provoke the ſilent duſt,
  Or flatt'ry ſoothe the dull cold ear of death?

Perhaps in this neglected ſpot is laid
   Some heart once pregnant with celeſtial fire;
Hands, that the rod of empire might have ſway'd,
   Or waked to extaſy the living lyre:

But knowledge to their eyes her ample page
   Rich with the ſpoils of time did ne'er unroll;
Chill penury repreſs'd their noble rage,
   And froze the genial current of the ſoul.

Full many a gem of pureſt ray ſerene
   The dark unfathom'd caves of ocean bear:
Full many a flower is born to bluſh unſeen,
   And waſte its ſweetneſs on the deſert air.

Some village-Hampden, that, with dauntleſs breaſt,
   The little tyrant of his fields withſtood,
Some mute inglorious Milton here may reſt,
   Some Cromwell guiltleſs of his country's blood.

Th' applaufe of lift'ning fenates to command,
The threats of pain and ruin to defpife,
To fcatter plenty o'er a fmiling land,
And read their hiftory in a nation's eyes,

Their lot forbad: nor circumfcribed alone
Their growing virtues, but their crimes confined;
Forbad to wade through flaughter to a throne,
And fhut the gates of mercy on mankind,

The ftruggling pangs of confcious truth to hide,
To quench the blufhes of ingenuous fhame,
Or heap the fhrine of luxury and pride
With incenfe kindled at the Mufe's flame.

Far from the madding crowd's ignoble ftrife,
Their fober wifhes never learn'd to ftray;
Along the cool fequefter'd vale of life
They kept the noifelefs tenour of their way.

Yet ev'n theſe bones from inſult to protect
   Some frail memorial ſtill erected nigh,
With uncouth rhymes and ſhapeleſs ſculpture deck'd,
   Implores the paſſing tribute of a ſigh.

Their name, their years, ſpelt by th' unletter'd Muſe,
   The place of fame and elegy ſupply:
And many a holy text around ſhe ſtrews,
   That teach the ruſtic moraliſt to die.

For who, to dumb forgetfulneſs a prey,
   This pleaſing anxious being e'er reſign'd,
Left the warm precincts of the cheerful day,
   Nor caſt one longing ling'ring look behind?

On ſome fond breaſt the parting ſoul relies,
   Some pious drops the cloſing eye requires;
E'en from the tomb the voice of nature cries,
   E'en in our aſhes live their wonted fires.[3]

For thee, who, mindful of th' unhonour'd dead,
  Doſt in theſe lines their artleſs tale relate;
If chance, by lonely contemplation led,
  Some kindred ſpirit ſhall enquire thy fate,—

Haply ſome hoary-headed ſwain may ſay,
  "Oft have we ſeen him at the peep of dawn
Bruſhing with haſty ſteps the dews away,
  To meet the ſun upon the upland lawn:

"There at the foot of yonder nodding beech,
  That wreathes its old fantaſtic roots ſo high,
His liſtleſs length at noontide would he ſtretch,
  And pore upon the brook that babbles by.

"Hard by yon wood, now ſmiling as in ſcorn,
  Mutt'ring his wayward fancies he would rove;
Now drooping, woful-wan, like one forlorn,
  Or crazed with care, or croſs'd in hopeleſs love.

" One morn I miſs'd him on the cuſtom'd hill,
  Along the heath, and near his fav'rite tree;
Another came; nor yet beſide the rill,
  Nor up the lawn, nor at the wood was he:

" The next, with dirges due in ſad array
  Slow through the church-way path we ſaw him borne:—
Approach and read (for thou can'ſt read) the lay
  Graved on the ſtone beneath yon aged thorn."

THE EPITAPH.

Here reſts his head upon the lap of earth
  A youth, to fortune and to fame unknown:
Fair ſcience frown'd not on his humble birth,
  And melancholy mark'd him for her own.

Large was his bounty, and his ſoul ſincere,
  Heaven did a recompenſe as largely ſend:
He gave to mis'ry (all he had) a tear,
  He gain'd from heav'n ('twas all he wiſh'd) a friend.

No farther ſeek his merits to diſcloſe,
  Or draw his frailties from their dread abode,
(There they alike in trembling hope repoſe,[4])
  The boſom of his Father and his God.

A LONG STORY.[1]

IN Britain's iſle, no matter where,
An ancient pile of building ſtands:
The Huntingdons and Hattons there
Employ'd the pow'r of fairy hands

To raiſe the ceiling's fretted height,
Each pannel in achievements clothing,
Rich windows that exclude the light,
And paſſages, that lead to nothing.

Full oft within the ſpacious walls,
When he had fifty winters o'er him,
My grave Lord-Keeper[2] led the brawls;
The ſeals and maces danced before him.

His bushy beard, and shoe-strings green,
His high-crown'd hat, and satin doublet,
Moved the stout heart of England's queen,
Though Pope and Spaniard could not trouble it.

What, in the very first beginning!
Shame of the versifying tribe!
Your hist'ry whither are you spinning!
Can you do nothing but describe?

A house there is (and that's enough)
From whence one fatal morning issues
A brace of warriors, not in buff,
But rustling in their silks and tissues.

The first came cap-a-pee from France,
Her conqu'ring destiny fulfilling,
Whom meaner beauties eye askance,
And vainly ape her art of killing.

The other amazon kind heav'n
  Had arm'd with ſpirit, wit, and ſatire;
But Cobham had the poliſh giv'n,
  And tipp'd her arrows with good-nature.

To celebrate her eyes, her air—
  Coarſe panegyrics would but teaſe her;
Meliſſa is her " nom de guerre."
  Alas, who would not wiſh to pleaſe her!

With bonnet blue and capuchine,
  And aprons long, they hid their armour;
And veil'd their weapons, bright and keen,
  In pity to the country farmer.

Fame, in the ſhape of Mr. P—t,
  (By this time all the pariſh know it)
Had told that thereabouts there lurk'd
  A wicked imp they call a poet:

Who prowl'd the country far and near,
  Bewitch'd the children of the peaſants,
Dried up the cows, and lamed the deer,
  And ſuck'd the eggs, and kill'd the pheaſants.

My lady heard their joint petition,
  Swore by her coronet and ermine,
She'd iſſue out her high commiſſion
  To rid the manor of ſuch vermin.

The heroines undertook the taſk,
  Through lanes unknown, o'er ſtiles they ventured,
Rapp'd at the door, nor ſtay'd to aſk,
  But bounce into the parlour enter'd.

The trembling family they daunt,
  They flirt, they ſing, they laugh, they tattle,
Rummage his mother, pinch his aunt,
  And up ſtairs in a whirlwind rattle :

Each hole and cupboard they explore,
  Each creek and cranny of his chamber,
Run hurry-ſcurry round the floor,
  And o'er the bed and teſter clamber;

Into the drawers and china pry,
  Papers and books, a huge imbroglio!
Under a tea-cup he might lie,
  Or creaſed, like dogs-ears, in a folio.

On the firſt marching of the troops,
  The Muſes, hopeleſs of his pardon,
Convey'd him underneath their hoops
  To a ſmall cloſet in the garden.

So rumour ſays: (who will, believe.)
  But that they left the door ajar,
Where, ſafe and laughing in his ſleeve,
  He heard the diſtant din of war.

Short was his joy. He little knew
The pow'r of magic was no fable;
Out of the window, wisk, they flew,
But left a spell upon the table.

The words too eager to unriddle,
The poet felt a strange disorder;
Transparent bird-lime form'd the middle,
And chains invisible the border.

So cunning was the apparatus,
The powerful pot-hooks did so move him,
That, will he, nill he, to the great house
He went, as if the devil drove him.

Yet on his way (no sign of grace,
For folks in fear are apt to pray)
To Phœbus he preferr'd his case,
And begg'd his aid that dreadful day.

The godhead would have back'd his quarrel;
But with a blufh, on recollection,
Own'd that his quiver and his laurel
'Gainft four fuch eyes were no protection.

The court was fate, the culprit there,
Forth from their gloomy manfions creeping,
The lady Janes and Joans repair,
And from the gallery ftand peeping:

Such as in filence of the night
Come (fweep) along fome winding entry,
(Styack[3] has often feen the fight)
Or at the chapel-door ftand fentry:

In peak'd hoods and mantles tarnifh'd,
Sour vifages, enough to fcare ye,
High dames of honour once, that garnifh'd
The drawing-room of fierce Queen Mary.

The peeresſs comes. The audience ſtare,
  And doff their hats with due ſubmiſſion:
She curtſies, as ſhe takes her chair,
  To all the people of condition.

The bard, with many an artful fib,
  Had in imagination fenced him,
Diſproved the arguments of Squib,[4]
  And all that Groom[5] could urge againſt him.

But ſoon his rhetoric forſook him,
  When he the ſolemn hall had ſeen;
A ſudden fit of ague ſhook him,
  He ſtood as mute as poor Macleane.[6]

Yet ſomething he was heard to mutter,
  "How in the park beneath an old tree,
(Without deſign to hurt the butter,
  Or any malice to the poultry,)

" He once or twice had penn'd a ſonnet;
  Yet hoped, that he might ſave his bacon:
Numbers would give their oaths upon it,
  He ne'er was for a conj'rer taken."

The ghoſtly prudes with hagged face
  Already had condemn'd the ſinner.
My lady roſe, and with a grace—
  She ſmiled, and bid him come to dinner.

" Jeſu-Maria! Madam Bridget,
  Why, what can the Viſcounteſs mean?"
(Cried the ſquare-hoods in woful fidget)
  " The times are alter'd quite and clean!

" Decorum's turn'd to mere civility;
  Her air and all her manners ſhow it.
Commend me to her affability!
  Speak to a commoner and a poet!"

[Here five hundred ſtanzas are loſt.]

And ſo God ſave our noble king,
  And guard us from long-winded lubbers,
That to eternity would ſing,
  And keep my lady from her rubbers.

ODE

ON THE PLEASURE ARISING FROM VICISSITUDE.[1]

NOW the golden morn aloft
Waves her dew-beſpangled wing,
With vermeil cheek and whiſper ſoft
She woos the tardy ſpring:
Till April ſtarts, and calls around
The ſleeping fragrance from the ground;
And lightly o'er the living ſcene
Scatters his freſheſt, tendereſt green.

New-born flocks, in ruſtic dance,
  Friſking ply their feeble feet;
Forgetful of their wintry trance
  The birds his preſence greet:
But chief, the ſky-lark warbles high
His trembling thrilling extaſy;
And, leſſening from the dazzled ſight,
Melts into air and liquid light.

Riſe, my ſoul! on wings of fire,
  Riſe the rapt'rous choir among;
Hark! 'tis nature ſtrikes the lyre,
  And leads the gen'ral ſong:
"Warm let the lyric tranſport flow,
Warm as the ray that bids it glow;
And animates the vernal grove
With health, with harmony, and love."

Yesterday the sullen year
  Saw the snowy whirlwind fly;
Mute was the music of the air,
  The herd stood drooping by:
Their raptures now that wildly flow,
No yesterday nor morrow know;
'Tis man alone that joy descries
With forward, and reverted eyes.

Smiles on past misfortune's brow
  Soft reflection's hand can trace;
And o'er the cheek of sorrow throw
  A melancholy grace;
While hope prolongs our happier hour,
Or deepest shades, that dimly lower
And blacken round our weary way,
Gilds with a gleam of distant day.

Still, where rosy pleasure leads,
   See a kindred grief pursue;
Behind the steps that misery treads,
   Approaching comfort view:
The hues of bliss more brightly glow,
Chastised by sabler tints of woe;
And blended form, with artful strife,
The strength and harmony of life.

See the wretch, that long has tost
   On the thorny bed of pain,
At length repair his vigour lost,
   And breathe and walk again:
The meanest floweret of the vale,
The simplest note that swells the gale,
The common sun, the air, the skies,
To him are opening paradise.

Humble quiet builds her cell,
  Near the ſource whence pleaſure flows;
She eyes the clear cryſtalline well,
  And taſtes it as it goes.
" While" far below the " madding" crowd
" Ruſh headlong to the dangerous flood,"
Where broad and turbulent it ſweeps,
" And" periſh in the boundleſs deeps.

Mark where indolence and pride,
  " Sooth'd by flattery's tinkling ſound,"
Go, ſoftly rolling, ſide by ſide,
  Their dull but daily round:
" To theſe, if Hebe's ſelf ſhould bring
The pureſt cup from pleaſure's ſpring,
Say, can they taſte the flavour high
Of ſober, ſimple, genuine joy?

" Mark ambition's march ſublime
Up to power's meridian height;
While pale-eyed envy ſees him climb,
And ſickens at the ſight.
Phantoms of danger, death, and dread,
Float hourly round ambition's head;
While ſpleen, within his rival's breaſt,
Sits brooding on her ſcorpion neſt.

" Happier he, the peaſant, far,
From the pangs of paſſion free,
That breathes the keen yet wholeſome air
Of rugged penury.
He, when his morning taſk is done,
Can ſlumber in the noontide ſun;
And hie him home, at evening's cloſe,
To ſweet repaſt, and calm repoſe.

" He, unconſcious whence the bliſs,
Feels, and owns in carols rude,
That all the circling joys are his,
Of dear Viciſſitude.
From toil he wins his ſpirits light,
From buſy day the peaceful night;
Rich, from the very want of wealth,
In heaven's beſt treaſures, peace and health."

HYMN TO IGNORANCE.[1]

A FRAGMENT.

HAIL, horrors, hail! ye ever gloomy bowers,
Ye gothic fanes, and antiquated towers,
Where rufhy Camus' flowly-winding flood
Perpetual draws his humid train of mud:
Glad I revifit thy neglected reign,
Oh take me to thy peaceful fhade again.
But chiefly thee, whofe influence breathed from high
Augments the native darknefs of the fky;
Ah, ignorance! foft falutary power!
Proftrate with filial reverence I adore.
Thrice hath Hyperion roll'd his annual race,
Since weeping I forfook thy fond embrace.
Oh fay, fuccefsful doft thou ftill oppofe
Thy leaden ægis 'gainft our ancient foes?

Still ſtretch, tenacious of thy right divine,
The maſſy ſceptre o'er thy ſlumb'ring line?
And dews Lethean through the land diſpenſe
To ſteep in ſlumbers each benighted ſenſe?
If any ſpark of wit's deluſive ray
Break out, and flaſh a momentary day,
With damp, cold touch forbid it to aſpire,
And huddle up in fogs the dang'rous fire.
Oh ſay—ſhe hears me not, but, careleſs grown,
Lethargic nods upon her ebon throne.
Goddeſs! awake, ariſe! alas, my fears!
Can powers immortal feel the force of years?
Not thus of old, with enſigns wide unfurl'd,
She rode triumphant o'er the vanquiſh'd world;
Fierce nations own'd her unreſiſted might,
And all was ignorance, and all was night.
Oh! ſacred age! Oh! times for ever loſt!
(The ſchoolman's glory, and the churchman's boaſt.)
For ever gone—yet ſtill to fancy new,
Her rapid wings the tranſient ſcene purſue,

And bring the buried ages back to view.

High on her car, behold the grandam ride
Like old Sesostris with barbaric pride;
* * * a team of harness'd monarchs bend

*   *   *   *   *

THE ALLIANCE OF

EDUCATION AND GOVERNMENT.

A FRAGMENT.

ESSAY I.

——— Πόταγ', ὦ 'γαθέ· τὰν γὰρ ἀοιδὰν
Οὔτι πα εἰς Ἀΐδαν γε τὸν ἐκλελάθοντα φυλαξεῖς.

THEOCRITUS, *Id.* i. 63.

AS ſickly plants betray a niggard earth,
Whoſe barren boſom ſtarves her generous birth,
Nor genial warmth, nor genial juice retains,
Their roots to feed, and fill their verdant veins:
And as in climes, where winter holds his reign,
The ſoil, though fertile, will not teem in vain,
Forbids her gems to ſwell, her ſhades to riſe,
Nor truſts her bloſſoms to the churliſh ſkies:
So draw mankind in vain the vital airs,

Unform'd, unfriended, by thofe kindly cares,
That health and vigour to the foul impart,
Spread the young thought, and warm the opening heart:
So fond inftruction on the growing powers
Of nature idly lavifhes her ftores,
If equal juftice with unclouded face
Smile not indulgent on the rifing race,
And fcatter with a free, though frugal hand,
Light golden fhowers of plenty o'er the land:
But tyranny has fix'd her empire there,
To check their tender hopes with chilling fear,
And blaft the blooming promife of the year.
  This fpacious animated fcene furvey,
From where the rolling orb, that gives the day,
His fable fons with nearer courfe furrounds,
To either pole, and life's remoteft bounds,
How rude fo e'er th' exterior form we find,
Howe'er opinion tinge the varied mind,
Alike to all, the kind, impartial heav'n
The fparks of truth and happinefs has giv'n:

With ſenſe to feel, with memory to retain,
They follow pleaſure, and they fly from pain;
Their judgment mends the plan their fancy draws,
The event preſages, and explores the cauſe;
The ſoft returns of gratitude they know,
By fraud elude, by force repel the foe;
While mutual wiſhes, mutual woes endear
The ſocial ſmile, the ſympathetic tear.
   Say, then, through ages by what fate confined
To different climes ſeem different ſouls aſſign'd?
Here meaſured laws and philoſophic eaſe
Fix, and improve the poliſh'd arts of peace;
There induſtry and gain their vigils keep,
Command the winds, and tame th' unwilling deep:
Here force and hardy deeds of blood prevail;
There languid pleaſure ſighs in every gale.
Oft o'er the trembling nations from afar
Has Scythia breathed the living cloud of war;
And, where the deluge burſt, with ſweepy ſway
Their arms, their kings, their gods were roll'd away.

As oft have iſſued, hoſt impelling hoſt,
The blue-eyed myriads from the Baltic coaſt.
The proſtrate ſouth to the deſtroyer yields
Her boaſted titles, and her golden fields:
With grim delight the brood of winter view
A brighter day, and heav'ns of azure hue;
Scent the new fragrance of the breathing roſe,
And quaff the pendent vintage as it grows.
Proud of the yoke, and pliant to the rod,
Why yet does Aſia dread a monarch's nod,
While European freedom ſtill withſtands
Th' encroaching tide that drowns her leſſening lands;
And ſees far off, with an indignant groan,
Her native plains, and empires once her own?
Can opener ſkies and ſuns of fiercer flame
O'erpower the fire, that animates our frame;
As lamps, that ſhed at eve a cheerful ray,
Fade and expire beneath the eye of day?
Need we the influence of the northern ſtar
To ſtring our nerves and ſteel our hearts to war?

And, where the face of nature laughs around,
Muſt ſick'ning virtue fly the tainted ground?
Unmanly thought! what ſeaſons can control,
What fancied zone can circumſcribe the ſoul,
Who, conſcious of the ſource from whence ſhe ſprings,
By reaſon's light, on reſolution's wings,
Spite of her frail companion, dauntleſs goes
O'er Libya's deſerts and through Zembla's ſnows?
She bids each ſlumb'ring energy awake,
Another touch, another temper take,
Suſpends th' inferior laws that rule our clay:
The ſtubborn elements confeſs her ſway;
Their little wants, their low deſires, refine,
And raiſe the mortal to a height divine.

Not but the human fabric from the birth
Imbibes a flavour of its parent earth:
As various tracts enforce a various toil,
The manners ſpeak the idiom of their ſoil.
An iron-race the mountain-cliffs maintain,
Foes to the gentler genius of the plain:

For where unwearied ſinews muſt be found
With ſide-long plough to quell the flinty ground,
To turn the torrent's ſwift-deſcending flood,
To brave the ſavage ruſhing from the wood,
What wonder if to patient valour train'd,
They guard with ſpirit, what by ſtrength they gain'd?
And while their rocky ramparts round they ſee,
The rough abode of want and liberty,
(As lawleſs force from confidence will grow)
Inſult the plenty of the vales below?
What wonder, in the ſultry climes, that ſpread
Where Nile redundant o'er his ſummer-bed
From his broad boſom life and verdure flings,
And broods o'er Egypt with his wat'ry wings,
If with advent'rous oar and ready ſail
The duſky people drive before the gale;
Or on frail floats to neighb'ring cities ride,
That riſe and glitter o'er the ambient tide

* * * * *

When love could teach a monarch to be wiſe,
And goſpel-light firſt dawn'd from Bullen's eyes.[1]

STANZAS TO MR. BENTLEY.[1]

A FRAGMENT.

IN ſilent gaze the tuneful choir among,
Half pleaſed, half bluſhing, let the Muſe admire,
While Bentley leads her ſiſter-art along,
And bids the pencil anſwer to the lyre.

See, in their courſe, each tranſitory thought
Fix'd by his touch a laſting eſſence take;
Each dream, in fancy's airy colouring wrought
To local ſymmetry and life awake!

The tardy rhymes that uſed to linger on,
To cenſure cold, and negligent of fame,
In ſwifter meaſures animated run,
And catch a luſtre from his genuine flame.

Ah! could they catch his ſtrength, his eaſy grace,
   His quick creation, his unerring line;
The energy of Pope they might efface,
   And Dryden's harmony ſubmit to mine.

But not to one in this benighted age
   Is that diviner inſpiration giv'n,
That burns in Shakeſpeare's or in Milton's page,
   The pomp and prodigality of heav'n.

As when conſpiring in the diamond's blaze,
   The meaner gems that ſingly charm the ſight,
Together dart their intermingled rays,
   And dazzle with a luxury of light.

Enough for me, if to ſome feeling breaſt
   My lines a ſecret ſympathy "impart;"
And as their pleaſing influence "flows confeſt,"
   A ſigh of ſoft reflection "heaves the heart."[a]

*   *   *   *   *

SKETCH OF HIS OWN CHARACTER.

WRITTEN IN 1761, AND FOUND IN ONE OF HIS POCKET-BOOKS.

TOO poor for a bribe, and too proud to importune;
He had not the method of making a fortune:
Could love, and could hate, ſo was thought ſomewhat odd;
No very great wit, he believed in a God:
A poſt or a penſion he did not deſire,
But left church and ſtate to Charles Townſhend and Squire.

AMATORY LINES.[1]

WITH beauty, with pleaſure ſurrounded, to
languiſh—
To weep without knowing the cauſe of my
anguiſh:
To ſtart from ſhort ſlumbers, and wiſh for the morning—
To cloſe my dull eyes when I ſee it returning;
Sighs ſudden and frequent, looks ever dejected—
Words that ſteal from my tongue, by no meaning
connected!
Ah! ſay, fellow-ſwains, how theſe ſymptoms befell me?
They ſmile, but reply not—Sure Delia will tell me!

SONG.[1]

THYRSIS, when we parted, ſwore
Ere the ſpring he would return—
Ah! what means yon violet flower!
And the bud that decks the thorn!
'Twas the lark that upward ſprung!
'Twas the nightingale that ſung!

Idle notes! untimely green!
Why this unavailing haſte?
Weſtern gales and ſkies ſerene
Speak not always winter paſt.
Ceaſe, my doubts, my fears to move,
Spare the honour of my love.

IMPROMPTU,

SUGGESTED BY A VIEW, IN 1766, OF THE SEAT AND RUINS OF A DECEASED NOBLEMAN, AT KINGSGATE, KENT.[1]

OLD, and abandon'd by each venal friend,
Here H——d form'd the pious reſolution
To ſmuggle a few years, and ſtrive to mend
A broken character and conſtitution.

On this congenial ſpot he fix'd his choice;
Earl Goodwin trembled for his neighbouring ſand;
Here ſea-gulls ſcream, and cormorants rejoice,
And mariners, though ſhipwreck'd, dread to land.

Here reign the bluſtering North and blighting Eaſt,
No tree is heard to whiſper, bird to ſing;
Yet Nature could not furniſh out the feaſt,
Art he invokes new horrors ſtill to bring.

Here mouldering fanes and battlements ariſe,
Turrets and arches nodding to their fall,
Unpeopled monaſt'ries delude our eyes,
And mimic deſolation covers all.

" Ah!" ſaid the ſighing peer, " had B—te been true,
Nor [2]M—'s, R—'s, B—'s friendſhip vain,
Far better ſcenes than theſe had bleſt our view,
And realized the beauties which we feign:

" Purged by the ſword, and purified by fire,
Then had we ſeen proud London's hated walls;
Owls would have hooted in St. Peter's choir,
And foxes ſtunk and litter'd in St. Paul's."

THE CANDIDATE:

OR, THE CAMBRIDGE COURTSHIP.[1]

WHEN ſly Jemmy Twitcher had ſmugg'd up his face,
With a lick of court white-waſh, and pious grimace,
A wooing he went, where three ſiſters of old
In harmleſs ſociety guttle and ſcold.
"Lord! ſiſter," ſays Phyſic to Law, "I declare,
Such a ſheep-biting look, ſuch a pick-pocket air!
Not I for the Indies:—You know I'm no prude,—
But his noſe is a ſhame,—and his eyes are ſo lewd!
Then he ſhambles and ſtraddles ſo oddly—I fear—

No—at our time of life 'twould be ſilly, my dear."
  "I don't know," ſays Law, "but methinks for his look,
'Tis juſt like the picture in Rocheſter's book;
Then his character, Phyzzy,—his morals—his life—
When ſhe died, I can't tell, but he once had a wife.
They ſay he's no Chriſtian, loves drinking and w——g,
And all the town rings of his ſwearing and roaring!
His lying and filching, and Newgate-bird tricks;—
Not I—for a coronet, chariot and ſix."
  Divinity heard, between waking and dozing,
Her ſiſters denying, and Jemmy propoſing:
From table ſhe roſe, and with bumper in hand,
She ſtroked up her belly, and ſtroked down her band—
"What a pother is here about wenching and roaring!
Why, David loved catches, and Solomon w——g:
Did not Iſrael filch from th' Egyptians of old
Their jewels of ſilver and jewels of gold?
The prophet of Bethel, we read, told a lie:
He drinks—ſo did Noah;—he ſwears—ſo do I:

To reject him for ſuch peccadillos, were odd ;
Beſides, he repents—for he talks about G**—

[*To* Jemmy.]

‘ Never hang down your head, you poor penitent elf,
Come buſs me—I'll be Mrs. Twitcher myſelf.’”

*   *   *   *   *

PROPERTIUS, LIB. III. ELEG. III. v. 41.

ME juvat in primâ coluiſſe Helicona juventâ,
Muſarumque choris implicuiſſe manus.
Me juvat et multo mentem vincire Lyæo,
Et caput in verna ſemper habere roſa.
Atque ubi jam Venerem gravis interceperit ætas,
Sparſerit et nigras alba ſenecta comas :

EXTRACTS.

PROPERTIUS, LIB. III. ELEG. III. v. 41.

IMITATED.

LONG as of youth the joyous hours remain,
Me may Caſtalia's ſweet receſs detain,
Faſt by the umbrageous vale lull'd to repoſe,
Where Aganippe warbles as it flows;
Or rouſed by ſprightly ſounds from out the trance,
I'd in the ring knit hands, and join the Muſes' dance.
Give me to ſend the laughing bowl around,
My ſoul in Bacchus' pleaſing fetters bound;
Let on this head unfading flowers reſide,
There bloom the vernal roſe's earlieſt pride;
And when, our flames commiſſion'd to deſtroy,
Age ſtep 'twixt Love and me, and intercept the joy;
When my changed head theſe locks no more ſhall know,
And all its jetty honours turn to ſnow;

Tum mihi naturæ libeat perdiſcere mores,
   Quis deus hanc mundi temperet arte domum :
Qua venit exoriens, qua deficit; unde coactis
   Cornibus in plenum menſtrua Luna redit:
Unde ſalo ſuperant venti: quid flamine captet
   Eurus, et in nubes unde perennis aqua:
Si ventura dies, mundi quæ ſubruat arces:
   Purpureus pluvias cur bibat arcus aquas:
Aut cur Perrhæbi tremuere cacumina Pindi,
   Solis et atratis luxerit orbis equis :

Then let me rightly ſpell of Nature's ways;
To Providence, to HIM my thoughts I'd raiſe,
Who taught this vaſt machine its ſteadfaſt laws,
That firſt, eternal, univerſal cauſe;
Search to what regions yonder ſtar retires,
That monthly waning hides her paly fires,
And whence, anew revived, with ſilver light
Relumes her creſcent orb to cheer the dreary night:
How riſing winds the face of ocean ſweep,
Where lie the eternal fountains of the deep,
And whence the cloudy magazines maintain
Their wintry war, or pour the autumnal rain;
How flames perhaps, with dire confuſion hurl'd,
Shall ſink this beauteous fabrick of the world;
What colours paint the vivid arch of Jove;
What wondrous force the ſolid earth can move,
When Pindus' ſelf approaching ruin dreads,
Shakes all his pines, and bows his hundred heads;
Why does yon orb, ſo exquiſitely bright,
Obſcure his radiance in a ſhort-lived night;

Cur ſerus verſare boves, et plauſtra Bootes:
  Pleiadum ſpiſſo cur coit imbre chorus:
Curve ſuos fines altum non exeat æquor,
  Plenus et in partes quatuor annus eat:
Sub terris ſi jura deum, et tormenta Gigantum:
  Tiſiphones atro ſi furit angue caput:
Aut Alcmæoniæ furiæ, aut jejunia Phinei;
  Num rota, num ſcopuli, num ſitis inter aquas:
Num tribus infernum cuſtodit faucibus antrum
  Cerberus, et Tityo jugera pauca novem:
An ficta in miſeras deſcendit fabula gentes,
  Et timor haud ultra, quam rogus eſſe poteſt.
Exitus hic vitæ ſuperet mihi.

Whence the Seven-Sisters' congregated fires,
And what Bootes' lazy waggon tires;
How the rude surge its sandy bounds control;
Who measured out the year, and bade the seasons roll;
If realms beneath those fabled torments know,
Pangs without respite, fires that ever glow,
Earth's monster brood stretch'd on their iron bed,
The hissing terrors round Alecto's head,
Scarce to nine acres Tityus' bulk confined,
The triple dog that scares the shadowy kind,
All angry heaven inflicts, or hell can feel,
The pendent rock, Ixion's whirling wheel,
Famine at feasts, or thirst amid the stream;
Or are our fears the enthusiast's empty dream,
And all the scenes, that hurt the grave's repose,
But pictured horror and poetic woes.
These soft inglorious joys my hours engage;
Be love my youth's pursuit, and science crown my age.

1738. Æt. 22.

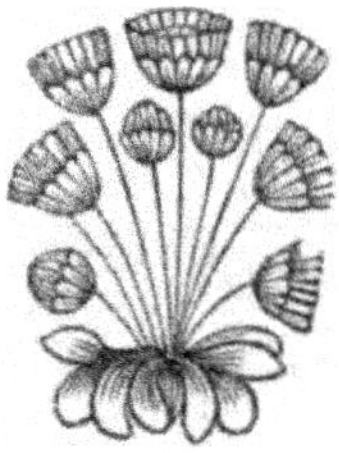

TASSO GERUS. LIB. CANT. XIV. ST. 32.

DISMISS'D at length, they break through all delay
To tempt the dangers of the doubtful way;
And firſt to Aſcalon their ſteps they bend,
Whoſe walls along the neighbouring ſea extend,
Nor yet in proſpect roſe the diſtant ſhore;
Scarce the hoarſe waves from far were heard to roar,
When thwart the road a river roll'd its flood
Tempeſtuous, and all further courſe withſtood;
The torrent ſtream his ancient bounds diſdains,
Swoll'n with new force, and late-deſcending rains.
Irreſolute they ſtand; when lo, appears
The wondrous Sage: vigorous he ſeem'd in years,
Awful his mien, low as his feet there flows
A veſtment unadorn'd, though white as new-fall'n ſnows;

Againſt the ſtream the waves ſecure he trod,
His head a chaplet bore, his hand a rod.
As on the Rhine, when Boreas' fury reigns,
And winter binds the floods in icy chains,
Swift ſhoots the village-maid in ruſtic play
Smooth, without ſtep, adown the ſhining way,
Fearleſs in long excurſion loves to glide,
And ſports and wantons o'er the frozen tide.
So moved the Seer, but on no harden'd plain;
The river boil'd beneath, and ruſh'd toward the main.
Where fix'd in wonder ſtood the warlike pair,
His courſe he turn'd, and thus relieved their care:
" Vaſt, oh my friends, and difficult the toil
To ſeek your hero in a diſtant ſoil!
No common helps, no common guide ye need,
Art it requires, and more than winged ſpeed.
What length of ſea remains, what various lands,
Oceans unknown, inhoſpitable ſands!
For adverſe fate the captive chief has hurl'd
Beyond the confines of our narrow world:

Great things and full of wonder in your ears
I ſhall unfold; but firſt diſmiſs your fears;
Nor doubt with me to tread the downward road
That to the grotto leads, my dark abode."
  Scarce had he ſaid, before the warriors' eyes
When mountain-high the waves diſparted riſe;
The flood on either hand its billows rears,
And in the midſt a ſpacious arch appears.
Their hands he ſeized, and down the ſteep he led
Beneath the obedient river's inmoſt bed;
The watery glimmerings of a fainter day
Diſcover'd half, and half conceal'd their way;
As when athwart the duſky woods by night
The uncertain creſcent gleams a ſickly light.
Through ſubterraneous paſſages they went,
Earth's inmoſt cells, and caves of deep deſcent;
Of many a flood they view'd the ſecret ſource,
The birth of rivers riſing to their courſe,
Whate'er with copious train its channel fills,
Floats into lakes, and bubbles into rills;

The Po was there to ſee, Danubius' bed,
Euphrates' fount, and Nile's myſterious head.
Further they paſs, where ripening minerals flow,
And embryon metals undigeſted glow,
Sulphureous veins and living ſilver ſhine,
Which ſoon the parent ſun's warm powers refine,
In one rich maſs unite the precious ſtore,
The parts combine and harden into ore:
Here gems break through the night with glittering beam,
And paint the margin of the coſtly ſtream,
All ſtones of luſtre ſhoot their vivid ray,
And mix attemper'd in a various day;
Here the ſoft emerald ſmiles of verdant hue,
And rubies flame, with ſapphire's heavenly blue,
The diamond there attracts the wondrous ſight,
Proud of its thouſand dies and luxury of light.

1738. Æt. 22.

POEMATA.

HYMENEAL

ON THE MARRIAGE OF HIS ROYAL HIGHNESS THE PRINCE OF WALES.[1]

IGNARÆ noſtrûm mentes, et inertia corda,
Dum curas regum, et ſortem miſeramur iniquam,
Quæ ſolio affixit, vetuitque caleſcere flammâ
Dulci, quæ dono divûm, gratiſſima ſerpit
Viſcera per, molleſque animis lene implicat æſtus ;
Nec teneros ſenſus, Veneris nec præmia nôrunt,
Eloquiumve oculi, aut facunda ſilentia linguæ :
Scilicet ignorant lacrymas, ſævoſque dolores,
Dura rudimenta, et violentæ exordia flammæ ;
Scilicet ignorant, quæ flumine tinxit amaro

Tela Venus, cæcique armamentaria Divi,
Irasque, insidiasque, et tacitum sub pectore vulnus;
Namque sub ingressu, primoque in limine Amoris
Luctus et ultrices posuere cubilia Curæ;
Intus habent dulces Risus, et Gratia sedem,
Et roseis resupina toris, roseo ore Voluptas:
Regibus huc faciles aditus; communia spernunt
Ostia, jamque expers duris custodibus istis
Panditur accessus, penetraliaque intima Templi.

Tuque Oh! Angliacis, Princeps, spes optima regnis,
Ne tantum, ne finge metum: quid imagine captus
Hæres, et mentem pictura pascis inani?
Umbram miraris: nec longum tempus, et ipsa
Ibit in amplexus, thalamosque ornabit ovantes.
Ille tamen tabulis inhians longum haurit amorem,
Affatu fruitur tacito, auscultatque tacentem
Immemor artificis calami, risumque, ruboremque
Aspicit in fucis, pictæque in virginis ore:
Tanta Venus potuit; tantus tenet error amantes.

Naſcere, magna Dies, qua ſeſe AUGUSTA Britanno
Committat Pelago, patriamque relinquat amœnam;
Cujus in adventum jam nunc tria regna ſecundos
Attolli in plauſus, dulcique accenſa furore
Incipiunt agitare modos, et carmina dicunt:
Ipſe animo ſedenim juvenis comitatur euntem,
Explorat ventos, atque auribus aëra captat,
Atque auras, atque aſtra vocat crudelia; pectus
Intentum exultat, ſurgitque arrecta cupido;
Incuſat ſpes ægra fretum, ſolitoque videtur
Latior effundi pontus, fluctuſque morantes.

Naſcere, Lux major, qua ſeſe AUGUSTA Britanno
Committat juveni totam, propriamque dicabit;
At citius (precor) Oh! cedas melioribus aſtris;
Nox finem pompæ, finemque imponere curis
Poſſit, et in thalamos furtim deducere nuptam;
Sufficiat requiemque viris, et amantibus umbras:
Adſit Hymen, et ſubridens cum matre Cupido
Accedant, ſternantque toros, ignemque miniſtrent;

Ilicet haud pictæ incandeſcit imagine formæ
Ulterius juvenis, verumque agnoſcit amorem.

Sculptile ſicut ebur, faciemque arſiſſe venuſtam
Pygmaliona canunt: ante hanc ſuſpiria ducit,
Alloquiturque amens, flammamque et vulnera narrat;
Implorata Venus juſſit cum vivere ſignum,
Fœmineam inſpirans animam; quæ gaudia ſurgunt,
Audiit ut primæ naſcentia murmura linguæ,
Luctari in vitam, et paulatim volvere ocellos
Sedulus, aſpexitque novâ ſplendeſcere flammâ;
Corripit amplexu vivam, jamque oſcula jungit
Acria confeſtim, recipitque rapitque; prioris
Immemor ardoris, Nymphæque oblitus eburneæ.

THO. GRAY. Pet. Coll.

LUNA HABITABILIS.[1]

DUM Nox rorantes, non incomitata per auras
Urget equos, tacitoque inducit ſidera lapſu;
Ultima, ſed nulli ſoror inficianda ſororum,
Huc mihi, Muſa; tibi patet alti janua cœli,
Aſtra vides, nec te numeri, nec nomina fallunt.
Huc mihi, Diva veni; dulce eſt per aperta ſerena
Vere frui liquido, campoque errare ſilenti;
Vere frui dulce eſt; modo tu dignata petentem
Sis comes, et mecum gelidâ ſpatiere ſub umbrâ.
Scilicèt hos orbes, cœli hæc decora alta putandum eſt,
Noctis opes, nobis tantum lucere; virûmque
Oſtentari oculis, noſtræ laquearia terræ,
Ingentes ſcenas, vaſtique aulæa theatri?
Oh! quis me pennis æthræ ſuper ardua ſiſtet
Mirantem, propiuſque dabit convexa tueri;

Teque adeo, undè fluens reficit lux mollior arva
Pallidiorque dies, triſtes ſolata tenebras?
Sic ego, ſubridens Dea ſic ingreſſa viciſſim:
Non pennis opus hìc, ſupera ut ſimul illa petamus:
Diſce, Puer, potiùs cœlo deducere Lunam;
Neu crede ad magicas te invitum accingier artes,
Theſſalicoſve modos; ipſam deſcendere Phœben
Conſpicies novus Endymion; ſeque offeret ultrò
Viſa tibi ante oculos, et notâ major imago.
Quin tete admoveas (tumuli ſuper aggere ſpectas),
Compoſitum tubulo; ſimul imum invade canalem
Sic intentâ acie, cœli ſimul alta pateſcent
Atria; jamque, auſus Lunaria viſere regna,
Ingrediêre ſolo, et caput inter nubila condes.
Ecce autem! vitri ſe in vertice ſiſtere Phœben
Cernis, et Oceanum, et crebris Freta conſita terris
Panditur *ille* atram faciem caligine condens
Sublustri; refugitque oculos, fallitque tuentem;
Integram Solis lucem quippè haurit aperto
Fluctu avidus radiorum, et longos imbibit ignes:

Verum *his*, quæ, maculis variata nitentibus, auro
Cœrula discernunt, celso sese insula dorso
Plurima protrudit, prætentaque littora saxis;
Liberior datur his quoniàm natura, minusque
Lumen depascunt liquidum; sed tela diei
Detorquent, retròque docent se vertere flammas.

Hinc longos videas tractus, terrasque jacentes
Ordine candenti, et claros se attollere montes;
Montes queîs Rhodope assurgat, quibus Ossa nivali
Vertice: tum scopulis infrà pendentibus antra
Nigrescunt clivorum umbrâ, nemorumque tenebris.
Non rores illi, aut desunt sua nubila mundo;
Non frigus gelidum, atque herbis gratissimus imber;
His quoque nota ardet picto Thaumantias arcu,
Os roseum Auroræ, propriique crepuscula cœli.

Et dubitas tantum certis cultoribus orbem
Destitui? exercent agros, sua mœnia condunt
Hi quoque, vel Martem invadunt, curantque triumphos
Victores: sunt hic etiam sua præmia laudi;
His metus, atque amor, et mentem mortalia tangunt.

Quin, uti nos oculis jam nunc juvat ire per arva,
Lucentesque plagas Lunæ, pontumque profundum;
Idem illos etiàm ardor agit, cum se aureus effert
Sub sudum globus, et terrarum ingentior orbis;
Scilicèt omne æquor tum lustrant, scilicèt omnem
Tellurem, gentesque polo sub utroque jacentes;
Et quidam æstivi indefessus ad ætheris ignes
Pervigilat, noctem exercens, cœlumque fatigat;
Jam Galli apparent, jam se Germania latè
Tollit, et albescens pater Apenninus ad auras;
Jam tandem in Borean, en! parvulus Anglia nævus
(Quanquam aliis longè fulgentior) extulit oras;
Formosum extemplò lumen, maculamque nitentem
Invisunt crebri Proceres, serùmque tuendo;
Hærent, certatimque suo cognomine signant:
Forsitan et Lunæ longinquus in orbe Tyrannus
Se dominum vocat, et nostrâ se jactat in aulâ.
Terras possim alias propiori sole calentes
Narrare, atque alias, jubaris queîs parcior usus,
Lunarum chorus, et tenuis penuria Phœbi;

Nî, meditans eadem hæc audaci evolvere cantu,
Jam pulſet citharam ſoror, et præludia tentet.
Non tamen has proprias laudes, nec facta ſilebo
Jampridèm in fatis, patriæque oracula famæ.
Tempus erit, ſurſùm totos contendere cœtus
Quo cernes longo excurſu, primoſque colonos
Migrare in lunam, et notos mutare Penates:
Dum ſtupet obtutu tacito vetus incola, longèque
Inſolitas explorat aves, claſſemque volantem.
Ut quondàm ignotum marmor, campoſque natantes
Tranavit Zephyros viſens, nova regna, Columbus;
Litora mirantur circùm, mirantur et undæ
Incluſas acies ferro, turmaſque biformes,
Monſtraque fœta armis, et non imitabile fulmen.
Fœdera mox icta, et gemini commercia mundi,
Agminaque aſſueto glomerata ſub æthere cerno.
Anglia, quæ pelagi jamdudum torquet habenas,
Exercetque frequens ventos, atque imperat undæ;
Aëris attollet faſces, vetereſque triumphos
Hùc etiam feret, et victis dominabitur auris.

ALCAIC ODE,

WRITTEN IN THE ALBUM OF THE GRANDE CHARTREUSE, IN DAUPHINY, AUGUST, 1741.

OH Tu, ſeveri Religio loci,
Quocunque gaudes nomine (non leve
Nativa nam certè fluenta
Numen habet, vetereſque ſylvas;
Præſentiorem et conſpicimus Deum
Per invias rupes, fera per juga,
Clivoſque præruptos, ſonantes
Inter aquas, nemorumque noctem;
Quàm ſi repoſtus ſub trabe citreâ
Fulgeret auro, et Phidiacâ manu)
Salve vocanti ritè, feſſo et
Da placidam juveni quietem.

Quod ſi invidendis ſedibus, et frui
Fortuna ſacrâ lege ſilentii
Vetat volentem, me reſorbens
In medios violenta fluctus:

Saltem remoto des, Pater, angulo
Horas ſenectæ ducere liberas;
Tutumque vulgari tumultu
Surripias, hominumque curis.

DE PRINCIPIIS COGITANDI.

LIBER PRIMUS. AD FAVONIUM.

UNDE Animus ſcire incipiat; quibus inchoet orſa
Principiis ſeriem rerum, tenuemque catenam
Mnemoſyne: Ratio unde rudi ſub pectore tardum
Augeat imperium; et primum mortalibus ægris
Ira, Dolor, Metus, et Curæ naſcantur inanes,
Hinc canere aggredior. Nec dedignare canentem,
O decus! Angliacæ certe O lux altera gentis!
Si quà primus iter monſtras, veſtigia conor
Signare incertâ, tremulâque inſiſtere plantâ.
Quin potius duc ipſe (potes namque omnia) ſanctum
Ad limen (ſi ritè adeo, ſi pectore puro,)

Obſcuræ reſerans Naturæ ingentia clauſtra.
Tu cæcas rerum cauſas, fontemque ſeverum
Pande, Pater; tibi enim, tibi, veri magne Sacerdos,
Corda patent hominum, atque altæ penetralia Mentis.
  Tuque aures adhibe vacuas, facileſque, Favonî,
(Quod tibi creſcit opus) ſimplex nec deſpice carmen,
Nec vatem: non illa leves primordia motus,
Quanquam parva, dabunt. Lætum vel amabile quicquid
Uſquam oritur, trahit hinc ortum; nec ſurgit ad auras,
Quin ea conſpirent ſimul, eventuſque ſecundent.
Hinc variæ vitaï artes, ac mollior uſus,
Dulce et amicitiæ vinclum: Sapientia dia
Hinc roſeum accendit lumen, vultuque ſereno
Humanas aperit mentes, nova gaudia monſtrans,
Deformeſque fugat curas, vanoſque timores:
Scilicet et rerum creſcit pulcherrima Virtus.
Illa etiam, quæ te (mirùm) noctеſque dieſque
Aſſiduè fovet inſpirans, linguamque ſequentem
Temperat in numeros, atque horas mulcet inertes;
Aurea non aliâ ſe jactat origine Muſa.

Principio, ut magnum fœdus Natura creatrix
Firmavit, tardis juſſitque inoleſcere membris
Sublimes animas; tenebroſo in carcere partem
Noluit æthercam longo torpere veterno:
Nec per ſe proprium paſſa exercere vigorem eſt,
Ne ſociæ molis conjunctos ſperneret artus,
Ponderis oblita, et cœleſtis conſcia flammæ.
Idcircò innumero ductu tremere undique fibras
Nervorum inſtituit: tum toto corpore miſcens
Implicuit latè ramos, et ſenſile textum,
Implevitque humore ſuo, (ſeu lympha vocanda,
Sive aura eſt) tenuis certè, atque leviſſima quædam
Vis verſatur agens, parvoſque infuſa canales
Perfluit; aſſiduè externis quæ concita plagis,
Mobilis, incuſſique fidelis nuntia motûs,
Hinc indè accensâ contage relabitur uſque
Ad ſuperas hominis ſedes, arcemque cerebri.
Namque illìc poſuit ſolium, et ſua templa ſacravit
Mens animi: hanc circum coëunt, denſoque feruntur
Agmine notitiæ, ſimulacraque tenuia rerum:

Ecce autem naturæ ingens aperitur imago
Immenſæ, variique patent commercia mundi.
 Ac uti longinquis deſcendunt montibus amnes
Velivolus Tamiſis, flaventiſque Indus arenæ,
Euphrateſque, Taguſque, et opimo flumine Ganges,
Undas quiſque ſuas volvens, curſuque ſonoro
In mare prorumpunt : hos magno acclinis in antro
Excipit Oceanus, natorumque ordine longo
Dona recognoſcit ventientûm, ultròque ſerenat
Cæruleam faciem, et diffuſo marmore ridet :
Haud aliter ſpecies properant ſe inferre novellæ
Certatim menti, atque aditus quino agmine complent.
 Primas tactus agit partes, primuſque minutæ
Laxat iter cæcum turbæ, recipitque ruentem.
Non idem huic modus eſt, qui fratribus : amplius ille
Imperium affectat ſenior, penituſque medullis,
Viſceribuſque habitat totis, pelliſque recentem
Funditur in telam, et latè per ſtamina vivit.
Necdum etiam matris puer eluctatus ab alvo
Multiplices ſolvit tunicas, et vincula rupit ;

Sopitus molli ſomno, tepidoque liquore
Circumfuſus adhuc: tactûs tamen aura laceſſit
Jamdudum levior ſenſus, animamque reclufit.
Idque magis, ſimul ac ſolitum blandumque calorem
Frigore mutavit cœli, quod verberat acri
Impete inaſſuetos artus: tum ſævior adſtat
Humanæque comes vitæ Dolor excipit; ille
Cunctantem fruſtrà et tremulo multa ore querentem
Corripit invadens, ferreiſque amplectitur ulnis.
Tum ſpecies primùm patefacta eſt candida Lucis
(Uſque vices adeò Natura bonique, malique,
Exæquat, juſtâque manu ſua damna rependit)
Tum primùm, ignotoſque bibunt nova lumina ſoles.

Carmine quo, Dea, te dicam, gratiſſima cœli
Progenies, ortumque tuum; gemmantia rore
Ut per prata levi luſtras, et floribus halans
Purpureum Veris gremium, ſcenamque virentem
Pingis, et umbriferos colles, et cærula regna?
Gratia te, Veneriſque Lepos, et mille Colorum,
Formarumque chorus ſequitur, motuſque decentes.

At caput inviſum Stygiis Nox atra tenebris
Abdidit, horrendæque ſimul Formidinis ora,
Pervigileſque æſtus Curarum, atque anxius Angor:
Undique lætitiâ florent mortalia corda,
Purus et arridet largis fulgoribus Æther.

Omnia nec tu ideò invalidæ ſe pandere Menti
(Quippe nimis teneros poſſet vis tanta diei
Perturbare, et inexpertos confundere viſus)
Nec capere infantes animos, neu cernere credas
Tam variam molem, et miræ ſpectacula lucis:
Neſcio quâ tamen hæc oculos dulcedine parvos
Splendida percuſſit novitas, traxitque ſequentes;
Nonne videmus enim, latis inſerta feneſtris
Sicubi ſe Phœbi diſpergant aurea tela,
Sive lucernarum rutilus colluxerit ardor,
Extemplo hùc obverti aciem, quæ fixa repertos
Haurit inexpletùm radios, fruiturque tuendo.

Altior huic verò ſenſu, majorque videtur
Addita, Judicioque arctè connexa poteſtas,
Quod ſimul atque ætas volventibus auxerit annis,

Hæc ſimul, aſſiduo depaſcens omnia viſu,
Perſpiciet, vis quanta loci, quid polleat ordo,
Juncturæ quis honos, ut res accendere rebus
Lumina conjurant inter ſe, et mutua fulgent.
Nec minor in geminis viget auribus inſita virtus,
Nec tantum in curvis quæ pervigil excubet antris
Hinc atque hinc (ubi Vox tremefecerit oſtia pulſu
Aëriis invecta rotis) longèque recurſet:
Scilicet Eloquio hæc ſonitus, hæc fulminis alas.
Et mulcere dedit dictis et tollere corda,
Verbaque metiri numeris, verſuque ligare
Repperit, et quicquid diſcant Libethrides undæ,
Calliope quotiès, quotiès Pater ipſe canendi
Evolvat liquidum carmen, calamove loquenti
Inſpiret dulces animas, digitiſque figuret.
At medias fauces, et linguæ humentia templa
Guſtus habet, quà ſe inſinuet jucunda ſaporum
Luxuries, dona Autumni, Bacchique voluptas.
Naribus interea conſedit odora hominum vis,
Docta leves captare auras, Panchaïa quales

Vere novo exhalat, Floræve quod oſcula fragrant
Roſcida, cum Zephyri furtìm ſub veſperis horâ
Reſpondet votis, mollemque aſpirat amorem.
Tot portas altæ capitis circumdedit arci
Alma Parens, ſensûſque vias per membra recluſit;
Haud ſolas: namque intùs agit vivata facultas,
Quâ ſeſe explorat, contemplatuſque repentè
Ipſe ſuas animus vires, momentaque cernit.
Quid velit, aut poſſit, cupiat, fugiatve, viciſsìm
Percipit imperio gaudens; neque corpora fallunt
Morigera ad celeres actus, ac numina mentis.
Qualis Hamadryadum quondam ſi fortè ſororum
Una, novos peragrans ſaltus, et devia rura;
(Atque illam in viridi ſuadet procumbere ripâ
Fontis pura quies, et opaci frigoris umbra)
Dum prona in latices ſpeculi de margine pendet,
Mirata eſt ſubitam venienti occurrere Nympham:
Mox eoſdem, quos ipſa, artus, eadem ora gerentem
Unà inferre gradus, unà ſuccedere ſylvæ
Aſpicit alludens; ſeſeque agnoſcit in undis.

Sic ſenſu interno rerum ſimulacra ſuarum
Mens ciet, et proprios obſervat conſcia vultus.
Nec verò ſimplex ratio, aut jus omnibus unum
Conſtat imaginibus. Sunt quæ bina oſtia nôrunt;
Hæ privos ſervant aditus; ſine legibus illæ
Paſsìm, quà data porta, ruunt, animoque propinquant.
Reſpice, cui à cunis triſtes extinxit ocellos,
Sæva et in eternas merſit natura tenebras:
Illi ignota dies lucet, vernuſque colorum
Offuſus nitor eſt, et vivæ gratia formæ.
Corporis at filum, et motus, ſpatiumque, locique
Intervalla datur certo dignoſcere tactu:
Quandoquidem his iter ambiguum eſt, et janua duplex,
Excluſæque oculis ſpecies irrumpere tendunt
Per digitos. Atqui ſolis conceſſa poteſtas
Luminibus blandæ eſt radios immittere lucis.

Undique proporrò ſociis, quacunque pateſcit
Notitiæ campus, miſtæ laſciva feruntur
Turba voluptatis comites, formæque dolorum
Terribiles viſu, et portâ glomerantur in omni.

Nec vario minus introïtu magnum ingruit Illud,
Quo facere et fungi, quo res existere circùm
Quamque sibi proprio cum corpore scimus, et ire
Ordine, perpetuoque per ævum flumine labi.
  Nunc age quo valeat pacto, quâ sensilis arte
Affectare viam, atque animi tentare latebras
Materies (dictis aures adverte faventes)
Exsequar. Imprimìs spatii quam multa per æquor
Millia multigenis pandant se corpora seclis,
Expende. Haud unum invenies, quod mente licebit
Amplecti, nedum propiùs deprendere sensu,
Molis egens certæ, aut solido sine robore, cujus
Denique mobilitas linquit, texturave partes,
Ulla nec orarum circumcæsura coërcet.
Hæc conjuncta adeò totâ compage fatetur
Mundus, et extremo clamant in limine rerum,
(Si rebus datur extremum) primordia. Firmat
Hæc eadem tactus (tactum quis dicere falsum
Audeat?) hæc oculi nec lucidus arguit orbis.
  Inde potestatum enasci densissima proles;

Nam quodcunque ferit viſum, tangive laborat,
Quicquid nare bibis, vel concava concipit auris,
Quicquid lingua ſapit, credas hoc omne, neceſſe eſt
Ponderibus, textu, diſcurſu, mole, figurâ
Particulas præſtare leves, et ſemina rerum.
Nunc oculos igitur paſcunt, et luce miniſtrâ
Fulgere cuncta vides, ſpargique coloribus orbem,
Dum de ſole trahunt alias, aliaſque ſupernè
Detorquent, retròque docent ſe vertere flammas.
Nunc trepido inter ſe fervent corpuſcula pulſu,
Ut tremor æthera per magnum, latèque natantes
Aurarum fluctus avidi vibrantia clauſtra
Auditûs queat allabi, ſonitumque propaget.
Cominùs interdum non ullo interprete per ſe
Nervorum invadunt teneras quatientia fibras,
Senſiferumque urgent ultrò per viſcera motum.

* * * * *

LIBER QUARTUS.

HACTENUS haud ſegnis Naturæ arcana retexi
Muſarum interpres, primuſque Britanna per arva
Romano liquidum deduxi flumine rivum.
Cum Tu opere in medio, ſpes tanti et cauſa laboris,
Linquis, et æternam fati te condis in umbram!
Vidi egomet duro graviter concuſſa dolore
Pectora, in alterius non unquam lenta dolorem;
Et languere oculos vidi, et palleſcere amantem
Vultum, quo nunquam Pietas niſi rara, Fideſque,
Altus amor Veri, et purum ſpirabat Honeſtum.
Viſa tamen tardi demùm inclementia morbi
Ceſſare eſt, reducemque iterum roſeo ore Salutem
Speravi, atque unà tecum, dilecte Favoni!
Credulus heu longos, ut quondàm, fallere Soles:

Heu ſpes nequicquam dulces, atque irrita vota!
Heu mæſtos Soles, ſine te quos ducere flendo
Per deſideria, et queſtus jam cogor inanes!
At Tu, ſancta anima, et noſtri non indiga luctûs,
Stellanti templo, ſincerique ætheris igne,
Unde orta es, fruere; atque ô ſi ſecura, nec ultra
Mortalis, notos olìm miſerata labores
Reſpectes, tenueſque vacet cognoſcere curas;
Humanam ſi fortè altâ de ſede procellam
Contemplêre, metus, ſtimuloſque cupidinis acres,
Gaudiaque et gemitus, parvoque in corde tumultum
Irarum ingentem, et ſævos ſub pectore fluctus;
Reſpice et has lacrymas, memori quas ictus amore
Fundo; quod poſſum, juxtà lugere ſepulchrum
Dum juvat, et mutæ vana hæc jactare favillæ.

* * * * *

EXTRACTS.

RIME DI PETRARCA.

SONETTO 170.[1]

LASSO, ch' i' ardo, ed altri non mel crede!
Si crede ogni uom, ſe non ſola colei
Ch' è ſovr' ogni altra, e ch' i' ſola vorrei:
Ella non par che 'l creda, e sì ſel vede.
Infinita bellezza e poca fede,
Non vedete voi 'l cor negli occhi miei?
Se non foſſe mia ſtella, i' pur devrei
Al fonte di pietà trovar mercede.
Queſt' aider mio, di che vi cal sì poco,
E i voſtri onori in mie rime diffuſi
Ne porian infiammar fors' ancor mille:
Ch' i' veggio nel penſier, dolce mio foco,
Fredda una lingua, e duo begli occhi chiuſi,
Rimaner dopo noi pien di faville.

UROR, io; veros at nemo credidit ignes:
Quin credunt omnes; dura ſed illa negat,
Illa negat, ſoli volumus cui poſſe probare;
Quin videt, et viſos improba diſſimulat.
Ah, duriſſima mî, ſed et, ah, pulcherrima rerum!
Nonne animam in miſerâ, Cynthia, fronte vides?
Omnibus illa pia eſt; et, ſi non fata vetâſſent,
Tam longas mentem flecteret ad lacrymas.
Sed tamen has lacrymas, hunc tu, quem ſpreveris, ignem,
Carminaque auctori non bene culta ſuo,
Turba futurorum non ignorabit amantûm:
Nos duo, cumque erimus parvus uterque cinis,
Jamque faces, eheu! oculorum, et frigida lingua,
Hæ ſine luce jacent, immemor illa loqui;
Infelix muſa æternos ſpirabit amores,
Ardebitque urnâ multa favilla meâ.

ΠΑΥΛΟΥ Σιλεντιαρίου εἰς Βάκχην ἐν Βυζαντίῳ.

Ἔκφρονα τὴν Βάκχην οὐχ' ἡ φύσις ἀλλ' ἡ τέχνη
Θήκατο, καὶ μανίην ἐγκατέμιξε λίθῳ.

ΠΟΣΕΙΔΙΠΠΟΥ εἰς στήλην Ἀλεξάνδρου τοῦ Μακεδόνος.

Λύσιππε πλάστα Σικυώνιε, θαρσαλέη χεὶρ,
Δάϊε τεχνῖτα, πῦρ τοι ὁ χαλκὸς ὁρῇ
Ὃν κατ' Ἀλεξάνδρου μορφᾶς χέες· οὐκέτι μεμπτοὶ
Πέρσαι· συγγνώμη βουσὶ λέοντα φυγεῖν.

FROM THE ANTHOLOGIA GRÆCA.

EDIT. HEN. STEPH. 1566.

IN BACCHÆ FURENTIS STATUAM.[1]

CREDITE, non viva eſt Mænas; non ſpirat imago:
Artificis rabiem miſcuit ære manus.

IN ALEXANDRUM, ÆRE EFFICTUM.[2]

QUANTUM audet, Lyſippe, manus tua! ſurgit in ære
Spiritus, atque oculis bellicus ignis adeſt:
Spectate hos vultus, miſeriſque ignoſcite Perſis:
Quid mirum, imbelles ſi leo ſparſit oves?

ΑΝΤΙΦΙΛΟΥ Βυζαντίου εἰς εἰκόνα Μηδείας.

Τὰν ὀλοὰν Μήδειαν ὅτ᾽ ἔγραφε Τιμομάχου χεὶρ,
Ζάλῳ καὶ τέκνοις ἀντιμεθελκομέναν,
Μυρίον ἄρατο μόχθον, ἵν᾽ ἤθεα δισσὰ χαράξῃ,
Ὧν τὸ μὲν εἰς ὀργὰν νεῦε, τὸ δ᾽ εἰς ἔλεον.
Ἄμφω δ᾽ ἐπλήρωσεν· ὅρα τύπον· ἐν γὰρ ἀπειλᾷ
Δάκρυον, ἐν δ᾽ ἐλέῳ θυμὸς ἀναστρέφεται.
Ἀρκεῖ δ᾽ ἁ μέλλησις, ἔφα σοφός· αἷμα δὲ τέκνων
Ἔπρεπε Μηδείῃ, κοὐ χερὶ Τιμομάχου.

Εἰς ἄγαλμα Νιόβης.

Ἐκ ζωῆς με θεοὶ τεῦξαν λίθον· ἐκ δὲ λίθοιο
Ζωὴν Πραξιτέλης ἔμπαλιν εἰργάσατο.

ΛΟΥΚΙΑΝΟΥ εἰς ἄγαλμα Ἀφροδίτης.

Σοὶ μορφῆς ἀνέθηκα τεῆς περικαλλὲς ἄγαλμα,
Κύπρι, τεῆς μορφῆς φέρτερον οὐδὲν ἔχων.

IN MEDEÆ IMAGINEM, NOBILE TIMOMACHI OPUS.[3]

EN ubi Medeæ varius dolor æſtuat ore,
Jamque animum nati, jamque maritus, habent!
Succenſet, miſeret, medio exardeſcit amore,
Dum furor inque oculo gutta minante tremit.
Cernis adhuc dubiam; quid enim? licet impia matris
Colchidos, at non ſit dextera Timomachi.

IN NIOBES STATUAM.[4]

FECERAT e vivâ lapidem me Jupiter; at me
Praxiteles vivam reddidit e lapide.

IN VENERIS STATUAM.[5]

TE tibi, ſancta, fero, nudam; formoſius ipsâ
Cum tibi, quod ferrem, te, Dea, nil habui.

Εἰς Ἔρωτα κοιμώμενον.

Εὕδεις ἀγρύπνους ἐπάγων θνητοῖσι μερίμνας;
Εὕδεις ἀτηρὴς, ὦ τέκος Ἀφρογενοῦς,
Οὐ πεύκην πυρόεσσαν ἐπηρμένος, οὐδ᾽ ἀφύλακτον
Ἐκ κέραος ψάλλων ἀντιτόνοιο βέλος;
Ἄλλοι θαρσείτωσαν· ἐγὼ δ᾽, ἀγέρωχε, δέδοικα
Μή μοι καὶ κνώσσων πικρὸν ὄνειρον ἴδῃς.

ΠΛΑΤΩΝΟΣ εἰς Ἔρωτα ἐν ἄλσει κοιμώμενον· εὑρέθη δὲ ὑπὸ ὑδάτων.

Ἄλσος δ᾽ ὡς ἱκόμεσθα βαθύσκιον, εὕρομεν ἔνδον
Πορφυρέοις μήλοισιν ἐοικότα παῖδα Κυθήρης.
Οὐδ᾽ ἔχεν ἰοδόκον φαρέτρην, οὐ καμπύλα τόξα·
Ἀλλὰ τὰ μὲν δένδρεσσιν ὑπ᾽ εὐπετάλοισι κρέμαντο,
Αὐτὸς δ᾽ ἐν καλύκεσσι ῥόδων πεπεδημένος ὕπνῳ,
Εὗδεν μειδιόων, ξουθαὶ δ᾽ ἐφύπερθε μέλισσαι
Κηροχύτοις ἐντὸς λαγαροῖς ἐπὶ χείλεσι βαίνον.

IN AMOREM DORMIENTEM.[6]

DOCTE puer vigiles mortalibus addere curas,
    Anne poteſt in te ſomnus habere locum?
Laxi juxta arcus, et fax ſuſpenſa quieſcit,
    Dormit et in pharetrâ clauſa ſagitta ſuâ;
Longè mater abeſt; longè Cythereïa turba:
    Verùm auſint alii te prope ferre pedem,
Non ego; nam metui valdè, mihi, perfide, quiddam
    Forſan et in ſomnis ne meditere mali.

ITUR[7] in Idalios tractus, felicia regna,
    Fundit ubi denſam myrtea ſylva comam,
Intus Amor teneram viſus ſpirare quietem,
    Dum roſeo roſeos imprimit ore toros;
Sublimem procul a ramis pendere pharetram,
    Et de languidulâ ſpicula lapſa manu,
Vidimus, et riſu molli diducta labella
    Murmure quæ aſſiduo pervolitabat apis.

MAPIANOY σχολαστικοῦ εἰς βαλανεῖον.

Τάσδ' ὑπὸ τὰς πλατάνους ἁπαλῷ πεπεδημένος ὕπνῳ
Εὗδεν Ἔρως, νύμφαις λαμπάδα παρθέμενος.
Νύμφαι δ' ἀλλήλῃσι, τί μέλλομεν; αἴθε δὲ τούτῳ
Σβέσσαμεν (εἶπον) ὁμοῦ πῦρ κραδίης μερόπων.
Λαμπὰς δ' ὡς ἔφλεξε καὶ ὕδατα, θερμὸν ἐκεῖθεν
Νύμφαι ἐρωτιάδες λουτροχοοῦσιν ὕδωρ.

ΛΟΥΚΙΛΛΙΟΥ.

Μῦν Ἀσκληπιάδης ὁ φιλάργυρος εἶδεν ἐν οἴκῳ,
Καὶ, τί ποιεῖς, φησὶν, φίλτατε μῦ, παρ' ἐμοί;
Ἡδὺ δ' ὁ μῦς γελάσας, μηδὲν φίλε, φησὶ, φοβηθῇς·
Οὐχι τροφῆς παρὰ σοὶ χρήζομεν, ἀλλὰ μονῆς.

IN FONTEM AQUÆ CALIDÆ.[8]

SUB platanis puer Idalius prope fluminis undam
Dormiit, in ripâ depoſuitque facem.
Tempus adeſt, ſociæ, Nympharum audentior una,
Tempus adeſt, ultra quid dubitamus? ait.
Ilicet incurrit, peſtem ut divûmque hominumque
Lampada collectis exanimaret aquis:
Demens! nam nequiit ſævam reſtinguere flammam
Nympha, ſed ipſa ignes traxit, et inde calet.

IRREPSISSE[9] ſuas murem videt Argus in ædes,
Atque ait, heus, a me nunquid, amice, velis?
Ille autem ridens, metuas nihil, inquit; apud te,
O bone, non epulas, hoſpitium petimus.

ῬΟΥΦΙΝΟΥ.

Πέμπω σοὶ, Ῥοδόκλεια, τόδε στέφος, ἄνθεσι πλέξας,
Αὐτὸς ὑφ' ἡμετέραις δρεψάμενος παλάμαις.
Εστι κρίνον, ῥοδέη τε κάλυξ, νοτερή τ' ἀνεμώνη,
Καὶ νάρκισσος ὑγρὸς, καὶ κυαναυγὲς ἴον.
Ταῦτα στεψαμένη, λῆξον μεγάλαυχος ἐοῦσα.
Ἀνθεῖς, καὶ λήγεις καὶ σὺ καὶ ὁ στέφανος.

ΠΟΣΕΙΔΙΠΠΟΥ.

Λίσσομ', ἔρως, τὸν ἄγρυπνον ἐμοὶ πόθον Ἡλιοδώρας
Κοίμισον, αἰδεσθεὶς μοῦσαν ἐμὴν ἱκέτιν.
Νὴ γὰρ δὴ τὰ σὰ τόξα, τὰ μὴ δεδιδαγμένα βάλλειν
Ἄλλον, ἀεὶ δ' ἐπ' ἐμοὶ πτηνὰ χέοντα βέλη,
Εἰ καί με κτείνῃς, λείψω φωνὴν προϊέντα
Γράμματ', ἔρωτος ὅρα, ξεῖνε, μιαιφονίην.

HANC[10] tibi Rufinus mittit, Rodoclea, coronam,
Has tibi decerpens texerat ipſe roſas;
Eſt viola, eſt anemòne, eſt ſuave-rubens hyacynthus,
Miſtaque Narciſſo lutea caltha ſuo:
Sume; ſed aſpiciens, ah, fidere deſine formæ;
Qui pinxit, brevis eſt, ſertaque teque, color.

AD AMOREM.[11]

PAULISPER vigiles, oro, compeſce dolores,
Reſpue nec muſæ ſupplicis aure preces;
Oro brevem lacrymis veniam, requiemque furori:
Ah, ego non poſſum vulnera tanta pati!
Intima flamma, vides, miſeros depaſcitur artus,
Surgit et extremis ſpiritus in labiis:
Quòd ſi tam tenuem cordi eſt exſolvere vitam,
Stabit in opprobrium ſculpta querela tuum.
Juro perque faces iſtas, arcumque ſonantem,
Spiculaque hoc unum figere docta jecur;
Heu fuge crudelem puerum, ſævaſque ſagittas!
Huic fuit exitii cauſa, viator, Amor.

NOTES TO THE POEMS.

NOTES.

Page 3, note 1.

THE original manuſcript title given by Gray to this Ode was " Noontide." It appeared for the firſt time in Dodſley's Collection, vol. ii. p. 271, under the title of " Ode."

P. 4, note 2.—" A bank *o'ercanopied* with luſcious woodbine."—*Mids. N. Dr.* Act. ii. Sc. 2.

P. 4, note 3.— " How low, how indigent the proud,
How little are the great!"—*Dodſley*.

P. 4, note 4.—" Sporting with *quick glance*, ſhow to the *ſun* their waved coats dropp'd with gold."—*Par. L.* vii. 405-6.

" While inſects from the threſhold preach," Green, in the Grotto. Dodſley, Miſc. v. p. 161.

P. 7, note 1.—This Ode firſt appeared in Dodſley, Col. vol. ii. p. 274, with ſome variations.

P. 7, note 2.— " The penſive Selima reclined,
Demureſt of the tabby kind."—*Dodſley*.

P. 8, note 3.—" Two beauteous forms."—*Dodſley*.

P. 8, note 4.—" *A foe* to fiſh."—*Dodſley*.

P. 8, note 5.—*Looks.*] Eyes.—MS.

P. 9, note 6.— "nor *Harry* heard.
What favourite has a friend?"—Dodſley.

P. 9, note 7.—Strikes.—MS.

P. 11, note 1.—This, as Maſon informs us, was the *firſt Engliſh* production of Gray which appeared in print. It was publiſhed in folio, in 1747, and appeared again in Dodſley, Col. vol. ii. p. 267, without the name of the author.

P. 11, note 2.—King Henry the Sixth, founder of the College.

P. 12, note 3.—" And bees their honey *redolent of ſpring,*" Dryden's *Fable on the Pythag. Syſtem.*

P. 12, note 4.—" To chaſe the hoop's eluſive ſpeed."—MS.

P. 17, note 1.—This Hymn firſt appeared in Dodſley, Col. vol iv. together with the " Elegy in a Country Churchyard."

P. 21, note 1.—Finiſhed in 1754. Printed together with the " Bard, an Ode," Aug. 8, 1757.—MS.

When the author firſt publiſhed this and the following Ode, he was adviſed, even by his friends, to ſubjoin ſome few explanatory notes; but had too much reſpect for the underſtanding of his readers to take that liberty.

P. 21, note 2.—" Awake, my glory: awake, lute and harp."—*David's Pſalms.*

Pindar ſtyles his own poetry, with its muſical accompaniments, Αἰολὶς μολπὴ, Αἰολίδες χορδαὶ, Αἰολίδων πνοαὶ αὐλῶν, Æolian ſong, Æolian ſtrings, the breath of the Æolian flute.

The ſubject and ſimile, as uſual with Pindar, are united. The various ſources of poetry, which gives life and luſtre to all it touches, are here deſcribed; its quiet majeſtic progreſs enriching every ſubject (otherwiſe dry and barren) with a pomp of diction and luxuriant harmony of numbers; and its more rapid and irreſiſtible courſe when ſwoln and hurried away by the conflict of tumultuous paſſions.

P. 22, note 3.—Power of harmony to calm the turbulent ſallies of the ſoul. The thoughts are borrowed from the firſt Pythian of Pindar.

P. 22, note 4.—This is a weak imitation of ſome beautiful lines in the ſame ode. Pyth. i. ver. 10.

P. 22, note 5.—Power of harmony to produce all the graces of motion in the body.

P. 23, note 6.— Μαρμαρυγὰς θηεῖτο ποδῶν· θαύμαζε δὲ θυμῷ.
Hom. Od. Θ. ver. 265.

P. 23, note 7.— Λάμπει δ' ἐπὶ πορφυρέῃσι
Παρείῃσι φῶς ἔρωτος.
Phrynicus apud Athenæum.

P. 23, note 8.—To compenſate the real and imaginary ills of life, the Muſe was given to mankind by the ſame Providence that ſends the day, by its cheerful preſence, to diſpel the gloom and terrors of the night.

P. 24, note 9.—" Or ſeen the morning's well appointed ſtar
Come marching up the eaſtern hills afar."—*Cowley.*

P. 24, note 10.—Extenſive influence of poetic genius over the remoteſt and moſt uncivilized nations: its connection with liberty, and the virtues that naturally attend on it. [See the Erſe, Norwegian, and Welſh fragments, the Lapland and American ſongs.]

" Tutta lontana dal camin del ſole."—*Petr. Canz.* ii.

P. 25, note 11.—Progreſs of Poetry from Greece to Italy, and from Italy to England. Chaucer was not unacquainted with the writings of Dante or of Petrarch. The Earl of Surrey and Sir Thomas Wyatt had travelled in Italy, and formed their taſte there. Spenſer imitated the Italian writers; Milton improved on them: but this ſchool expired ſoon after the Reſtoration, and a new one aroſe on the French model, which has ſubſiſted ever ſince.

P. 26, note 12.—" Nature's darling." Shakeſpeare.

" The flowery May, who from her *green lap* throws
The yellow cowſlip, and the pale primroſe."
Milton, Son. on May Morn.

P. 26, note 13.—*Milton*, *P. L.* vi. 771.

P. 26, note 14.—" Flammantia mœnia mundi."—*Lucret.* i. 74.

" For the ſpirit of the living creature was in the wheels. And above the firmament that was over their heads, was the likeneſs of a throne, as the appearance of a ſapphire ſtone. This was the appearance of the glory of the Lord."—*Ezek.* i. 20. 26. 28.

P. 27, note 15.—'Οφθαλμῶν μὲν ἄμερσε· δίδου δ' ἡδεῖαν ἀοιδήν.

Hom. Od. Θ. ver. 64.

P. 27, note 16.—" Haſt thou clothed his neck with thunder?"—*Job.* This verſe and the foregoing are meant to expreſs the ſtately march and ſounding energy of Dryden's rhymes.

P. 27, note 17.—" Words that weep, and tears that ſpeak."

Cowley, *Prophet*, vol. i. p. 113.

We have had in our language no other odes of the ſublime kind, than that of Dryden on St. Cecilia's Day; for Cowley, who had his merit, yet wanted judgment, ſtyle, and harmony, for ſuch a taſk. That of Pope is not worthy of ſo great a man. Mr. Maſon indeed, of late days, has touched the true chords, and with a maſterly hand, in ſome of his choruſes; above all in the laſt of Caractacus:

" Hark! heard ye not yon footſtep dread?" &c.

P. 27, note 18.—Διὸς πρὸς ὄρνιχα θεῖον, *Olymp.* ii. 159. Pindar compares himſelf to that bird, and his enemies to ravens that croak and clamour in vain below, while it purſues its flight, regardleſs of their noiſe.

P. 29, note 1.—This ode is founded on a tradition current in Wales, that Edward the Firſt, when he completed the conqueſt of that country, ordered all the Bards that fell into his hands to be put to death.

P. 29, note 2.—" Mocking the air with colours idly ſpread."

King John, Act v. Sc. 1.

P. 29, note 3.—The hauberk was a texture of ſteel ringlets, or rings interwoven, forming a coat of mail that ſat cloſe to the body, and adapted itſelf to every motion.

P. 29, note 4.—"The crefted adder's pride."—*Dryden, Indian Queen.*

P. 29, note 5.—Snowdon was a name given by the Saxons to that mountainous tract which the Welfh themfelves call Craigian-eryri: it included all the highlands of Caernarvonfhire and Merionethfhire, as far eaft as the river Conway. R. Hygden, fpeaking of the caftle of Conway, built by King Edward the Firft, fays, "Ad ortum amnis Conway ad clivum montis Erery;" and Matthew of Weftminfter, (ad ann. 1283) "Apud Aberconway ad pedes montis Snowdoniæ fecit erigi caftrum forte."

P. 30, note 6.—Gilbert de Clare, furnamed the Red, earl of Gloucefter and Hertford, fon-in-law to King Edward.

Edmond de Mortimer, Lord of Wigmore.

They both were Lord Marchers, whofe lands lay on the borders of Wales, and probably accompanied the king in this expedition.

P. 30, note 7.—The image was taken from a well-known picture of Raphael, reprefenting the Supreme Being in the vifion of Ezekiel. There are two of thefe paintings, both believed to be originals, one at Florence, the other in the Duke of Orleans' collection at Paris.

P. 31, note 8.—The fhores of Caernarvonfhire oppofite the ifle of Anglefey.

P. 31, note 9.—Camden and others obferve, that eagles ufed annually to build their aerie among the rocks of Snowdon, which from thence (as fome think) were named by the Welfh Craigian-eryri, or the crags of the eagles. At this day (I am told) the higheft point of Snowdon is called the Eagle's Neft. That bird is certainly no ftranger to this ifland, as the Scots, and the people of Cumberland, Weftmoreland, &c. can teftify: it even has built its neft upon the peak of Derbyfhire. [See *Willoughby's Ornithol.* by Ray.]

P. 31, note 10.—"As dear to me as are the ruddy drops
That vifit my fad heart."—*Jul. Cæfar,* Act ii. Sc. 1.

P. 32, note 11.—Edward the Second, cruelly butchered in Berkley Caftle.

P. 32, note 12.—Ifabel of France, Edward the Second's adulterous queen.

P. 32, note 13.—Triumphs of Edward the Third in France.

P. 33, note 14.—Death of that king, abandoned by his children, and even robbed in his laſt moments by his courtiers and his miſtreſs.

P. 33, note 15.—Edward the Black Prince, dead ſome time before his father.

P. 33, note 16.—Magnificence of Richard the Second's reign. See Froiſſard and other contemporary writers.

P. 34, note 17.—Richard the Second, as we are told by Archbiſhop Scroop and the confederate Lords in their manifeſto, by Thomas of Walſingham, and all the older writers, was ſtarved to death. The ſtory of his aſſaſſination by Sir Piers of Exon is of much later date.

For the profuſion of Richard II. ſee *Harding, Chron.* quoted in the Preface to *Maſon's Hoccleve*, p. 5; *Daniel, Civil Wars*, iii. 87; and *Pennant, London*, p. 89, 4to.

P. 34, note 18.—Ruinous wars of York and Lancaſter.

P. 34, note 19.—Henry the Sixth, George Duke of Clarence, Edward the Fifth, Richard Duke of York, &c., believed to be murdered ſecretly in the Tower of London. The oldeſt part of that ſtructure is vulgarly attributed to Julius Cæſar.

P. 34, note 20.—Margaret of Anjou, a woman of heroic ſpirit, who ſtruggled hard to ſave her huſband and her crown.

Henry the Fifth.

P. 34, note 21.—Henry the Sixth, very near being canonized. The line of Lancaſter had no right of inheritance to the crown.

P. 34, note 22.—The white and red roſes, devices of York and Lancaſter.

P. 34, note 23.—The ſilver boar was the badge of Richard the Third; whence he was uſually known in his own time by the name of the Boar.

P. 35, note 24.—Eleanor of Caſtile died a few years after the conqueſt of Wales. The heroic proof ſhe gave of her affection for her lord is well known. The monuments of his regret and ſorrow for the loſs of her, are ſtill to be ſeen at Northampton, Gaddington, Waltham, and other places.

P. 35, note 25.—It was the common belief of the Welſh nation, that King Arthur was ſtill alive in Fairyland, and would return again to reign over Britain.

Both Merlin and Talieſſin had propheſied, that the Welſh ſhould regain their ſovereignty over this iſland; which ſeemed to be accompliſhed in the houſe of Tudor.

P. 36, note 26.—Speed, relating an audience given by Queen Elizabeth to Paul Dzialinſki, ambaſſador of Poland, ſays, "And thus ſhe, lion-like riſing, daunted the malapert orator no leſs with her ſtately port and majeſtical deporture, than with the tartneſſe of her princelie checkes."

P. 36, note 27.—Talieſſin, chief of the bards, flouriſhed in the ſixth century. His works are ſtill preſerved, and his memory held in high veneration among his countrymen.

P. 36, note 28.—"Fierce wars and faithful loves ſhall moralize my ſong." Spenſer, Proëme to the *F. Q.*

P. 36, note 29.—Shakeſpeare.

P. 37, note 30.—The ſucceſſion of poets after Milton's time.

P. 37, note 31.—The original argument of this ode, as Mr. Gray had ſet it down in one of the pages of his common-place book, was as follows: "The army of Edward I., as they march through a deep valley, (and approach Mount Snowdon, MS.) are ſuddenly ſtopped by the appearance of a venerable figure ſeated on the ſummit of an inacceſſible rock, who, with a voice more than human, reproaches the king with all the miſery and deſolation (deſolation and miſery, MS.) which he had brought on his country; foretells the misfortunes of the Norman race, and with prophetic ſpirit declares, that all his cruelty ſhall never extinguiſh the noble ardour of poetic genius in this iſland; and that men ſhall never be wanting to celebrate true virtue and valour in immortal ſtrains, to expoſe vice and infamous pleaſure, and boldly cenſure tyranny and oppreſſion. His ſong ended, he precipitates himſelf from the mountain, and is ſwallowed up by the river that rolls at its foot."

"Fine (ſays Mr. Maſon) as the concluſion of this ode is at preſent, I think it would have been ſtill finer, if he could have executed it according to this plan; but, unhappily for his purpoſe, inſtances of Engliſh poets were wanting. Spenſer had that enchanting flow of verſe which was peculiarly calculated to *celebrate virtue and valour;* but he choſe to celebrate them, not literally, but in allegory. Shakeſpeare, who had talents for everything, was undoubtedly capable *of expoſing vice and infamous pleaſure;* and the drama was a proper vehicle for his ſatire; but we do not ever find that he profeſſedly made this his object; nay, we know that, in one inimitable character, he has ſo contrived as to make vices of the worſt kind, ſuch as cowardice, drunkenneſs, diſhoneſty, and lewdneſs, not only laughable, but almoſt amiable; for with all theſe ſins on his head, who can help liking Falſtaff? Milton, of all our great poets, was the only one *who boldly cenſured tyranny and oppreſſion:* but he choſe to deliver this cenſure, not in poetry, but in proſe. Dryden was a mere court paraſite to the moſt infamous of all courts. Pope, with all his laudable deteſtation of corruption and bribery, was a Tory; and Addiſon, though a Whig, and a fine writer, was unluckily not enough of a poet for his purpoſe. On theſe conſiderations Mr. Gray was neceſſitated to change his plan towards the concluſion: hence we perceive, that in the laſt epode he praiſes Spenſer only *for his allegory*, Shakeſpeare *for his powers of moving the paſſions*, and Milton *for his epic excellence.* I remember the ode lay unfiniſhed by him for a year or two on this very account; and I hardly believe that it would ever have had his laſt hand, but for the circumſtance of his hearing Parry play on the Welſh harp at a concert at Cambridge, (ſee Letter xxxv. ſect. iv.) which he often declared inſpired him with the concluſion.

"Mr. Smith, the muſical compoſer and worthy pupil of Mr. Handel, had once an idea of ſetting this ode, and of having it performed by way of ſerenata or oratorio. A common friend of his and Mr. Gray's intereſted himſelf much in this deſign, and drew out a clear analyſis of the ode, that Mr. Smith might more perfectly underſtand the poet's meaning. He converſed alſo with Mr. Gray on the ſubject, who gave him an idea for the overture, and marked alſo ſome paſſages in the ode, in order to aſcertain which ſhould be recitative, which air, what kind of air, and how accompanied. This deſign was, however, not executed; and therefore I ſhall only (in order to give the reader a taſte of Mr. Gray's muſical feelings) inſert in this place what his ſentiments were concerning the overture. 'It ſhould be ſo contrived as to be a proper introduction to the ode; it might conſiſt of two movements, the firſt deſcriptive of the horror and confuſion of battle, the laſt a march grave and majeſtic, but expreſſing the exultation and inſolent ſecurity of conqueſt. This movement ſhould be compoſed entirely of wind inſtruments, except the kettle-drum heard at intervals. The *da capo* of it muſt be ſuddenly broke in upon, and put to ſilence by the clang of the harp in a tumultuous rapid movement, joined with the voice, all at once, and not uſhered in by any ſymphony. The harmony may be ſtrengthened by any other ſtringed inſtrument; but the harp ſhould everywhere prevail, and form the continued running accompaniment, ſubmitting itſelf to nothing but the voice.'

"I cannot (adds Mr. Maſon) quit this and the preceding ode, without ſaying a word or two concerning the obſcurity which has been imputed to them, and the preference which, in conſequence, has been given to his Elegy. It ſeems as if the perſons, who hold this opinion, ſuppoſe that every ſpecies of poetry ought to be equally clear and intelligible: than which poſition nothing can be more repugnant to the ſeveral ſpecific natures of compoſition, and to the practice of ancient art. Not to take Pindar and his odes for an example, (though what I am here defending were written profeſſedly in imitation of him,) I would aſk, are all the writings of Horace, his Epiſtles, Satires, and Odes, equally perſpicuous? Among his odes, ſeparately conſidered, are there not remarkable differences of this very kind? Is the ſpirit and meaning of that which begins, 'Deſcende cœlo, et dic, age, tibiâ,' Ode iv. lib. 3, ſo readily comprehended as 'Perſicos odi, puer, apparatus,' Ode xxxviii. lib. 1? And is the latter a finer piece of lyrical compoſition on that account? Is 'Integer vitæ, ſceleriſque purus,' Ode xxii. lib. 1, ſuperior to 'Pindarum quiſquis ſtudet æmulari,' Ode ii. lib. 4: becauſe it may be underſtood at the firſt reading, and the latter not without much ſtudy and reflection? Now between theſe odes, thus compared, there is ſurely equal difference in point of perſpicuity, as between the Progreſs of Poeſy, and the Proſpect of Eton College; the Ode on the Spring, and the Bard. 'But,' ſay theſe objectors, 'the end of poetry is univerſally to pleaſe. Obſcurity, by taking off from our pleaſure, deſtroys that end.' I will grant that if the obſcurity be great, conſtant, and inſurmountable, this is certainly true; but if it be only found in particular paſſages, proceeding from the nature of the ſubject and the very genius of the compoſition, it does not rob us of our pleaſure, but ſuperadds a new one, which ariſes from conquering a difficulty; and the pleaſure which accrues from a difficult paſſage, when well underſtood, provided the paſſage itſelf be a fine one, is always more permanent than that which we diſcover at the firſt glance. The Lyric Muſe, like other fine ladies, requires to be courted, and retains her admirers the longer for not having yielded too readily to their ſolicitations. This argument, ending as it does in a ſort of ſimile, will, I am perſuaded, not only have its force with the intelligent readers (the ΣΥΝΕΤΟΙ), but alſo with the men of faſhion: as to critics of a lower claſs, it may be ſufficient to tranſcribe, for their improvement, an unfiniſhed remark, or rather maxim, which I found amongſt our author's papers; and which he probably wrote on occaſion of the common preference given to his Elegy. 'The *Goût dè comparíſon* (as Bruyere ſtyles it) is the only taſte of ordinary minds. They do not know the ſpecific excellence either of an author or a compoſition: for inſtance, they do not know that Tibullus ſpoke the language of nature and love; that Horace ſaw the vanities and follies of mankind with the moſt penetrating eye, and touched them to the quick; that Virgil ennobled even the moſt common images by the graces of a glowing, melodious, and well-adapted expreſſion; but they do know that Virgil was a better poet than Horace; and that Horace's Epiſtles do not run ſo well as the Elegies of Tibullus.'"

P. 39, note 1.—This Ode was performed in the Senate-Houſe at Cambridge, July 1, 1769, at the Inſtallation of His Grace Auguſtus Henry Fitzroy, Duke of Grafton, Chancellor of the Univerſity. This Ode is printed with the diviſions adopted by the compoſer, Dr. Randall, then Profeſſor of Muſic at Cambridge.

P. 41, note 2.—Mary de Valentia, Counteſs of Pembroke, daughter of Guy de Chatillon, Comte de St. Paul in France; of whom tradition ſays, that her huſband, Audemar de Valentia, Earl of Pembroke, was ſlain at a tournament on the day of his nuptials. She was the foundreſs of Pembroke College or Hall, under the name of Aula Mariæ de Valentia.

Elizabeth de Burg, Counteſs of Clare, was wife of John de Burg, ſon and heir of the Earl of Ulfter, and daughter of Gilbert de Clare, Earl of Gloucefter, by Joan of Acres, daughter of Edward the Firft. She founded Clare Hall.

P. 41, note 3.—Elizabeth Widville, wife of Edward the Fourth, hence called the paler rofe, as being of the Houfe of York. She added to the foundation of Margaret of Anjou.

P. 41, note 4.—Henry the Sixth and Eighth. The former the founder of King's, the latter the greateft benefactor to Trinity College.

P. 43, note 5.—Countefs of Richmond and Derby; the mother of Henry the Seventh, foundrefs of St. John's and Chrift's Colleges.

P. 43, note 6.—The Countefs was a Beaufort, and married to a Tudor: hence the application of this line to the Duke of Grafton, who claims defcent from both thefe families.

P. 44, note 7.—Lord Treafurer Burleigh was chancellor of the Univerfity in the reign of Queen Elizabeth.

P. 45, note 1.—To be found in the Orcades of Thormodus Torfæus; Hafniæ, 1697, folio; and alfo in Bartholinus, p. 617. lib. iii. c. 1. 4to. (The fong of the Weird Sifters, tranflated from the Norwegian, written about 1029. Wharton, MS.)

P. 45, note 2.—" How quick they wheel'd, and, flying, behind them fhot Sharp *fleet of arrowy fhow'r.*"—*Par. Reg.* iii. 324.

" The noife of battle hurtled in the air."—*Julius Cæfar,* Act ii. Sc. 2.

P. 51, note 1.—The original is to be found in Sæmund's *Edda,* and in Bartholinus, *De Caufis contemnendæ Mortis;* Hafniæ, 1689, quarto, Lib. iii. c. ii. p. 632. (See Warton, *Hift. of E. Poetry,* vol. i. p. xli. And Warton's Pope, vol. ii. p. 70. " This Ode, I think with Lord Orford, equal to any of Gray's.")

P. 51, note 2.—Hela, in the Edda, is defcribed with a dreadful countenance, and her body half flefh colour, and half blue.

P. 52, note 3.—The original word is *Valgalldr;* from *Valr* mortuus, and *Galldr* incantatio.

P. 54, note 4.—Women were looked upon by the Gothic nations as having a peculiar insight into futurity; and some there were that made profession of magic arts and divination. These travelled round the country, and were received in every house with great respect and honour. Such a woman bore the name of Volva Seidkona or Spakona. The dress of Thorbiorga, one of these prophetesses, is described at large in Eirik's *Rauda Sogu*, (apud Bartholin., lib. i. cap. iv. p. 688.) "She had on a blue vest spangled all over with stones, a necklace of glass beads, and a cap made of the skin of a black lamb lined with white cat-skin. She leaned on a staff adorned with brass, with a round head set with stones; and was girt with an Hunlandish belt, at which hung her pouch full of magical instruments. Her buskins were of rough calf-skin, bound on with thongs studded with knobs of brass, and her gloves of white cat-skin, the fur turned inwards," &c. They were also called *Fiolkyngi*, or *Fiolkunnug*, i.e. Multi-scia; and *Uisindakona*, i.e. Oraculorum Mulier; *Nornir*, i.e. Parcæ.

P. 59, note 1.—From Evans, *Spec. of the Welsh Poetry*, 1764, quarto, p. 25, where is a prose version of this Poem, and p. 127. Owen succeeded his father Griffith app Cynan in the principality of N. Wales, A.D. 1137. This battle was fought in the year 1157. Jones, *Relics*, vol. ii. p. 36.

P. 63, note 1.—See S. Turner's *Vindication of Ancient British Poems*, p. 50. Warton's *Engl. Poetry*, vol. i. p. lxiii.

P. 64, note 2.—This and the following short fragment ought to have appeared among the Posthumous Pieces of Gray; but it was thought preferable to insert them in this place, with the preceding fragment from the Gododin. See Jones, *Relics*, vol. i. p. 17.

P. 69, note 1.—This lady, the wife of Dr. John Clerke, physician at Epsom, died April 27, 1757; and was buried in the church of Beckenham, Kent.

P. 69, note 2.— "To hide her cares her only art,
Her pleasure, pleasures to impart,

In ling'ring pain, in death resign'd,
Her latest agony of mind
Was felt for him, who could not save
His all from an untimely grave."—MS.

P. 71, note 1.—This Epitaph was written at the request of Mr. Frederick Montagu, who intended to have inscribed it on a monument at Bellisle, at the siege of which Sir W. Williams was killed, 1761.

Sir William Peere Williams, bart., a captain in Burgoyne's dragoons.

P. 73, note 1.—The manuscript variations in this poem, in the Wharton papers, agree generally with those published by Mr. Mathias, vol. i. p. 65, in his edition of Gray's Works.

P. 73, note 2.— " squilla di lontano
Che paia 'l giorno pianger, che si muore."
Dante, Purgat. l. 8.

P. 78, note 3.—" Ch' i' veggio nel pensier, dolce mio fuoco,
Fredda una lingua, e due begli occhi chiusi
Rimaner doppo noi pien di faville."—*Petr.* Son. clxx.

P. 81, note 4.— " paventosa speme."—*Petr.* Son. cxiv.

P. 83, note 1.—Gray's Elegy in a Country Church-yard, previous to its publication, was handed about in manuscript; and had amongst other admirers the Lady Cobham, who resided at the mansion-house Stoke Pogeis. The performance inducing her to wish for the author's acquaintance, her relation, Miss Speed, and Lady Schaub, then at her house, undertook to effect it. These two ladies waited on the author at his aunt's solitary habitation, where he at that time resided; and not finding him at home, they left a card behind them. Mr. Gray, surprised at such a compliment, returned the visit. And as the beginning of this acquaintance bore some appearance of romance, he soon after gave a humorous account of it in the following copy of verses, which he entitled " A Long Story." Printed in 1753 with Mr. Bentley's designs, and repeated in a second edition. MS.

This Poem was rejected by Gray in the Collection published by himself.

P. 83, note 2.—Sir Chriſtopher Hatton, promoted by Queen Elizabeth for his graceful perſon and fine dancing.

P. 89, note 3.—*Styack*] The houſekeeper.

P. 90, note 4.—*Squib*] Groom of the chamber.

P. 90, note 5.—*Groom*] The ſteward.

P. 90, note 6.—*Macleane*] A famous highwayman hanged the week before.

P. 93, note 1.—Left unfiniſhed by Gray. With additions by Maſon, diſtinguiſhed by inverted commas.

P. 101, note 1.—See *Maſon's Memoirs*, vol. iii. p. 75. Suppoſed to be written about the year 1742, when Gray returned to Cambridge.

P. 110, note 1.—This couplet, which was intended to have been introduced in the Poem on the Alliance of Education and Government, is much too beautiful to be loſt. Maſon, vol. iii. p. 114.

P. 111, note 1.—Theſe were in compliment to Bentley, who drew a ſet of deſigns for Gray's poems, particularly a head-piece to the "Long Story."

P. 112, note 2.—The words within the inverted commas were ſupplied by Maſon.

P. 115, note 1.—The following Lines by Gray firſt appeared in Warton's edition of Pope, vol. i. p. 285.

P. 117, note 1.—Written at the requeſt of Miſs Speed, to an old air of Geminiani :—the thought from the French.

This Song is in this edition printed from the copy as it appears in H. Walpole's Letters to the Counteſs of Aileſbury. See his Works, vol. v. p. 561.

P. 119, note 1.—Written at Denton in the Spring of 1766.

P. 120, note 2.—Theſe initials ſtand for "Mungo's, Rigby's, Bradſhaw's."

P. 121, note 1.—These verses were written a short time previous to the election of a high-steward of the University of Cambridge, for which office the noble lord alluded to (Lord Sandwich) made an active canvass.

P. 135, note 1.—Printed in the Cambridge Collection, 1736, fol.

P. 139, note 1.—This copy of verses was written by desire of the College, in 1737.

P. 162, note 1.—From *Le Rime di Messer Petrarca*, p. 208. Parigi, 1838.

P. 165, note 1.—*Anthologia Græca*, p. 296.

P. 165, note 2.—Ibid. p. 314.

P. 167, note 3.—Ibid. p. 317.

P. 167, note 4.—Ibid. p. 315.

P. 167, note 5.—Ibid. p. 323.

P. 169, note 6.—Ibid. p. 332. Catullianam illam spirat mollitiem.

P. 169, note 7.—Ibid. p. 332. "Elegantissimum hercle fragmentum, quod sic Latinè nostro modo adumbravimus."

P. 171, note 8.—Ibid. p. 354.

P. 171, note 9.—Ibid. p. 186.

P. 173, note 10.—Ibid. p. 474.

P. 173, note 11.—Ibid. p. 452.

LETTERS.

Letter I.

MR. GRAY TO MR. WEST.

PERMIT me again to write to you, though I have ſo long neglected my duty, and forgive my brevity, when I tell you it is occaſioned wholly by the hurry I am in to get to a place where I expect to meet with no other pleaſure than the ſight of you; for I am preparing for London in a few days at furtheſt. I do not wonder in the leaſt at your frequent blaming my indolence, it ought rather to be called ingratitude, and I am obliged to your goodneſs for ſoftening ſo harſh an appellation. When we meet, it will, however, be my greateſt of pleaſures to know what you do, what you read, and how you ſpend your time, &c. &c. and to tell you what I do not read, and how I do not, &c. for almoſt all the employment of my hours may be beſt explained by negatives; take my word and experience upon it, doing nothing is a moſt amuſing buſineſs; and yet neither ſomething nor nothing gives me any pleaſure. When you have ſeen one of my days, you have ſeen a whole year of my life; they go round and round like the blind horſe in the mill, only he has the ſatisfaction of fancying he makes a progreſs and gets ſome ground; my eyes are open enough to ſee the ſame dull proſpect, and to know that having made four-and-twenty ſteps more, I ſhall be juſt where I was; I may, better than moſt people, ſay my life is but a ſpan, were I not afraid leſt you ſhould not believe that a perſon ſo ſhort-lived could write even ſo long a letter as this; in ſhort, I believe I muſt not ſend you the hiſtory of my own time, till I can ſend you that alſo of the reformation. However, as the moſt undeſerving people in the world muſt ſure have the vanity to wiſh ſomebody had a regard for them, ſo I need not wonder at my own, in being pleafed that you care about me. You need not doubt, therefore, of having a firft row in the front box of my little heart, and I believe you are not in danger of being crowded there; it is afking you to an old play, indeed, but you will be candid enough to excufe the whole piece for the fake of a few tolerable lines.

For this little while paft I have been playing with Statius; we yefterday had a game at quoits together; you will eafily forgive me for having broke his head, as you have a little pique to him. I fend you my tranflation which I did not engage in becaufe I liked that part of the Poem, nor do I now fend it to you becaufe I think it deferves it, but merely to fhow you how I mifpend my days.

* * * * *

P. PAPINII STATII THEBAIDOS LIB. VI. V. 646.

TUNC vocat, emiſſo ſi quis decernere diſco
Impiger, et vires velit oſtentare ſuperbas.
It juſſus Pterelas, et aënæ lubrica maſſæ
Pondera vix toto curvatus corpore juxta
Dejicit: inſpectant taciti, expenduntque laborem
Inachidæ. Mox turba ruunt: duo gentis Achææ,
Tres Ephyrëiadæ, Piſâ ſatus unus, Acarnan
Septimus: et plures agitabat gloria, ni ſe
Arduus Hippomedon caveâ ſtimulante tuliſſet
In medios, latèque ferens ſub pectore dextro
Orbem alium: Hunc potius, juvenes, qui mœnia ſaxis

THEN thus the King:—Adraſtus.
"Whoe'er the quoit can wield,
And furtheſt ſend its weight athwart the field,
Let him ſtand forth his brawny arm to boaſt."
Swift at the word, from out the gazing hoſt,
Young Pterelas with ſtrength unequal drew,
Labouring, the diſc, and to ſmall diſtance threw.
The band around admire the mighty maſs,
A ſlipp'ry weight, and form'd of poliſh'd braſs.
The love of honour bade two youths advance,
Achaians born, to try the glorious chance;
A third aroſe, of Acarnania he,
Of Piſa one, and three from Ephyre;
Nor more, for now Neſimachus's ſon,—(*Hippomedon,*)
By acclamations rouſed, came tow'ring on.
Another orb upheaved his ſtrong right hand,
Then thus: "Ye Argive flower, ye warlike band,

Frangere, qui Tyrias dejectum vaditis arces,
Hunc rapite: ast illud cui non jaculabile dextræ
Pondus? Et abreptum nullo conamine jecit
In latus. Absistunt procul, attonitique fatentur
Cedere: vix unus Phlegyas, acerque Menestheus
(Hos etiam pudor et magni tenuere parentes)
Promisere manum: concessit cetera pubes
Sponte, et adorato rediit ingloria disco.
Qualis Bistoniis clypeus Mavortis in arvis
Luce malâ Pangæa ferit, solemque refulgens
Territat, incussâque Dei grave mugit ab hastâ.
Pisæus Phlegyas opus inchoat, et simul omnes
Abstulit in se oculos exhausto corpore virtus
Promissa: ac primum terrâ discumque manumque
Asperat; excusso mox circum pulvere versat,
Quod latus in digitos, mediæ quod certius ulnæ
Conveniat; non artis egens: hic semper amori
Ludus erat, patriæ non tantum ubi laudis obiret
Sacra, sed alternis Alpheon utrimque solebat

Who truſt your arms ſhall raſe the Tyrian towers,
And batter Cadmus' walls with ſtony ſhowers,
Receive a worthier load; yon puny ball
Let youngſters toſs:"—
He ſaid, and ſcornful flung th' unheeded weight
Aloof; the champions, trembling at the ſight,
Prevent diſgrace, the palm deſpair'd reſign;
All but two youths th' enormous orb decline,
Theſe conſcious ſhame withheld, and pride of noble line.
As bright and huge the ſpacious circle lay,
With double light it beam'd againſt the day:
So glittering ſhows the Thracian Godhead's ſhield,
With ſuch a gleam affrights Pangæa's field,
When blazing 'gainſt the ſun it ſhines from far,
And, claſh'd, rebellows with the din of war.
Phlegyas the long-expected play began,
Summon'd his ſtrength, and call'd forth all the man.
All eyes were bent on his experienced hand;
For oft in Piſa's ſports, his native land
Admired that arm, oft on Alpheus' ſhore

Metiri ripis, et, quâ latiſſima diſtant,
Non unquam merſo tranſmittere flumina diſco.
Ergo operum fidens non protinus horrida campi
Jugera, ſed cœlo dextram metitur, humique
Preſſus utroque genu, collecto ſanguine diſcum
Ipſe ſuper ſeſe rotat, atque in nubila condit.
Ille citus ſublime petit, ſimiliſque cadenti
Creſcit in adverſum, tandemque exhauſtus ab alto
Tardior in terram redit, atque immergitur arvis.
Sic cadit, attonitis quoties avellitur aſtris,
Solis opaca ſoror: procul auxiliantia gentes
Æra crepant, fruſtràque timent: at Theſſala victrix
Ridet anhelantes audito carmine bigas.

* * * * *

The pond'rous braſs in exerciſe he bore;
Where flow'd the wideſt ſtream he took his ſtand;
Sure flew the diſc from his unerring hand,
Nor ſtopp'd till it had cut the further ſtrand.
And now in duſt the poliſh'd ball he roll'd,
Then graſp'd its weight, eluſive of his hold;
Now fitting to his gripe and nervous arm,
Suſpends the crowd with expectation warm;
Nor tempts he yet the plain, but hurl'd upright,
Emits the maſs, a prelude of his might;
Firmly he plants each knee, and o'er his head,
Collecting all his force, the circle ſped;
It towers to cut the clouds; now through the ſkies
Sings in its rapid way, and ſtrengthens as it flies;
Anon, with ſlacken'd rage comes quiv'ring down,
Heavy and huge, and cleaves the ſolid ground.
So from th' aſtoniſh'd ſtars, her nightly train,
The ſun's pale ſiſter, drawn by magic ſtrain,
Deſerts precipitant her darken'd ſphere:
In vain the nations with officious fear

*　　*　　*　　*　　*

Tertius Hippomedon valida ad certamina tardos
Molitur greſſus; namque illum corde ſub alto
Et caſus Phlegyæ monet, et fortuna Meneſthei.
Erigit aſſuetum dextræ geſtamen, et altè
Suſtentans, rigidumque latus, forteſque lacertos
Conſulit, ac vaſto contorquet turbine, et ipſe
Proſequitur: fugit horrendo per inania ſaltu,
Jamque procul meminit dextræ, ſervatque tenorem
Diſcus; nec dubiâ junctâve Meneſthea victum
Tranſabiit metâ: longe ſuper æmula ſigna
Conſedit, virideſque humeros, et opaca Theatri
Culmina, ceu latæ tremefecit mole ruinæ.

Their cymbals toſs, and ſounding braſs explore;
Th' Æmonian hag enjoys her dreadful hour,
And ſmiles malignant on the labouring power.
  Third in the labours of the diſc came on,
With ſturdy ſtep and ſlow, Hippomedon;
Artful and ſtrong he poiſed the well-known weight
By Phlegyas warn'd, and fired by Mneſtheus' fate,
That to avoid, and this to emulate.
His vigorous arm he tried before he flung,
Braced all his nerves, and every ſinew ſtrung;
Then, with a tempeſt's whirl, and wary eye,
Purſued his caſt, and hurl'd the orb on high;
The orb on high tenacious of its courſe,
True to the mighty arm that gave it force,
Far overleaps all bound, and joys to ſee
Its ancient lord ſecure of victory.
The theatre's green height and woody wall
Tremble ere it precipitates its fall;
The ponderous maſs ſinks in the cleaving ground,
While vales and woods and echoing hills rebound.

Quale vaporiferâ ſaxum Polyphemus ab Ætnâ
Lucis egente manû, tamen in veſtigia puppis
Auditæ, juxtaque inimicum exegit Ulixen.

*   *   *   *   *

Tunc genitus Talao victori tigrin inanem
Ire jubet, fulvo quæ circumfuſa nitebat
Margine, et extremos auro manſueverat ungues.

As when from Ætna's ſmoking ſummit broke,
The eyeleſs Cyclops heaved the craggy rock ;
Where Ocean frets beneath the daſhing oar,
And parting ſurges round the veſſel roar ;
'Twas there he aim'd the meditated harm,
And ſcarce Ulyſſes ſcaped his giant arm.
A tiger's pride the victor bore away,
With native ſpots and artful labour gay,
A ſhining border round the margin roll'd,
And calm'd the terrors of his claws in gold.

Cambridge, May 8, 1736.

Letter II.

MR. GRAY TO MR. WEST.

YOU muſt know that I do not take degrees, and, after this term, ſhall have nothing more of college impertinences to undergo, which I truſt will be ſome pleaſure to you, as it is a great one to me. I have endured lectures daily and hourly ſince I came laſt, ſupported by the hopes of being ſhortly at full liberty to give myſelf up to my friends and claſſical companions, who, poor ſouls! though I ſee them fallen into great contempt with moſt people here, yet I cannot help ſticking to them, and out of a ſpirit of obſtinacy (I think) love them the better for it; and indeed, what can I do elſe? Muſt I plunge into metaphyſics? Alas, I cannot ſee in the dark; nature has not furniſhed me with the optics of a cat. Muſt I pore upon mathematics? Alas, I cannot ſee in too much light; I am no eagle. It is very poſſible that two and two make four, but I would not give four farthings to demonſtrate this ever ſo clearly; and if theſe be the profits of life, give me the amuſements of it. The people I behold all around me, it ſeems, know all this and more, and yet I do not know one of them who inſpires me with any ambition of being like him. Surely it was of this place, now Cambridge, but formerly known by the name of Babylon, that the prophet ſpoke when he ſaid, "the wild beaſts of the deſert ſhall dwell there, and their houſes ſhall be full of doleful creatures, and owls ſhall build there, and ſatyrs ſhall dance there; their forts and towers ſhall be a den for ever, a joy of wild aſſes; there ſhall the great owl make her neſt, and lay and hatch and gather under her ſhadow; it ſhall be a court of dragons; the ſcreech owl alſo ſhall reſt there, and find for herſelf a place of reſt." You ſee here is a pretty collection of deſolate animals, which is verified in this town to a tittle, and perhaps it may alſo allude to your habitation, for you know all types may be taken by abundance of handles; however, I defy your owls to match mine.

If the default of your ſpirits and nerves be nothing but the effect of the hyp, I have no more to ſay. We all muſt ſubmit to that wayward queen; I too in no ſmall degree own her ſway,

I feel her influence while I ſpeak her power.

But if it be a real diſtemper, pray take more care of your health, if not for your own at leaſt for our ſakes, and do not be ſo ſoon weary of this little world: I do not know what refined friendſhips you may have contracted in the other, but pray do not be in a hurry to ſee your acquaintance above; among your terreſtrial familiars, however, though I ſay it, that ſhould not ſay it, there poſitively is not one that has a greater eſteem for you than yours moſt ſincerely, &c.

Peterhouſe, December, 1736.

Letter III.

MR. GRAY TO MR. WALPOLE.

YOU can never weary me with the repetition of any thing that makes me ſenſible of your kindneſs; ſince that has been the only idea of any ſocial happineſs that I have almoſt ever received, and which (begging your pardon for thinking ſo differently from you in ſuch caſes) I would by no means have parted with for an exemption from all the uneaſineſs mixed with it: but it would be unjuſt to imagine my taſte was any rule for yours; for which reaſon my letters are ſhorter and leſs frequent than they would be, had I any materials but myſelf to entertain you with. Love and brown ſugar muſt be a poor regale for one of your goût, and, alas! you know I am by trade a grocer. Scandal (if I had any) is a merchandize you do not profeſs dealing in; now and then, indeed, and to oblige a friend, you may perhaps ſlip a little out of your pocket, as a decayed gentlewoman would a piece of right mecklin, or a little quantity of run tea, but this only now and then, not to make a practice of it. Monſters appertaining to this climate you have ſeen already, both wet and dry. So you perceive within how narrow bounds my pen is circumſcribed, and the whole contents of my ſhare in our correſpondence may be reduced under the two heads of 1ſt, you, 2ndly, I; the firſt is, indeed, a ſubject to expatiate upon, but you might laugh at me for talking about what I do not underſtand; the ſecond is ſo tiny, ſo tireſome, that you ſhall hear no more of it, than that it is ever yours.

Peterhouſe, December 23, 1736.

Letter IV.

MR. GRAY TO MR. WEST.

AFTER a month's expectation of you, and a fortnight's despair, at Cambridge, I am come to town, and to better hopes of seeing you. If what you sent me last be the product of your melancholy, what may I not expect from your more cheerful hours? For by this time the ill health that you complain of is (I hope) quite departed; though, if I were self-interested, I ought to wish for the continuance of any thing that could be the occasion of so much pleasure to me. Low spirits are my true and faithful companions; they get up with me, go to bed with me, make journeys and returns as I do; nay, and pay visits, and will even affect to be jocose, and force a feeble laugh with me; but most commonly we sit alone together, and are the prettiest insipid company in the world. However, when you come,

I believe they muſt undergo the fate of all humble companions, and be diſcarded. Would I could turn them to the ſame uſe that you have done, and make an Apollo of them. If they could write ſuch verſes with me, not hartſhorn, nor ſpirit of amber, nor all that furniſhes the cloſet of an apothecary's widow, ſhould perſuade me to part with them: But, while I write to you, I hear the bad news of Lady Walpole's death on Saturday night laſt. Forgive me if the thought of what my poor Horace muſt feel on that account, obliges me to have done in reminding you that I am yours, &c.

London, Aug. 22, 1737.

Letter V.

MR. GRAY TO MR. WALPOLE.

I WAS hindered in my laſt, and ſo could not give you all the trouble I would have done. The deſcription of a road, which your coach wheels have ſo often honoured, it would be needleſs to give you; ſuffice it that I arrived ſafe[1] at my Uncle's, who is a great hunter in imagination; his dogs take up every chair in the houſe, ſo I am forced to ſtand at this preſent writing; and though the gout forbids him galloping after them in the field, yet he continues ſtill to regale his ears and noſe with their comfortable noiſe and ſtink. He holds me mighty cheap, I perceive, for walking when I ſhould ride, and reading when I ſhould hunt. My comfort amidſt all this is, that I have at the diſtance of half a mile, through a green lane, a foreſt (the vulgar call it a common) all my own, at leaſt as good as ſo, for I ſpy no human thing in it but myſelf. It is a little chaos of mountains and precipices; mountains, it is true, that do not aſcend much above the clouds, nor are the declivities quite ſo amazing as Dover cliff; but juſt ſuch hills as people who love their necks as well as I do may venture to climb, and crags that give the eye as much pleaſure as if they were more dangerous: Both vale and hill are covered with moſt venerable beeches, and other very reverend vegetables, that, like moſt other ancient people, are always dreaming out their old ſtories to the winds,

And as they bow their hoary tops relate,
In murm'ring ſounds, the dark decrees of fate;
While viſions, as poetic eyes avow,
Cling to each leaf, and ſwarm on every bough.

At the foot of one of theſe ſquats ME I (il penſeroſo), and there grow to the trunk for a whole morning. The timorous hare and ſportive ſquirrel gambol around me like Adam in Paradiſe, before he had an Eve; but I think he did not uſe to read Virgil, as I commonly do there. In this ſituation I often converſe with my Horace, aloud too, that is talk to you, but I do not remember that I ever heard you anſwer me. I beg pardon for taking all the converſation to myſelf, but it is entirely your own fault. We have old Mr. Southern at a Gentleman's houſe a little way off, who often comes to ſee us; he is now ſeventy-ſeven years old, and has almoſt wholly loſt his memory; but is as agreeable as an old man can be, at leaſt I perſuade myſelf ſo when I look at him, and think of Iſabella and Oroonoko. I ſhall be in Town in about three weeks. Adieu.

September, 1737.

Letter VI.

MR. GRAY TO MR. WALPOLE.[2]

I SYMPATHIZE with you in the ſufferings which you foreſee are coming upon you. We are both at preſent, I imagine, in no very agreeable ſituation; for my part I am under the misfortune of having nothing to do, but it is a miſfortune which, thank my ſtars, I can pretty well bear. You are in a confuſion of wine, and roaring, and hunting, and tobacco, and, heaven be praiſed, you too can pretty well bear it; while our evils are no more I believe we ſhall not much repine. I imagine, however, you will rather chooſe to converſe with the living dead, that adorn the walls of your apartments, than with the dead living that deck the middles of them; and prefer a picture of ſtill life to the realities of a noiſy one, and as I gueſs, will imitate what you prefer, and for an hour or two at noon will ſtick yourſelf up as formal as if you had been fixed in your frame for theſe hundred years, with a pink or roſe in one hand, and a great ſeal ring on the other. Your name, I aſſure you, has been propagated in theſe countries by a convert of yours, one * *, he has brought over his whole family to you; they were before pretty good Whigs, but now they are abſolute Walpolians. We have hardly any body in the pariſh but knows exactly the dimenſions of the hall and ſaloon at Houghton, and begin to believe that the lanthorn[3] is not ſo great a conſumer of the fat of the land as diſaffected perſons have ſaid: For your reputation, we keep to ourſelves your not hunting nor drinking hogan, either of which here would be ſufficient to lay your honour in the duſt. To-morrow ſe'nnight I hope to be in Town, and not long after at Cambridge. I am, &c.

Burnham, Sept. 1737.

Letter VII.

MR. WEST TO MR. GRAY.

RECEIVING no anſwer to my laſt letter, which I writ above a month ago, I muſt own I am a little uneaſy. The ſlight ſhadow of you which I had in Town, has only ſerved to endear you to me the more. The moments I paſt with you made a ſtrong impreſſion upon me. I ſingled you out for a friend, and I would have you know me to be yours, if you deem me worthy.—Alas, Gray, you cannot imagine how miſerably my time paſſes away. My health, and nerves, and ſpirits are, thank my ſtars, the very worſt, I think in Oxford. Four and twenty hours of pure unalloyed health together, are as unknown to me as the 400,000 characters in the Chineſe vocabulary. One of my complaints has of late been ſo over-civil as to viſit me regularly once a month—jam certus conviva. This is a painful nervous head-ach, which perhaps you have ſometimes heard me ſpeak of before. Give me leave to ſay, I find no phyſic comparable to your letters. If, as it is ſaid in Eccleſiaſticus, " Friendſhip be the phyſic of the mind," preſcribe to me, dear Gray, as often and as much as you think proper, I ſhall be a moſt obedient patient.

Non ego
Fidis iraſcar medicis, offendar amicis.

I venture here to write you down a Greek epigram,[4] which I lately turned into Latin, and hope you will excuſe it.

ΠΟΣΕΙΔΙΠΠΟΥ.

Τὸν τριετῆ παίζοντα περὶ φρέαρ Ἀστυάνακτα
  Εἴδωλον μορφᾶς κωφὸν ἐπεσπάσατο.
Ἐκ δ' ὕδατος τὸν παῖδα διάβροχον ἥρπασε μάτηρ,
  Σκεπτομένα ζωᾶς εἴ τινα μοῖραν ἔχει.
Νύμφας δ' οὐκ ἐμίηνεν ὁ νήπιος, ἀλλ' ἐπὶ γούνων
  Ματρὸς κοιμηθεὶς τὸν βαθὺν ὕπνον ἔχει.

Perſpicui puerum ludentem in margine rivi;
  Immerſit vitreæ limpidus error aquæ:
At gelido ut mater moribundum e flumine traxit
  Credula, & amplexu funus inane fovet;

Paulatim puer in dilecto pectore, ſomno
Languidus, æternùm lumina compoſuit.

Adieu! I am going to my tutor's lectures on one Puffendorff, a very juriſprudent author as you ſhall read on a ſummer's day. Believe me yours, &c.

Chriſt Church, Dec. 2, 1738.

Letter VIII.

MR. GRAY TO MR. WEST.

LITERAS mi Favonî! abs te demum, nudiuſtertiùs credo, accepi planè mellitas, niſi fortè quà de ægritudine quâdam tuâ dictum: atque hoc ſane mihi habitum eſt non paulò acerbiùs, quod te capitis morbo implicitum eſſe intellexi; oh morbum mihi quam odioſum! qui de induſtria id agit, ut ego in ſingulos menſes, dii boni, quantis jocunditatibus orbarer! quàm ex animo mihi dolendum eſt, quod

Medio de fonte leporum
Surgit amari aliquid.

Salutem mehercule, nolo, tam parvipendas, atq; amicis tam improbè conſulas: quanquam tute fortaſſis—æſtuas anguſto limite mundi, viamq; (ut dicitur) affectas Olympo, nos tamen non eſſe tam ſublimes, utpote qui hiſce in ſordibus & fæce diutius paululum verſari volumus, reminiſcendum eſt: illæ tuæ Muſæ, ſi te ament modo, derelinqui pauliſper non nimis ægrè patientur: indulge, amabo te, pluſquam ſoles, corporis exercitationibus: magis te campus habeat, aprico magis te dedas otio, ut ne id ingenium quod tam cultum curas, diligenter nimis dum foves, officioſarum matrum ritu, interimas. Vide quæſo, quam *ἰατρικῶς* tecum agimus,

ἠδ᾽ ἐπιθήσω
Φάρμαχ᾽ ἅ κεν παύσῃσι μελαινάων ὀδυνάων.[5]

ſi de his pharmacis non ſatis liquet; ſunt feſtivitates meræ, ſunt facetiæ & riſus; quos ego equidem ſi adhibere nequeo, tamen ad præcipiendum (ut medicorum fere mos eſt) certè ſatis ſim; id, quod poeticè ſub finem epiſtolæ luſiſti, mihi gratiſſimum quidem accidit; admodum latinè coctum & conditum tetraſticon, græcam tamen illam *ἀφελείαν* mirificè ſapit: tu quod reſtat, vide, ſodes, hujuſce hominis ignorantiam; cum, unde hoc tibi ſit depromptum, (ut fatear,) prorſus neſcio: ſane ego equidem nihil in capſis reperio quo tibi minimæ partis ſolutio fiat. Vale, & me ut ſoles, ama.

A. D. 11, Kalend. Februar.

Letter IX.

MR. GRAY TO MR. WEST.

BARBARAS ædes aditure mecum
Quas Eris ſemper fovet inquieta,
Lis ubi latè ſonat, et togatum
Æſtuat agmen;

Dulcius quanto, patulis ſub ulmi
Hoſpitæ ramis temerè jacentem
Sic libris horas, tenuique inertes
Fallere Musâ?

Sæpe enim curis vagor expeditâ
Mente; dum, blandam meditans Camænam,
Vix malo rori, meminive feræ
Cedere nocti;

Et, pedes quò me rapiunt, in omni
Colle Parnaſſum videor videre
Fertilem ſylvæ, gelidamque in omni
Fonte Aganippen.

Riſit et Ver me, facileſque Nymphæ
Nare captantem, nec ineleganti,
Manè quicquid de violis eundo
Surripit aura :

Me reclinatum teneram per herbam ;
Quà leves curſus aqua cunque ducit,
Et moras dulci ſtrepitu lapillo
Nectit in omni.

Hæ novo noſtrum ferè pectus anno
Simplices curæ tenuere, cœlum
Quamdiu ſudum explicuit Favonî
Purior hora :

Otia et campos nec adhuc relinquo,
Nec magis Phœbo Clytie fidelis;
(Ingruant venti licet, et ſeneſcat
Mollior æſtas.)

Namque, ceu, lætos hominum labores
Prataque et montes recreante curru,
Purpurâ tractus oriens Eoos
Veſtit, et auro;

Sedulus ſervo veneratus orbem
Prodigum ſplendoris; amœniori
Sive dilectam meditatur igne
Pingere Calpen;

Uſque dum, fulgore magis magis jam
Languido circum, variata nubes
Labitur furtim, viridiſque in umbras
Scena receſſit.

O ego felix, vice ſi (nec unquam
Surgerem rurſus) ſimili cadentem
Parca me lenis ſineret quieto
Fallere Letho!

Multa flagranti radiiſque cincto
Integris ah! quam nihil inviderem,
Cum Dei ardentes medius quadrigas
Sentit Olympus.

Ohe! amicule noſter, et unde, ſodes tu μεσοπάτακτος adeò repente evaſiſti? jam rogitaturum credo. Neſcio hercle, ſic planè habet. Quicquid enim nugarum ἐπὶ σχολῆς inter ambulandum in palimpſeſto ſcriptitavi, hiſce te maxumè impertiri viſum eſt, quippe quem probare, quod meum eſt, aut certè ignoſcere ſolitum probè novi: bonâ tuâ veniâ ſit ſi fortè videar in fine ſubtriſtior; nam riſui jamdudum ſalutem dixi; etiam paulò mœſtitiæ ſtudioſiorem factum ſcias, promptumque, Καινοῖς παλαιὰ δακρύοις στένειν κακά.

O lacrymarum fons, tenero ſacros
Ducentium ortus ex animo; quater
Felix! in imo qui ſcatentem
Pectore te, pia Nympha, ſenſit.

Sed de me ſatis. Cura ut valeas.

Jun. 1738.

Letter X.

MR. GRAY TO MR. WALPOLE.

MY dear Sir, I ſhould ſay Mr. Inſpector General of the Exports and Imports;[6] but that appellation would make but an odd figure in conjunction with the three familiar monoſyllables above written, for

> Non benè conveniunt nec in unâ ſede morantur
> Majeſtas & amor.[7]

Which is, being interpreted, Love does not live at the Cuſtom-houſe; however, by what ſtyle, title, or denomination ſoever you chooſe to be dignified or diſtinguiſhed hereafter, theſe three words will ſtick by you like a burr, and you can no more get quit of theſe and your chriſtian name than St. Anthony could of his pig. My motions at preſent (which you are pleaſed to aſk after) are much like thoſe of a pendulum or (Dr. Longically ſpeaking[8]) oſcillatory. I ſwing from Chapel or Hall home, and from home to Chapel or Hall. All the ſtrange incidents that happen in my journeys and returns I ſhall be ſure to acquaint you with; the moſt wonderful is, that it now rains exceedingly, this has refreſhed the proſpect, as the way for the moſt part lies between green fields on either hand, terminated with buildings at ſome diſtance, caſtles, I preſume, and of great antiquity. The roads are very good, being, as I ſuſpect, the works of Julius Cæſar's army, for they ſtill preſerve, in many places, the appearance of a pavement in pretty good repair, and, if they were not ſo near home, might perhaps be as much admired as the Via Appia; there are at preſent ſeveral rivulets to be croſſed, and which ſerve to enliven the view all around. The country is exceeding fruitful in ravens and ſuch black cattle; but, not to tire you with my travels, I abruptly conclude. Yours, &c.

Auguſt, 1738.

Letter XI.

MR. GRAY TO MR. WEST.

I AM coming away all ſo faſt, and leaving behind me without the leaſt remorſe, all the beauties of Sturbridge Fair. Its white bears may roar, its apes may ring their hands, and crocodiles cry their eyes out, all's one for that; I ſhall not once viſit them, nor ſo much as take my leave. The univerſity has publiſhed a ſevere edict againſt ſchiſmatical congregations, and created half-a-dozen new little procterlings to ſee its orders executed, being under mighty apprehenſions leſt Henley[9] and his gilt tub ſhould come to the Fair and ſeduce their young ones; but their pains are to ſmall purpoſe, for lo, after all, he is not coming.

I am at this inſtant in the very agonies of leaving college, and would not wiſh the worſt of my enemies a worſe ſituation. If you knew the duſt, the old boxes, the bedſteads, and tutors that are about my ears, you would look upon this letter as a great effort of my reſolution and unconcernedneſs in the midſt of evils. I fill up my paper with a looſe ſort of verſion of that ſcene in Paſtor Fido that begins, Care ſelve beati.

Sept. 1738.

Letter XII.

MR. GRAY TO HIS MOTHER.

Amiens, April 1, N. S. 1739.

AS we made but a very ſhort journey to-day, and came to our inn early, I ſit down to give you ſome account of our expedition. On the 29th (according to the ſtyle here) we left Dover at twelve at noon, and with a pretty briſk gale, which pleaſed every body mighty well, except myſelf, who was extremely ſick the whole time; we reached Calais by five: The weather changed, and it began to ſnow hard the minute we got into the harbour, where we took the boat and ſoon landed. Calais is an exceeding old, but very pretty town, and we hardly ſaw any thing there that was not ſo new and ſo different from England, that it ſurpriſed us agreeably. We went the next morning to the great Church, and were at high Maſs (it being Eaſter Monday).

We ſaw alſo the Convents of the Capuchins, and the Nuns of St. Dominic; with theſe laſt we held much converſation, eſpecially with an Engliſh Nun, a Mrs. Davis, of whoſe work I ſent you by the return of the Pacquet, a letter-caſe to remember her by. In the afternoon we took a poſt-chaiſe (it ſtill ſnowing very hard) for Boulogne, which was only eighteen miles further. This chaiſe is a ſtrange ſort of conveyance, of much greater uſe than beauty, reſembling an ill-ſhaped chariot, only with the door opening before inſtead of the ſide; three horſes draw it, one between the ſhafts, and the other two on each ſide, on one of which the poſtillion rides, and drives too: This vehicle will, upon occaſion, go fourſcore miles a-day, but Mr. Walpole, being in no hurry, chooſes to make eaſy journies of it, and they are eaſy ones indeed, for the motion is much like that of a ſedan; we go about ſix miles an hour, and commonly change horſes at the end of it: It is true they are no very graceful ſteeds, but they go well, and through roads which they ſay are bad for France, but to me they ſeem gravel walks and bowling-greens; in ſhort, it would be the fineſt travelling in the world, were it not for the inns, which are moſtly terrible places indeed. But to deſcribe our progreſs ſomewhat more regularly, we came into Boulogne when it was almoſt dark, and went out pretty early on Tueſday morning; ſo that all I can ſay about it is, that it is a large, old, fortified town, with more Engliſh in it than French. On Tueſday we were to go to Abbéville, ſeventeen leagues, or fifty-one ſhort Engliſh miles; but by the way we dined at Montreuil, much to our hearts' content, on ſtinking mutton cutlets, addled eggs, and ditch water. Madame the hoſteſs made her appearance in long lappets of bone lace and a ſack of linſey-woolſey. We ſupped and lodged pretty well at Abbéville, and had time to ſee a little of it before we came out this morning. There are ſeventeen convents in it, out of which we ſaw the chapels of Minims and the Carmelite Nuns. We are now come further thirty miles to Amiens, the chief city of the province of Picardy. We have ſeen the cathedral, which is juſt what that of Canterbury muſt have been before the Reformation. It is about the ſame ſize, a huge Gothic building, beſet on the outſide with thouſands of ſmall ſtatues, and within adorned with beautiful painted windows, and a vaſt number of chapels dreſſed out in all their finery of altar-pieces, embroidery, gilding, and marble. Over the high altar are preſerved, in a very large wrought ſhrine of maſſy gold, the relicks of St. Firmin, their patron ſaint. We went alſo to the chapels of the Jeſuits and Urſuline Nuns, the latter of which is very richly adorned. To-morrow we ſhall lie at Clermont, and next day reach Paris. The country we have paſſed through hitherto has been flat, open, but agreeably diverſified with villages, fields well-cultivated, and little rivers. On every hillock is a windmill, a crucifix, or a Virgin Mary dreſſed in flowers, and a ſarcenet robe; one ſees not many people or carriages on the road; now and then indeed you meet a ſtrolling friar, a countryman with his great muff, or a woman riding aſtride on a little aſs, with ſhort petticoats, and a great head-dreſs of blue wool. * *

Letter XIII.

MR. GRAY TO MR. WEST.

Paris, April 12, 1739.

ENFIN donc me voici à Paris. Mr. Walpole is gone out to ſupper at Lord Conway's, and here I remain alone, though invited too. Do not think I make a merit of writing to you preferably to a good ſupper; for theſe three days we have been here, have actually given me an averſion to eating in general. If hunger be the beſt ſauce to meat, the French are certainly the worſt cooks in the world; for what tables we have ſeen have been ſo delicately ſerved, and ſo profuſely, that, after riſing from one of them, one imagines it impoſſible ever to eat again. And now, if I tell you all I have in my head, you will believe me mad, mais n'importe, courage, allons! for if I wait till my head grow clear and ſettle a little, you may ſtay long enough for a letter. Six days have we been coming hither, which other people do in two; they have not been diſagreeable ones; through a fine, open country, admirable roads, and in an eaſy conveyance; the inns not abſolutely intolerable, and images quite unuſual preſenting themſelves on all hands. At Amiens we ſaw the fine cathedral, and eat pâté de perdrix; paſſed through the park of Chantilly by the Duke of Bourbon's palace, which we only beheld as we paſſed; broke down at Luſarche; ſtopt at St. Denis, ſaw all the beautiful monuments of the Kings of France, and the vaſt treaſures of the abbey, rubies, and emeralds as big as ſmall eggs, crucifixes, and vows, crowns and reliquaries, of ineſtimable value; but of all their curioſities the thing the moſt to our taſtes, and which they indeed do the juſtice to eſteem the glory of their collection, was a vaſe of an entire onyx, meaſuring at leaſt five inches over, three deep, and of great thickneſs. It is at leaſt two thouſand years old, the beauty of the ſtone and ſculpture upon it (repreſenting the myſteries of Bacchus) beyond expreſſion admirable; we have dreamed of it ever ſince. The jolly old Benedictine, that ſhowed us the treaſures, had in his youth been ten years a ſoldier; he laughed at all the relics, was very full of ſtories, and mighty obliging. On Saturday evening we got to Paris, and were driving through the ſtreets a long while before we knew where we were. The minute we came, voilà Milors Holderneſſe, Conway and his brother; all ſtayed ſupper, and till two o'clock in the morning, for here nobody ever ſleeps; it is not the way: Next day go to dine at my Lord Holderneſſe's, there was the Abbé Prevôt, author of the Cleveland, and ſeveral other pieces much eſteemed: The reſt were Engliſh. At night we went to the Pandore; a ſpectacle literally, for it is nothing but a beautiful piece of machinery of three ſcenes. The firſt repreſents the chaos, and by degrees the ſeparation of the elements. The ſecond, the temple of Jupiter, the giving of the box to Pandora. The third, the opening of the box, and all the miſchiefs that enſued. An abſurd deſign, but executed in the higheſt perfection, and that in one of the fineſt theatres in the world; it is the grande ſalle des machines in the Palais des Tuileries. Next day dined at Lord Waldegrave's; then to the opera. Imagine to yourſelf for the drama four acts[1] entirely unconnected with each other, each founded on ſome little hiſtory, ſkilfully taken out of an ancient author, e.g. Ovid's Metamorphoſes, &c. and with great addreſs converted into a French piece of gallantry. For inſtance, that which I ſaw, called the Ballet de la Paix, had its firſt act built upon the ſtory of Nireus. Homer having ſaid he was the handſomeſt man of his time, the poet, imagining ſuch a one could not want a miſtreſs, has given him one. Theſe two come in and ſing ſentiment in lamentable ſtrains, neither air nor recitative; only, to one's great joy, they are every now and then interrupted by a dance, or (to one's great ſorrow) by a chorus that borders the ſtage from one end to the other, and ſcreams, paſt all power of ſimile to repreſent. The ſecond act was Baucis and Philemon. Baucis is a beautiful young ſhepherdeſs, and Philemon her ſwain. Jupiter falls in love with her, but nothing will prevail upon her; ſo it is all mighty well, and the chorus ſing and dance the praiſes of Conſtancy. The two other acts were about

Iphis and Ianthe, and the judgment of Paris. Imagine, I ſay, all this tranſacted by cracked voices, trilling diviſions upon two notes and a half, accompanied by an orcheſtra of humſtrums, and a whole houſe more attentive than if Farinelli ſung, and you will almoſt have formed a juſt notion of the thing. Our aſtoniſhment at their abſurdity you can never conceive; we had enough to do to expreſs it by ſcreaming an hour louder than the whole dramatis perſonæ. We have alſo ſeen twice the Comédie Françoiſe; firſt, the Mahomet Second, a tragedy that has had a great run of late; and the thing itſelf does not want its beauties, but the actors are beyond meaſure delightful. Mademoiſelle Gauſſin (M. Voltaire's Zara) has with a charming (though little) perſon the moſt pathetic tone of voice, the fineſt expreſſion in her face, and moſt proper action imaginable. There is alſo a Dufrêne, who did the chief character, a handſome man and a prodigious fine actor. The ſecond we ſaw was the Philoſophe marié, and here they performed as well in comedy; there is a Mademoiſelle Quinault, ſomewhat in Mrs. Clive's way, and a Monſieur

Grandval, in the nature of Wilks, who is the genteeleſt thing in the world. There are ſeveral more would be much admired in England, and many (whom we have not ſeen) much celebrated here. Great part of our time is ſpent in ſeeing churches and palaces full of fine pictures, &c. the quarter of which is not yet exhauſted. For my part, I could entertain myſelf this month merely with the common ſtreets and the people in them. * * *

Letter XIV.

MR. GRAY TO MR. WEST.

Paris, May 22, 1739.

AFTER the little particulars aforeſaid I ſhould have proceeded to a journal of our tranſactions for this week paſt, ſhould have carried you poſt from hence to Verſailles, hurried you through the gardens to Trianon, back again to Paris, ſo away to Chantilly. But the fatigue is perhaps more than you can bear, and moreover I think I have reaſon to ſtomach your laſt piece of gravity. Suppoſing you were in your ſobereſt mood, I am ſorry you ſhould think me capable of ever being ſo diſſipé, ſo evaporé, as not to be in a condition of reliſhing any thing you could ſay to me. And now, if you have a mind to make your peace with me, arouſe ye from your megrims and your melancholies, and (for exerciſe is good for you) throw away your nightcap, call for your jack-boots, and ſet out with me, laſt Saturday evening, for Verſailles—and ſo at eight o'clock, paſſing through a road ſpeckled with vines, and villas, and hares, and partridges, we arrive at the great avenue, flanked on either hand with a double row of trees about half a mile long, and with the palace itſelf to terminate the view; facing which, on each ſide of you, is placed a ſemi-circle of very handſome buildings, which form the ſtables. Theſe we will not enter into, becauſe you know we are no jockeys. Well! and is this the great front of Verſailles? What a huge heap of littleneſs! it is compoſed, as it were, of three courts, all open to the eye at once, and gradually diminiſhing till you come to the royal apartments, which on this ſide preſent but half a dozen windows and a balcony. This laſt is all that can be called a front, for the reſt is only great wings. The hue of all this maſs is black, dirty red, and yellow; the firſt proceeding from ſtone changed by age; the ſecond, from a mixture of brick; and the laſt, from a profuſion of tarniſhed gilding. You cannot ſee a more diſagreeable tout-enſemble; and, to finiſh the matter, it is all ſtuck over in many places with ſmall buſts of a tawny hue between every two windows. We paſs through this to go into the garden, and here the caſe is indeed altered; nothing can be vaſter and more magnificent than the back front; before it a very ſpacious terrace ſpreads itſelf, adorned with two large baſons; theſe are bordered and lined (as moſt of the others) with white marble, with handſome ſtatues of bronze reclined on their edges. From hence you deſcend a huge flight of ſteps into a ſemi-circle formed by woods, that are cut all around into niches, which are filled with beautiful copies of all the famous antique ſtatues in white marble. Juſt in the midſt is the baſon of Latona; ſhe and her children are ſtanding on the top of a rock in the middle, on the ſides of which are the peaſants, ſome half, ſome totally changed into frogs, all which throw out water at her in great plenty. From this place runs on the great alley, which brings you into a complete round, where is the baſon of Apollo, the biggeſt in the gardens. He is riſing in his car out of the water, ſurrounded by nymphs and tritons, all in bronze, and finely executed, and these, as they play, raise a perfect storm about him; beyond this is the great canal, a prodigious long piece of water, that terminates the whole: All this you have at one coup d'œil in entering the garden, which is truly great. I cannot say as much of the general taste of the place: every thing you behold savours too much of art; all is forced, all is constrained about you; statues and vases sowed every where without distinction; sugar loaves and minced pies of yew; scrawl work of box, and little squirting jets-d'eau, besides a great sameness in the walks, cannot help striking one at first sight, not to mention the silliest of labyrinths, and all Æsop's fables in water; since these were designed in usum Delphini only. Here then we walk by moonlight, and hear the ladies and the nightingales sing. Next morning, being Whitsunday, make ready to go to the Installation of nine Knights du Saint Esprit, Cambis is one:[2] high mass celebrated with music, great crowd, much incense, King, Queen, Dauphin, Mesdames, Cardinals, and Court: Knights arrayed by his Majesty; reverences before the altar, not bows, but curtsies;

ſtiff hams: much tittering among the ladies; trumpets, kettle-drums and fifes. My dear Weſt, I am vaſtly delighted with Trianon, all of us with Chantilly; if you would know why, you muſt have patience, for I can hold my pen no longer, except to tell you that I ſaw Britannicus laſt night; all the characters, particularly Agrippina and Nero, done to perfection; to-morrow Phædra and Hippolitus. We are making you a little bundle of petites pièces; there is nothing in them, but they are acting at preſent; there are too Crebillon's Letters, and Amuſemens ſur le langage des Bêtes, ſaid to be of one Bougeant, a Jeſuit; they are both eſteemed, and lately come out. This day ſe'nnight we go to Rheims.

Letter XV.

MR. GRAY TO HIS MOTHER.

Rheims, June 21, N.S. 1739.

WE have now been ſettled almoſt three weeks in this city, which is more conſiderable upon account of its ſize and antiquity, than from the number of its inhabitants, or any advantages of commerce. There is little in it worth a ſtranger's curioſity, beſides the cathedral church, which is a vaſt Gothic building of a ſurpriſing beauty and lightneſs, all covered over with a profuſion of little ſtatues, and other ornaments. It is here the Kings of France are crowned by the Archbiſhop of Rheims, who is the firſt Peer, and the Primate of the kingdom: The holy veſſel made uſe of on that occaſion, which contains the oil, is kept in the church of St. Nicaſius hard by, and is believed to have been brought by an angel from heaven at the coronation of Clovis, the firſt chriſtian king. The ſtreets in general have but a melancholy aſpect, the houſes all old; the public walks run along the ſide of a great moat under the ramparts, where one hears a continual croaking of frogs; the country round about is one great plain covered with vines, which at this time of the year afford no very pleaſing proſpect, as being not above a foot high. What pleaſures the place denies to the ſight, it makes up to the palate; ſince you have nothing to drink but the beſt champaigne in the world, and all ſort of proviſions equally good. As to other pleaſures, there is not that freedom of converſation among the people of faſhion here, that one ſees in other parts of France; for though they are not very numerous in this place, and conſequently muſt live a good deal together, yet they never come to any great familiarity with one another. As my Lord Conway had ſpent a good part of his time among them, his brother, and we with him, were ſoon introduced into all their aſſemblies: As ſoon as you enter, the lady of the houſe preſents each of you a card, and offers you a party at quadrille; you ſit down, and play forty deals without intermiſſion, excepting one quarter of an hour, when every body riſes to eat of what they call the goûter, which ſupplies the place of our tea, and is a ſervice of wine, fruits, cream, ſweetmeats, crawfiſh, and cheeſe. People take what they like, and ſit down again to play; after that, they make little parties to go to the walks together, and then all the company retire to their ſeparate habitations. Very ſeldom any ſuppers or dinners are given; and this is the manner they live among one another; not ſo much out of any averſion they have to pleaſure, as out of a ſort of formality they have contracted by not being much frequented by people who have lived at Paris. It is ſure they do not hate gaiety any more than the reſt of their country-people, and can enter into diverſions, that are once propoſed, with a good grace enough: for inſtance, the other evening we happened to be got together in a company of eighteen people, men and women of the beſt faſhion here, at a garden in the town to walk; when one of the ladies bethought herſelf of aſking, Why ſhould not we ſup here? Immediately the cloth was laid by the ſide of a fountain under the trees, and a very elegant ſupper ſerved up; after which another ſaid, Come, let us ſing; and directly began herſelf: From ſinging we inſenſibly fell to dancing, and ſinging in a round; when ſomebody mentioned the violins, and immediately a company of them was ordered: Minuets were begun in the open air, and then came country-dances, which held till four o'clock next morning; at which hour the gayeſt lady there propoſed, that ſuch as were weary ſhould get into their coaches, and the reſt of them ſhould dance before them with the muſic in the van; and in this manner we paraded through all the principal ſtreets of the city, and waked every body in it. Mr. Walpole had a mind to make a cuſtom of the thing, and would have given a ball in the ſame manner next week; but the women did not come into it; ſo I believe it will drop, and they will return to their dull cards, and uſual formalities. We are not to ſtay above a month longer here, and ſhall then go to Dijon, the chief city of Burgundy, a very ſplendid and very gay town; at leaſt ſuch is the preſent deſign.

Letter XVI.

MR. GRAY TO HIS FATHER.

Dijon, Friday, Sept. 11, N. S. 1739.

WE have made three ſhort days journey of it from Rheims hither, where we arrived the night before laſt: The road we have paſſed through has been extremely agreeable: it runs through the moſt fertile part of Champaigne by the ſide of the river Marne, with a chain of hills on each hand at ſome diſtance, entirely covered with woods and vineyards, and every now and then the ruins of ſome old caſtle on their tops; we lay at St. Dizier the firſt night, and at Langres the ſecond, and got hither the next evening time enough to have a full view of this city in entering it: It lies in a very extenſive plain covered with vines and corn, and conſequently is plentifully ſupplied with both. I need not tell you that it is the chief city of Burgundy, nor that it is of great antiquity; confidering which one fhould imagine it ought to be larger than one finds it. However, what it wants in extent, is made up in beauty and cleanlinefs, and in rich convents and churches, moft of which we have feen. The palace of the States is a magnificent new building, where the Duke of Bourbon is lodged when he comes every three years to hold that affembly, as governor of the Province. A quarter of a mile out of the town is a famous Abbey of Carthufians, which we are juft returned from feeing. In their chapel are the tombs of the ancient Dukes of Burgundy, that were fo powerful, till at the death of Charles the Bold, the laft of them, this part of his dominions was united by Lewis XI. to the crown of France. To-morrow we are to pay a vifit to the Abbot of the Ciftercians, who lives a few leagues off, and who ufes to receive all ftrangers with great civility; his Abbey is one of the richeft in the kingdom; he keeps open houfe always, and lives with great magnificence. We have feen enough of this town already to make us regret the time we fpent at Rheims; it is full of people of condition, who feem to form a much more agreeable ſociety than we found in Champaigne; but as we ſhall ſtay here but two or three days longer, it is not worth while to be introduced into their houſes. On Monday or Tueſday we are to ſet out for Lyons, which is two days journey diſtant, and from thence you ſhall hear again from me.

Letter XVII.

MR. GRAY TO MR. WEST.

Lyons, Sept. 18, N.S. 1739.

SÇAVEZ-VOUS bien, mon cher ami, que je vous hais, que je vous déteſte? voilà des termes un peu forts; and that will ſave me, upon a juſt computation, a page of paper and ſix drops of ink; which, if I confined myſelf to reproaches of a more moderate nature, I ſhould be obliged to employ in uſing you according to your deſerts. What: to let any body reſide three months at Rheims, and write but once to them! Pleaſe to conſult Tully de Amicit. page 5, line 25, and you will find it ſaid in expreſs terms, "Ad amicum inter Remos relegatum menſe uno quinquies ſcriptum eſto;" nothing more plain or leſs liable to falſe interpretations. Now becauſe, I ſuppoſe, it will give you pain to know we are in being, I take this opportunity to tell you that we are at the ancient and celebrated Lugdunum, a city ſituated upon the confluence of the Rhône[3] and Saône (Arar, I ſhould ſay), two people, who though of tempers extremely unlike, think fit to join hands here, and make a little party to travel to the Mediterranean in company; the lady comes gliding along through the fruitful plains of Burgundy, incredibili lenitate, ita ut oculis in utram partem fluit judicari non poſſit; the gentleman runs all rough and roaring down from the mountains of Switzerland to meet her; and with all her ſoft airs ſhe likes him never the worſe; ſhe goes through the middle of the city in ſtate, and he paſſes incog. without the walls, but waits for her a little below. The houſes here are ſo high, and the ſtreets ſo narrow, as would be ſufficient to render Lyons the diſmalleſt place in the world, but the number of people, and the face of commerce diffuſed about it, are, at leaſt, as ſufficient to make it the livelieſt: between theſe two ſufficiencies, you will be in doubt what to think of it; ſo we ſhall leave the city, and proceed to its environs, which are beautiful beyond expreſſion: it is ſurrounded with mountains, and thoſe mountains all bedropped and beſpeckled with houſes, gardens, and plantations of the rich Bourgeois, who have from thence a proſpect of the city in the vale below on one, hand, on the other the rich plains of the Lyonnois, with the rivers winding among them, and the Alps, with the mountains of Dauphiné, to bound the view. All yeſterday morning we were buſied in climbing up Mount Fourvière, where the ancient city ſtood perched at ſuch a height, that nothing but the hopes of gain could certainly ever perſuade their neighbours to pay them a viſit: Here are the ruins of the Emperors' palaces, that reſided here, that is to ſay, Auguſtus and Severus; they conſiſt in nothing but great maſſes of old wall, that have only their quality to make them reſpected. In a vineyard of the Minims are remains of a theatre; the Fathers, whom they belong to, hold them in no eſteem at all, and would have ſhowed us their ſacriſty and chapel inſtead of them: The Urſuline Nuns have in their garden ſome Roman baths, but we having the misfortune to be men, and heretics, they did not think proper to admit us. Hard by are eight arches of a moſt magnificent aqueduct, ſaid to be erected by Antony, when his legions were quartered here: There are many other parts of it diſperſed up and down the country, for it brought the water from a river many leagues off in La Forez. Here are remains, too, of Agrippa's ſeven great roads which met at Lyons; in ſome places they lie twelve feet deep in the ground: In ſhort, a thouſand matters that you ſhall not know, till you give me a deſcription of the Païs de Tombridge, and the effect its waters have upon you.

Letter XVIII.

MR. GRAY TO HIS MOTHER.

Lyons, Oct. 13, N.S. 1739.

IT is now almoſt five weeks ſince I left Dijon, one of the gayeſt and moſt agreeable little cities of France, for Lyons, its reverſe in all theſe particulars. It is the ſecond in the kingdom in bigneſs and rank, the ſtreets exceſſively narrow and naſty; the houſes immenſely high and large; (that, for inſtance, where we are lodged, has twenty-five rooms on a floor, and that for five ſtories;) it ſwarms with inhabitants like Paris itſelf, but chiefly a mercantile people, too much given up to commerce, to think of their own, much leſs of a ſtranger's diverſions. We have no acquaintance in the town, but ſuch Engliſh as happen to be paſſing through here, in their way to Italy and the ſouth, which at preſent happen to be near thirty in number. It is a fortnight ſince we ſet out from hence upon a little excurſion to Geneva. We took the longeſt road, which lies through Savoy, on purpoſe to ſee a famous monaſtery, called the Grande Chartreuſe, and had no reaſon to think our time loſt. After having travelled ſeven days very ſlow (for we did not change horſes, it being impoſſible for a chaiſe to go poſt in theſe roads) we arrived at a little village, among the mountains of Savoy, called Echelles; from thence we proceeded on horſes, who are uſed to the way, to the mountain of the Chartreuſe: It is ſix miles to the top; the road runs winding up it, commonly not ſix feet broad; on one hand is the rock, with woods of pine[+]-trees hanging over head; on the other, a monſtrous precipice, almoſt perpendicular, at the bottom of which rolls a torrent, that ſometimes tumbling among the fragments of ſtone that have fallen from on high, and ſometimes precipitating itſelf down vaſt deſcents with a noiſe like thunder, which is ſtill made greater by the echo from the mountains on each ſide, concurs to form one of the moſt ſolemn, the moſt romantic, and the moſt aſtoniſhing ſcenes I ever beheld: Add to this the ſtrange views made by the crags and cliffs on the other hand; the caſcades that in many places throw themſelves from the very ſummit down into the vale, and the river below; and many other particulars impoſſible to deſcribe; you will conclude we had no occaſion to repent our pains. This place St. Bruno choſe to retire to, and upon its very top founded the aforeſaid convent, which is the ſuperior of the whole order. When we came there, the two fathers, who are commiſſioned to entertain ſtrangers, (for the reſt muſt neither ſpeak one to another, nor to any one elſe,) received us very kindly; and ſet before us a repaſt of dried fiſh, eggs, butter and fruits, all excellent in their kind, and extremely neat. They preſſed us to ſpend the night there, and to ſtay ſome days with them; but this we could not do, ſo they led us about their houſe, which is, you muſt think, like a little city; for there are 100 fathers, beſides 300 ſervants, that make their clothes, grind their corn, preſs their wine, and do every thing among themſelves: The whole is quite orderly and ſimple; nothing of finery, but the wonderful decency, and the ſtrange ſituation, more than ſupply the place of it. In the evening we deſcended by the ſame way, paſſing through many clouds that were then forming themſelves on the mountain's ſide. Next day we continued our journey by Chambéry, which, though the chief city of the duchy, and reſidence of the king of Sardinia, when he comes into this part of his dominions, makes but a very mean and inſignificant appearance; we lay at Aix, once famous for its hot baths, and the next night at Annecy; the day after, by noon, we got to Geneva. I have not time to ſay anything about it, nor of our ſolitary journey back again. * * *

Letter XIX.

MR. GRAY TO HIS FATHER.

Lyons, Oct. 25, N. S. 1739.

IN my laſt I gave you the particulars of our little journey to Geneva: I have only to add, that we ſtayed about a week, in order to ſee Mr. Conway ſettled there: I do not wonder ſo many Engliſh chooſe it for their reſidence; the city is very ſmall, neat, prettily built, and extremely populous; the Rhône runs through the middle of it, and it is ſurrounded with new fortifications, that give it a military compact air; which, joined to the happy, lively countenances of the inhabitants, and an exact diſcipline always as ſtrictly obſerved as in time of war, makes the little republic appear a match for a much greater power; though perhaps Geneva, and all that belongs to it, are not of equal extent with Windſor and its two parks. To one that has paſſed through Savoy, as we did, nothing can be more ſtriking than the contraſt, as ſoon as he approaches the town. Near the gates of Geneva runs the torrent Arve, which ſeparates it from the King of Sardinia's dominions; on the other ſide of it lies a country naturally, indeed, fine and fertile; but you meet with nothing in it but meagre, ragged, bare-footed peaſants, with their children, in extreme miſery and naſtineſs; and even of theſe no great numbers; You no ſooner have croſſed the ſtream I have mentioned, but poverty is no more; not a beggar, hardly a diſcontented face to be ſeen; numerous and well-dreſſed people ſwarming on the ramparts; drums beating, ſoldiers, well clothed and armed, exerciſing; and folks, with buſineſs in their looks, hurrying to and fro; all contribute to make any perſon, who is not blind, ſenſible what a difference there is between the two governments, that are the cauſes of one view and the other. The beautiful lake, at one end of which the town is ſituated; its extent; the ſeveral ſtates that border upon it; and all its pleaſures, are too well known for me to mention them. We ſailed upon it as far as the dominions of Geneva extend, that is, about two leagues and a half on each ſide; and landed at ſeveral of the little houſes of pleaſure, that the inhabitants have built all about it, who received us with much politeneſs. The ſame night we eat part of a trout, taken in the lake, that weighed thirty-ſeven pounds; as great a monſter as it appeared to us, it was eſteemed there nothing extraordinary, and they aſſured us, it was not uncommon to catch them of fifty pounds; they are dreſſed here and ſent poſt to Paris upon ſome great occaſions; nay, even to Madrid, as we were told. The road we returned through was not the ſame we came by: We croſſed the Rhône at Seyſſel, and paſſed for three days among the mountains of Bugey, without meeting with any thing new: At laſt we came out into the plains of La Breſſe, and ſo to Lyons again. Sir Robert has written to Mr. Walpole, to deſire he would go to Italy; which he has reſolved to do; ſo that all the ſcheme of ſpending the winter in the ſouth of France is laid aſide, and we are to paſs it in a much finer country. You may imagine I am not ſorry to have this opportunity of ſeeing the place in the world that beſt deſerves it: Beſides as the Pope (who is eighty-eight, and has been lately at the point of death) cannot probably laſt a great while, perhaps we may have the fortune to be preſent at the election of a new one, when Rome will be in all its glory. Friday next we certainly begin our journey; in two days we ſhall come to the foot of the Alps, and ſix more we ſhall be in paſſing them. Even here the winter is begun; what then muſt it be among thoſe vaſt ſnowy mountains where it is hardly ever ſummer? We are, however, as well armed as poſſible againſt the cold, with muffs, hoods, and maſks of beaver, fur-boots, and bear-ſkins. When we arrive at Turin, we ſhall reſt after the fatigues of the journey. * * *

Letter XX.

MR. GRAY TO HIS MOTHER.

Turin, Nov. 7, N. S. 1739.

I AM this night arrived here, and have juſt ſet down to reſt me after eight days tireſome journey: For the three firſt we had the ſame road we before paſſed through to go to Geneva; the fourth we turned out of it, and for that day and the next travelled rather among than upon the Alps; the way commonly running through a deep valley by the ſide of the river Arc, which works itſelf a paſſage, with great difficulty and a mighty noiſe, among vaſt quantities of rocks, that have rolled down from the mountain tops. The winter was ſo far advanced, as in great meaſure to ſpoil the beauty of the proſpect; however, there was ſtill ſomewhat fine remaining amidſt the ſavageneſs and horror of the place: The ſixth we began to go up ſeveral of theſe mountains; and as we were paſſing one, met with an odd accident enough: Mr. Walpole had a little fat black ſpaniel, that he was very fond of, which he ſometimes uſed to ſet down, and let it run by the chaiſe ſide. We were at that time in a very rough road, not two yards broad at moſt; on one ſide was a great wood of pines, and on the other a vaſt precipice; it was noon-day, and the ſun ſhone bright, when all of a ſudden, from the wood-ſide (which was as ſteep upwards, as the other part was downwards) out ruſhed a great wolf, came cloſe to the head of the horſes, ſeized the dog by the throat, and ruſhed up the hill again with him in his mouth. This was done in leſs than a quarter of a minute; we all ſaw it, and yet the ſervants had not time to draw their piſtols, or do any thing to ſave the dog. If he had not been there, and the creature had thought fit to lay hold of one of the horſes; chaiſe, and we, and all muſt inevitably have tumbled above fifty fathoms perpendicular down the precipice. The ſeventh we came to Lanebourg, the laſt town in Savoy; it lies at the foot of the famous mount Cenis, which is ſo ſituated as to allow no room for any way but over the very top of it. Here the chaiſe was forced to be pulled to pieces, and the baggage and that to be carried by mules: We ourſelves were wrapped up in our furs, and ſeated upon a ſort of matted chair without legs, which is carried upon poles in the manner of a bier, and ſo begun to aſcend by the help of eight men. It was ſix miles to the top, where a plain opens itſelf about as many more in breadth, covered perpetually with very deep ſnow, and in the midſt of that a great lake of unfathomable depth, from whence a river takes its riſe, and tumbles over monſtrous rocks quite down the other ſide of the mountain. The deſcent is ſix miles more, but infinitely more ſteep than the going up; and here the men perfectly fly down with you, ſtepping from ſtone to ſtone with incredible ſwiftneſs in places where none but they could go three paces without falling. The immenſity of the precipices, the roaring of the river and torrents that run into it, the huge crags covered with ice and ſnow, and the clouds below you and about you, are objects it is impoſſible to conceive without ſeeing them;

and though we had heard many ſtrange deſcriptions of the ſcene, none of them at all came up to it. We were but five hours in performing the whole, from which you may judge of the rapidity of the men's motion. We are now got into Piedmont, and ſtopped a little while at La Ferriere, a ſmall village about three quarters of the way down, but ſtill among the clouds, where we began to hear a new language ſpoken round about us; at laſt we got quite down, went through the Pas de Suſe, a narrow road among the Alps, defended by two fortreſſes, and lay at Boſſolens: Next evening through a fine avenue of nine miles in length, as ſtraight as a line, we arrived at this city, which, as you know, is the capital of the Principality, and the reſidence of the King of Sardinia. * * * We ſhall ſtay here, I believe, a fortnight, and proceed for Genoa, which is three or four days journey to go poſt. I am, &c.

Letter XXI.

MR. GRAY TO MR. WEST.

Turin, Nov. 16, N. S. 1739.

AFTER eight days journey through Greenland, we arrived at Turin. You approach it by a handſome avenue of nine miles long, and quite ſtraight. The entrance is guarded by certain vigilant dragons, called Douaniers, who mumbled us for ſome time. The city is not large, as being a place of ſtrength, and conſequently confined within its fortifications; it has many beauties and ſome faults; among the firſt are ſtreets all laid out by the line, regular uniform buildings, fine walks that ſurround the whole, and in general a good lively clean appearance: But the houſes are of brick plaſtered, which is apt to want repairing; the windows of oiled paper, which is apt to be torn; and every thing very ſlight, which is apt to tumble down.

There is an excellent Opera, but it is only in the Carnival: Balls every night, but only in the Carnival: Maſquerades too, but only in the Carnival. This Carnival laſts only from Chriſtmas to Lent; one half of the remaining part of the year is paſſed in remembering the laſt, the other in expecting the future Carnival. We cannot well ſubſiſt upon ſuch ſlender diet, no more than upon an execrable Italian Comedy, and a Puppet-Show, called Rappreſentatione d'un' anima dannata, which, I think, are all the preſent diverſions of the place; except the Marquiſe de Cavaillac's Converſazione, where one goes to ſee people play at Ombre and Taroc, a game with 72 cards all painted with ſuns, and moons, and devils, and monks. Mr. Walpole has been at court; the family are at preſent at a country palace, called La Venerie. The palace here in town is the very quinteſſence of gilding and looking-glaſs; inlaid floors, carved panels, and painting, wherever they could ſtick a bruſh. I own, I have not, as yet, anywhere met with thoſe grand and ſimple works of Art, that are to amaze one, and whoſe ſight one is to be the better for:

But thoſe of Nature have aſtoniſhed me beyond expreſſion. In our little journey up to the Grande Chartreuſe, I do not remember to have gone ten paces without an exclamation, that there was no reſtraining: Not a precipice, not a torrent, not a cliff, but is pregnant with religion and poetry. There are certain ſcenes that would awe an atheiſt into belief, without the help of other argument. One need not have a very fantaſtic imagination to ſee ſpirits there at noon-day; You have death perpetually before your eyes, only ſo far removed, as to compoſe the mind without frighting it. I am well perſuaded St. Bruno was a man of no common genius, to chooſe ſuch a ſituation for his retirement; and perhaps ſhould have been a diſciple of his, had I been born in his time. You may believe Abelard and Heloïſe were not forgot upon this occaſion: If I do not miſtake, I ſaw you too every now and then at a diſtance along the trees; il me ſemble, que j'ai vu ce chien de viſage là quelque part. You ſeemed to call to me from the other ſide of the precipice, but the noiſe of the river below was ſo great, that I really could not diſtinguiſh what you ſaid; it ſeemed to have a cadence like verſe. In your next you will be ſo good to let me know what it was. The week we have ſince paſſed among the Alps, has not equalled the ſingle day upon that mountain, becauſe the winter was rather too far advanced, and the weather a little foggy. However, it did not want its beauties; the ſavage rudeneſs of the view is inconceivable without ſeeing it: I reckoned in one day, thirteen caſcades, the leaſt of which was, I dare ſay, one hundred feet in height. I had Livy in the chaiſe with me, and beheld his "Nives cœlo propè immiſtæ, tecta informia impoſita rupibus, pecora jumentaque torrida frigore, homines intonſi & inculti, animalia inanimaque omnia rigentia gelu; omnia confragoſa, præruptaque."[5] The creatures that inhabit them are, in all reſpects, below humanity; and moſt of them, eſpecially women, have the tumidum guttur, which they call goſcia. Mont Cenis, I confeſs, carries the permiſſion mountains have of being frightful rather too far; and its horrors were accompanied with too much danger to give one time to reflect upon their beauties. There is a family of the Alpine monſters I have mentioned, upon its very top, that in the middle of winter calmly lay in their ſtock of proviſions and firing, and ſo are buried in their hut for a month or two under the ſnow. When we were down it, and got a little way into Piedmont, we began to find " Apricos quoſdam colles, rivoſque prope ſylvas, & jam humano cultu digniora loca."[6] I read Silius Italicus too, for the firſt time; and wiſhed for you according to cuſtom. We ſet out for Genoa in two days time.

Letter XXII.

MR. GRAY TO MR. WEST.

Genoa, Nov. 21, 1739.

Horridos tractus, Boreæq; linquens
Regna Taurini fera, molliorem
Advehor brumam, Genuæq; amantes
Litora ſoles.

AT leaſt if they do not, they have a very ill taſte: for I never beheld anything more amiable: Only figure to yourſelf a vaſt ſemicircular baſin, full of fine blue ſea, and veſſels of all ſorts and ſizes, ſome ſailing out, ſome coming in, and others at anchor; and all round it palaces, and churches peeping over one another's heads, gardens, and marble terraces full of orange and cypreſs trees, fountains, and trellis-works covered with vines, which altogether compoſe the grandeſt of theatres. This is the firſt coup d'œil, and is almoſt all I am yet able to give you an account of, for we arrived late laſt night. To-day was, luckily, a great feſtival, and in the morning we reſorted to the church of the Madonna delle Vigne, to put up our little oriſons; (I believe I forgot to tell you, that we have been ſome time converts to the holy Catholic church;) we found our Lady richly dreſſed out, with a crown of diamonds on her own head, another upon the child's, and a conſtellation of wax lights burning before them: Shortly after came the Doge, in his robes of crimſon damaſk, and a cap of the ſame, followed by the Senate in black. Upon his approach began a fine concert of muſic, and among the reſt two eunuchs' voices, that were a perfect feaſt to ears that had heard nothing but French operas for a year. We liſtened to this, and breathed nothing but incenſe for two hours. The Doge is a very tall, lean, ſtately old figure, called Conſtantino Balbi; and the Senate ſeem to have been made upon the ſame model. They ſaid their prayers, and heard an abſurd white friar preach, with equal devotion.

After this we went to the Annonciata, a church built by the family Lomellini, and belonging to it; which is, indeed, a moſt ſtately ſtructure, the inſide wholly marble of various kinds, except where gold and painting take its place. From hence to the Palazzo Doria. I ſhould make you ſick of marble, if I told you how it was laviſhed here upon the porticoes, the baluſtrades, and terraces, the loweſt of which extends quite to the ſea. The inſide is by no means anſwerable to the outward magnificence; the furniture ſeems to be as old as the founder of the family.[7] There great emboſſed ſilver tables tell you, in bas-relief, his victories at ſea; how he entertained the Emperor Charles, and how he refuſed the ſovereignty of the Commonwealth when it was offered him; the reſt is old-faſhioned velvet chairs, and Gothic tapeſtry. The reſt of the day has been ſpent, much to our hearts' content, in curſing French muſic and architecture, and in ſinging the praiſes of Italy. We find this place ſo very fine, that we are in fear of finding nothing finer. We are fallen in love with the Mediterranean ſea, and hold your lakes and your rivers in vaſt contempt. This is

"The happy country where huge lemons grow,"

as Waller ſays; and I am ſorry to think of leaving it in a week for Parma, although it be

The happy country where huge cheeſes grow.

Letter XXIII.

MR. GRAY TO HIS MOTHER.

Bologna, Dec. 9, N.S. 1739.

OUR journey hither has taken up much lefs time than I expected. We left Genoa (a charming place, and one that deferved a longer ftay,) the week before laft; croffed the mountains, and lay that night at Tortona, the next at St. Giovanni, and the morning after came to Piacenza. That city (though the capital of a Duchy) made fo frippery an appearance, that inftead of fpending fome days there, as had been intended, we only dined, and went on to Parma; ftayed there all the following day, which was paffed in vifiting the famous works of Correggio in the Dome, and other churches. The fine gallery of pictures, that once belonged to the Dukes of Parma, is no more here; the King of Naples has carried it all thither, and the city had not merit enough to detain us any longer, ſo we proceeded through Reggio to Modena; this, though the reſidence of its Duke, is an ill-built melancholy place, all of brick, as are moſt of the towns in this part of Lombardy: He himſelf lives in a private manner, with very little appearance of a court about him; he has one of the nobleſt collections of paintings in the world, which entertained us extremely well the reſt of that day and a part of the next; and in the afternoon we came to Bologna. So now you may wiſh us joy of being in the dominions of his Holineſs. This is a populous city, and of great extent: All the ſtreets have porticoes on both ſides, ſuch as ſurround a part of Covent Garden, a great relief in ſummer-time in ſuch a climate; and from one of the principal gates to a church of the Virgin, [where is a wonder-working picture, at three miles diſtance,] runs a corridor of the ſame ſort, lately finiſhed, and indeed a moſt extraordinary performance. The churches here are more remarkable for their paintings than architecture, being moſtly old ſtructures of brick; but the palaces are numerous, and fine enough to ſupply us with ſomewhat worth ſeeing from morning till night. The country of Lombardy, hitherto, is one of the moſt beautiful imaginable; the roads broad, and exactly ſtraight, and on either hand vaſt plantations of trees, chiefly mulberries and olives, and not a tree without a vine twining about it, and ſpreading among its branches. This ſcene, indeed, which muſt be the moſt lovely in the world during the proper ſeaſon, is at preſent all deformed by the winter, which here is rigorous enough for the time it laſts; but one ſtill ſees the ſkeleton of a charming place, and reaps the benefit of its product, for the fruits and proviſions are admirable; in ſhort, you find every thing that luxury can deſire in perfection. We have now been here a week, and ſhall ſtay ſome little time longer. We are at the foot of the Apennine mountains; it will take up three days to croſs them, and then we ſhall come to Florence, where we ſhall paſs the Chriſtmas. Till then we muſt remain in a ſtate of ignorance as to what is doing in England, for our letters are to meet us there: If I do not find four or five from you alone, I ſhall wonder.

Letter XXIV.

MR. GRAY TO HIS MOTHER.

Florence, Dec. 19, N.S. 1739.

WE ſpent twelve days at Bologna, chiefly (as moſt travellers do) in ſeeing ſights; for as we knew no mortal there, and as it is no eaſy matter to get admiſſion into any Italian houſe, without very particular recommendations, we could ſee no company but in public places; and there are none in that city but the churches. We ſaw, therefore, churches, palaces, and pictures from morning to night; and the 15th of this month ſet out for Florence, and began to croſs the Apennine mountains; we travelled among and upon them all that day, and, as it was but indifferent weather, were commonly in the middle of thick clouds, that utterly deprived us of a ſight of their beauties: For this vaſt chain of hills has its beauties, and all the valleys are cultivated; even the mountains themſelves are many of them ſo within a little of their very tops. They are not ſo horrid as the Alps, though pretty near as high; and the whole road is admirably well kept, and paved throughout, which is a length of fourſcore miles, and more: We left the Pope's dominions, and lay that night in thoſe of the Grand Duke at Fiorenzuola, a paltry little town, at the foot of Mount Giogo, which is the higheſt of them all. Next morning we went up it; the poſt-houſe is upon its very top, and uſually involved in clouds, or half-buried in the ſnow. Indeed there was none of the laſt at the time we were there, but it was ſtill a diſmal habitation. The deſcent is moſt exceſſively ſteep, and the turnings very ſhort and frequent; however, we performed it without any danger, and in coming down could dimly diſcover Florence, and the beautiful plain about it, through the miſts, but enough to convince us, it muſt be one of the nobleſt proſpects upon earth in ſummer. That afternoon we got thither; and Mr. Mann,[8] the reſident, had ſent his ſervant to meet us at the gates, and conduct us to his houſe. He is the beſt and moſt obliging perſon in the world. The next night we were introduced at the Prince of Craon's[9] aſſembly (he has the chief power here in the Grand Duke's abſence). The princeſs, and he, were extremely civil to the name of Walpole, ſo we were aſked to ſtay ſupper, which is as much as to ſay, you may come and ſup here whenever you pleaſe; for after the firſt invitation this is always underſtood. We have alſo been at the Counteſs Suarez's, a favourite of the late Duke, and one that gives the firſt movement to every thing gay that is going forward here. The news is every day expected from Vienna of the Great Ducheſs's delivery; if it be a boy, here will be all ſorts of balls, maſquerades, operas, and illuminations; if not, we muſt wait for the Carnival, when all thoſe things come of courſe. In the mean time it is impoſſible to want entertainment; the famous gallery, alone, is an amuſement for months; we commonly paſs two or three hours every morning in it, and one has perfect leiſure to conſider all its beauties. You know it contains many hundred antique ſtatues, ſuch as the whole world cannot match, beſides the vaſt collection of paintings, medals, and precious ſtones, ſuch as no other prince was ever maſter of; in ſhort, all that the rich and powerful houſe of Medicis has in ſo many years got together. And beſides this city abounds with ſo many palaces and churches, that you can hardly place yourſelf anywhere without having ſome fine one in view, or at leaſt ſome ſtatue or fountain, magnificently adorned; theſe undoubtedly are far more numerous than Genoa can pretend to; yet, in its general appearance, I cannot think that Florence equals it in beauty. Mr. Walpole is juſt come from being preſented to the Electreſs Palatine Dowager; ſhe is a ſiſter of the late Great Duke's; a ſtately old lady, that never goes out but to church, and then ſhe has guards, and eight horſes to her coach. She received him with much ceremony, ſtanding under a huge black canopy, and, after a few minutes talking, ſhe aſſured him of her good will, and diſmiſſed him: She never ſees any body but thus in form; and ſo ſhe paſſes her life, poor woman! * * *

Letter XXV.

MR. GRAY TO MR. WEST.

Florence, Jan. 15, 1740.

I THINK I have not yet told you how we left that charming place Genoa: How we croſſed a mountain of green marble, called Buchetto: How we came to Tortona, and waded through the mud to come to Caſtel St. Giovanni, and there eat muſtard and ſugar with a diſh of crows' gizzards: Secondly, how we paſſed the famous plains;

Qua Trebie glaucas ſalices interſecat undâ,
  Arvaque Romanis nobilitata malis.
Viſus adhuc amnis veteri de clade rubere,
  Et ſuſpirantes ducere mœſtus aquas;
Maurorumque ala, et nigræ increbeſcere turmæ,
  Et pulſa Auſonidum ripa ſonare fugâ.

Nor, thirdly, how we paſſed through Piacenza, Parma, Modena, entered the territories of the Pope; ſtayed twelve days at Bologna; croſſed the Appennines, and afterwards arrived at Florence. None of theſe things have I told you, nor do I intend to tell you, till you aſk me ſome queſtions concerning them. No not even of Florence itſelf, except that it is as fine as poſſible, and has every thing in it that can bleſs the eyes. But, before I enter into particulars, you muſt make your peace both with me and the Venus de Medicis, who, let me tell you, is highly and juſtly offended at you for not inquiring, long before this, concerning her ſymmetry and proportions. * * *

Letter XXVI.

MR. GRAY TO MR. WHARTON.

Proposals for Printing by Subscription, in

THIS LARGE LETTER,

THE TRAVELS OF T. G. Gent.

WHICH WILL CONSIST OF THE FOLLOWING PARTICULARS.

Chap. I.

THE Author arrives at Dover; his conversation with the Mayor of that Corporation. Sets out in the pacquet boat: grows very sick; the Author spews; a very minute account of all the circumstances thereof. His arrival at Calais; how the inhabitants of that country speak French, and are said to be all Papishes; the Author's reflections thereupon.

II.

How they feed him with ſoupe, and what ſoupe is. How he meets with a capucin, and what a capucin is. How they ſhut him up in a poſt-chaiſe and ſend him to Paris; he goes wondering along during ſix days; and how there are trees and houſes juſt as in England. Arrives at Paris without knowing it.

III.

Full account of the river Seine, and of the various animals and plants its borders produce. Deſcription of the little creature called an Abbé, its parts, and their uſes; with the reaſons why they will not live in England, and the methods that have been uſed to propagate them there. A cut of the inſide of a nunnery; its ſtructure wonderfully adapted to the uſe of the animals that inhabit it; a ſhort account of them, how they propagate without the help of a male: and how they eat up their own young ones, like cats and rabbits: ſuppoſed to have both ſexes in themſelves like a ſnail. Diſſection of a Ducheſs, with copper-plates, very curious.

IV.

Goes to the opera: grand orcheſtra of humſtrums, bagpipes, ſalt-boxes, tabors and pipes. Anatomy of a French ear, ſhowing the formation of it to be entirely different from that of an Engliſh one; and that ſounds have a directly contrary effect upon one and the other. Farinelli, at Paris, ſaid to have a fine manner, but no voice. Grand ballet, in which there is no ſeeing the dance for petticoats. Old women with flowers and jewels ſtuck in the curls of their grey hair. Red-heeled ſhoes and roll-ups innumerable; hoops and panniers immeaſurable, paint unſpeakable. Tables, wherein is calculated, with the utmoſt exactneſs, the ſeveral degrees of red, now in uſe, from the riſing bluſhes of an Advocate's wife, to the flaming crimſon of a princeſs of the Blood; done by a limner in great vogue.

V.

The author takes unto him a taylour; his character. How he covers him with ſilk and fringe, and widens his figure with buckram, a yard on each ſide. Waiſtcoat and breeches ſo ſtrait, he can neither breathe nor walk. How the barber curls him en bequille, and à la negligée, and ties a vaſt ſolitaire about his neck. How the milliner lengthens his ruffles to his fingers' ends, and ſticks his two arms into a muff. How he cannot ſtir; and how they cut him in proportion to his clothes.

VI.

He is carried to Verſailles, deſpiſes it infinitely. A diſſertation upon taſte. Goes to an Inſtallation in the Chapel Royal; enter the King and fifty fiddlers ſolus: kettle-drums and trumpets; queens and dauphins; princeſſes and cardinals; incenſe and the maſs; old knights making curtſies; Holy Ghoſts and fiery tongues.

VII.

Goes into the country to Rheims, in Champagne, ſtays there three months; what he did there (he muſt beg the reader's pardon but) he has really forgot.

VIII.

Proceeds to Lyons, vaſtneſs of that city. Can't ſee the ſtreets for houſes. How rich it is, and how much it ſtinks. Poem upon the confluence of the Rhone and the Saône, by a friend of the Author's; very pretty.

IX.

Makes a journey into Savoy, and in his way viſits the Grande Chartreuſe: he is ſet aſide upon a mule's back, and begins to climb up the mountains: rocks and torrents beneath, pine trees and ſnows above: horrors and terrors on all ſides. The Author dies of the fright.

X.

He goes to Geneva. His mortal antipathy to a preſbyterian, and the cure for it. Returns to Lyons; gets a ſurfeit with eating ortolans and lampreys; is adviſed to go into Italy for the benefit of the air.

XI.

Sets out the latter end of November to crofs the Alps. He is devoured by a wolf: and how it is to be devoured by a wolf: the feventh day he comes to the foot of Mount Cenis. How he is wrap'd up in bear-fkins and beaver-fkins; boots on his legs; caps on his head: muffs on his hands, and taffety over his eyes. He is placed on a bier and is carried to heaven by the favages blind-fold. How he lights among a certain fat nation called Clouds: how they are always in a fweat, and never fpeak but they ——; how they flock about him, and think him very odd for not doing fo too. He falls plump into Italy.

XII.

Arrives at Turin: goes to Genoa, and from thence to Placentia; croffes the river Tribia. The ghoft of Hannibal appears to him, and what it and he fay upon the occafion. Locked out of Parma on a cold winter's night; the Author, by an ingenious ftratagem, gains admittance.

Despises that city, and proceeds through Reggio to Modena. How the Duke and Duchess lie over their own stables, and go every night to a vile Italian Comedy; despises them and it, and proceeds to Bologna.

XIII.

Enters into the dominions of the Pope o'Rome. Meets the devil, and what he says on the occasion. Very publick and scandalous doings between the vine and the elm trees, and how the olive trees are shocked thereupon. Author longs for Bologna sausages and hams, and how he grows as fat as an hog.

XIV.

Observations on antiquities. The Author proves that Bologna was the ancient Tarentum; that the battle of Salamis, contrary to the vulgar opinion, was fought by land, and that not far from Ravenna; that the Romans were a colony of the Jews; and that Eneas was the same with Ehud.

XV.

Arrival at Florence. Is of opinion that the Venus of Medicis is a modern performance, and that a very indifferent one, and much inferior to the K. Charles at Charing-crofs. Account of the city and manners of the inhabitants. A learned Differtation on the true fituation of Gomorrah. . . .

And here will end the firft part of thefe inftructive and entertaining voyages. The Subfcribers are to pay twenty guineas, nineteen down, and the remainder upon delivery of the book. N. B. A few are printed on the fofteft royal brown paper, for the ufe of the curious.

My Dear, Dear Wharton,

(Which is a dear more than I give any body elfe. It is very odd to begin with a parenthefis, but) You may think me a beaft not having fooner wrote to you, and to be fure a beaft I am. Now, when one owns it, I don't fee what you have left to ſay. I take this opportunity to inform you (an opportunity I have had every week this twelvemonth) that I am arrived ſafe at Calais, and am at preſent at—Florence, a city in Italy, in I don't know how many degrees of N. latitude. Under the line I am ſure it is not, for I am at this inſtant expiring with cold. You muſt know, that not being certain what circumſtances of my hiſtory would particularly ſuit your curioſity, and knowing that all I had to ſay to you would overflow the narrow limits of many a good quire of paper, I have taken this method of laying before you the contents, that you may pitch upon what you pleaſe, and give me your orders accordingly to expatiate thereupon: for I conclude you will write to me: won't you? oh! yes, when you know that in a week I ſet out for Rome, and that the Pope is dead, and that I ſhall be (I ſhould ſay, God willing; and if nothing extraordinary intervene; and if I am alive and well; and in all human probability) at the coronation of a new one. Now, as you have no other correſpondent there, and as if you do not, I certainly ſhall not write again, (obſerve my impudence,) I take it to be your intereſt to ſend me a vaſt letter, full of all ſorts of news and politics, and ſuch other ingredients, as to you ſhall ſeem convenient with all decent expedition, only do not be too ſevere upon the Pretender; and if you like my ſtyle, pray ſay ſo. This is à la Françoiſe; and if you think it a little too fooliſh, and impertinent, you ſhall be treated alla Toſcana with a thouſand Signoria Illuſtriſſimas, in the mean time I have the honour to remain Your loſing frind tell deth,

T. Gray.

Florence, March 12, N. S. 1740.

P. S. This is à l'Angloiſe. I don't know where you are; if at Cambridge pray let me know all, how, and about it: and if my old friends, Thomſon or Clarke, fall in your way, ſay I am extremely theirs. But if you are in town, I entreat you to make my beſt compliments to Mrs. Wharton. Adieu. Yours, ſincerely, a ſecond time.

Letter XXVII.

MR. GRAY TO HIS MOTHER.

Florence, March 19, 1740.

THE Pope[1] is at laſt dead, and we are to ſet out for Rome on Monday next. The conclave is ſtill ſitting there, and likely to continue ſo ſome time longer, as the two French Cardinals are but juſt arrived, and the German ones are ſtill expected. It agrees mighty ill with thoſe that remain incloſed: Ottoboni is already dead of an apoplexy; Altieri and ſeveral others are ſaid to be dying, or very bad: Yet it is not expected to break up till after Eaſter. We ſhall lie at Sienna the firſt night, ſpend a day there, and in two more get to Rome. One begins to ſee in this country the firſt promiſes of an Italian ſpring, clear unclouded ſkies, and warm ſuns, ſuch as are not often felt in England; yet, for your ſake, I hope at preſent you have your proportion of them, and that all your froſts, and ſnows, and ſhort breaths are, by this time, utterly vaniſhed. I have nothing new or particular to inform you of; and, if you ſee things at home go on much in their old courſe, you muſt not imagine them more various abroad. The diverſions of a Florentine Lent are compoſed of a ſermon in the morning, full of hell and the devil; a dinner at noon, full of fiſh and meagre diet; and in the evening, what is called a Converſazione, a ſort of aſſembly at the principal people's houſes, full of I cannot tell what: Beſides this, there is twice a week a very grand concert. * * *

Letter XXVIII.

MR. GRAY TO HIS MOTHER.

Rome, April 2, N. S. 1740.

THIS is the third day ſince we came to Rome, but the firſt hour I have had to write to you in. The journey from Florence coſt us four days, one of which was ſpent at Sienna, an agreeable, clean, old city, of no great magnificence or extent; but in a fine ſituation, and good air. What it has moſt conſiderable is its cathedral, a huge pile of marble, black and white laid alternately, and laboured with a gothic niceneſs and delicacy in the old-faſhioned way. Within too are ſome paintings and ſculpture of conſiderable hands. The ſight of this, and ſome collections that were ſhewed us in private houſes, were a ſufficient employment for the little time we were to paſs there: and the next morning we ſet forward on our journey through a country very oddly compofed; for fome miles you have a continual fcene of little mountains cultivated from top to bottom with rows of olive-trees, or elfe elms, each of which has its vine twining about it, and mixing with the branches; and corn fown between all the ranks. This diverfified with numerous fmall houfes and convents, makes the moft agreeable profpect in the world: But, all of a fudden, it alters to black barren hills, as far as the eye can reach, that feem never to have been capable of culture, and are as ugly as ufelefs. Such is the country for fome time before one comes to Mount Radicofani, a terrible black hill, on the top of which we were to lodge that night. It is very high, and difficult of afcent; and at the foot of it we were much embarraffed by the fall of one of the poor horfes that drew us. This accident obliged another chaife, which was coming down, to ftop alfo; and out of it peeped a figure in a red cloak, with a handkerchief tied round its head, which, by its voice and mien, feemed a fat old woman: but upon its getting out, appeared to be Senefino, who was returning from Naples to Sienna, the place of his birth and reſidence. On the higheſt part of the mountain is an old fortreſs, and near it a houſe built by one of the Grand Dukes for a hunting-ſeat, but now converted into an inn; It is the ſhell of a large fabric, but ſuch an inſide, ſuch chambers, and accommodations, that your cellar is a palace in compariſon; and your cat ſups and lies much better than we did; for, it being a ſaint's eve, there was nothing but eggs. We devoured our meagre fare; and, after ſtopping up the windows with the quilts, were obliged to lie upon the ſtraw beds in our clothes. Such are the conveniences in a road, that is, as it were, the great thoroughfare of all the world. Juſt on the other ſide of this mountain, at Ponte-Centino, one enters the patrimony of the church; a moſt delicious country, but thinly inhabited. That night brought us to Viterbo, a city of a more lively appearance than any we had lately met with; the houſes have glaſs windows, which is not very uſual here; and moſt of the ſtreets are terminated by a handſome fountain. Here we had the pleaſure of breaking our faſt on the leg of an old hare and ſome broiled crows. Next morning, in deſcending Mount Viterbo, we firſt diſcovered (though at near thirty miles diſtance) the cupola of St. Peter's, and a little after began to enter on an old Roman pavement, with now and then a ruined tower, or a ſepulchre on each hand. We now had a clear view of the city, though not to the beſt advantage, as coming along a plain quite upon a level with it; however it appeared very vaſt, and ſurrounded with magnificent villas and gardens. We ſoon after croſſed the Tiber, a river that ancient Rome made more conſiderable than any merit of its own could have done: However, it is not contemptibly ſmall, but a good handſome ſtream; very deep, yet ſomewhat of a muddy complexion. The firſt entrance of Rome is prodigiouſly ſtriking. It is by a noble gate, deſigned by Michael Angelo, and adorned with ſtatues; this brings you into a large ſquare, in the midſt of which is a vaſt obeliſk of granite, and in front you have at one view two churches of a handſome architecture, and ſo much alike that they are called the twins; with three ſtreets, the middlemoſt of which is one of the longeſt in Rome. As high as my expectation was raised, I confess, the magnificence of this city infinitely surpasses it. You cannot pass along a street but you have views of some palace, or church, or square, or fountain, the most picturesque and noble one can imagine. We have not yet set about considering its beauties, ancient and modern, with attention; but have already taken a slight transient view of some of the most remarkable. St. Peter's I saw the day after we arrived, and was struck dumb with wonder. I there saw the Cardinal d'Auvergne, one of the French ones, who upon coming off his journey, immediately repaired hither to offer up his vows at the high altar, and went directly into the Conclave; the doors of which we saw opened to him, and all the other immured Cardinals came thither to receive him. Upon his entrance they were closed again directly. It is supposed they will not come to an agreement about a Pope till after Easter, though the confinement is very disagreeable. I have hardly philosophy enough to see the infinity of fine things, that are here daily in the power of any body that has money, without regretting the want of it; but cuſtom has the power of making things eaſy to one. I have not yet ſeen his majeſty of Great-Britain, &c. though I have the two boys in the gardens of the Villa Borgheſe, where they go a-ſhooting almoſt every day; it was at a diſtance, indeed, for we did not chooſe to meet them, as you may imagine. This letter (like all thoſe the Engliſh ſend or receive) will paſs through the hands of that family, before it comes to thoſe it was intended for. They do it more honour than it deſerves; and all they will learn from thence will be, that I deſire you to give my duty to my father, and wherever elſe it is due, and that I am, &c.

Letter XXIX.

MR. GRAY TO HIS MOTHER.

Rome, April 15, 1740. Good-Friday.

TO-DAY I am juſt come from paying my adoration at St. Peter's to three extraordinary relics, which are expoſed to public view only on theſe two days in the whole year, at which time all the confraternities in the city come in proceſſion to ſee them. It was ſomething extremely novel to ſee that vaſt church, and the moſt magnificent in the world, undoubtedly, illuminated (for it was night) by thouſands of little cryſtal lamps, diſpoſed in the figure of a huge croſs at the high altar, and ſeeming to hang alone in the air. All the light proceeded from this, and had the moſt ſingular effect imaginable as one entered the great door. Soon after came one after another, I believe, thirty proceſſions, all dreſſed in linen frocks, and girt with a cord, their heads covered with a cowl all over, only two holes to ſee through left. Some of them were all black, others red, others white, others party-coloured; theſe were continually coming and going with their tapers and crucifixes before them; and to each company, as they arrived and knelt before the great altar, were ſhown from a balcony at a great height, the three wonders, which are, you muſt know, the head of the ſpear which wounded Chriſt; St. Veronica's handkerchief, with the miraculous impreſſion of his face upon it; and a piece of the true croſs, on the ſight of which the people thump their breaſts, and kiſs the pavement with vaſt devotion. The tragical part of the ceremony is half a dozen wretched creatures, who with their faces covered, but naked to the waiſt, are in a ſide chapel diſciplining themſelves with ſcourges full of iron prickles; but really in earneſt, as our eyes can teſtify, which ſaw their backs and arms ſo raw we ſhould have taken it for a red ſatin doublet torn, and ſhewing the ſkin through, had we not been convinced of the contrary by the blood which was plentifully ſprinkled about them. It is late; I give you joy of Port-Bello, and many other things, which I hope are all true. * * *

Letter XXX.

MR. WALPOLE TO MR. WEST.

Rome, April 16, N. S. 1740.

I'LL tell you, Weſt, becauſe one is amongſt new things, you think one can always write new things. When I firſt came abroad every thing ſtruck me, and I wrote its hiſtory; but now I am grown ſo uſed to be ſurpriſed, that I don't perceive any flutter in myſelf when I meet with any novelties; curioſity and aſtoniſhment wear off, and the next thing is, to fancy that other people know as much of places as one's ſelf; or, at leaſt, one does not remember that they do not. It appears to me as odd to write to you of St. Peter's, as it would do to write to you of Weſtminſter Abbey. Beſides, as one looks at churches, &c. with a book of travels in one's hand, and ſees every thing particularized there, it would appear tranſcribing to write upon the ſame ſubjects. I know you will hate me for this declaration; I remember how ill I uſed to take it when any body ſerved me ſo that was travelling. Well, I will tell you ſomething if you will love me: you have ſeen prints of the ruins of the temple of Minerva Medica; you ſhall only hear its ſituation, and then figure what a villa might be laid out there.

'Tis in the middle of a garden: at a little diſtance are two ſubterraneous grottos, which were the burial-places of the liberti of Auguſtus. There are all the niches and covers of the urns with the inſcriptions remaining: and in one, very conſiderable remains of an ancient ſtucco ceiling, with paintings in groteſque.

Some of the walks would terminate upon the Caſtellum Aquæ Martiæ, St. John Lateran, and St[a] Maria Maggiore, beſides other churches: the walls of the garden would be two aqueducts, and the entrance through one of the old gates of Rome. This glorious ſpot is neglected, and only ſerves for a ſmall vineyard and kitchen garden.

I am very glad that I ſee Rome while it yet exiſts; before a great number of years are elapſed, I queſtion whether it will be worth ſeeing. Between the ignorance and poverty of the preſent Romans, every thing is neglected and falling to decay; the villas are entirely out of repair, and the palaces ſo ill kept, that half the pictures are ſpoiled by damp.

At the villa Ludoviſi is a large oracular head of red marble, coloſſal, and with vaſt foramina for the eyes and mouth: the man that ſhewed the palace ſaid it was *un ritratto della famiglia.* The Cardinal Corſini has ſo thoroughly puſhed on the miſery of Rome by impoveriſhing it, that there is no money but paper to be ſeen. He is reckoned to have amaſſed three millions of crowns. You may judge of the affluence the nobility live in, when I aſſure you that what the chief princes allow for their own eating is a teſtoon a-day (eighteen-pence); there are ſome extend their expenſe to five pauls, or half-a-crown. Cardinal Albani is called extravagant for laying out ten pauls for his dinner and ſupper. You may imagine they never have any entertainments: ſo far from it, they never have any company. The Princeſſes and Ducheſſes, particularly, lead the diſmalleſt of lives. Being the poſterity of Popes, though of worſe families than the ancient nobility, they expect greater reſpect than my ladies the Counteſſes and Marquiſes will pay them; conſequently they conſort not, but mope in a vaſt palace with two miſerable tapers, and two or three Monſignori, whom they are forced to court and humour, that they may not be entirely deſerted. Sundays they do iſſue forth in a vaſt unwieldy coach to the Corſo.

In ſhort, child, after ſun-ſet one paſſes one's time here very ill; and if I did not wiſh for you in the mornings, it would be no compliment to tell you that I do in the evening. Lord! how many Engliſh I could change for you, and yet buy you wondrous cheap! and then French and Germans I could fling into the bargain by dozens. Nations ſwarm here. You will have a great fat French Cardinal, garniſhed with thirty Abbés, roll into the area of St. Peter's, gape, turn ſhort, and talk of the Chapel of Verſailles. I heard one of them ſay t'other day, he had been at the *Capitale.* One aſked of courſe how he liked it—*Ah! il y a aſſez de belles choſes.*

Tell Aſheton I have received his letter; and will write next poſt; but I am in a violent hurry and have no more time; ſo Gray finiſhes this delicately.

Not ſo delicate; nor, indeed, would his conſcience ſuffer him to write to you, till he received de vos nouvelles, if he had not the tail of another perſon's letter to uſe by way of evaſion. I ſha'n't deſcribe, as being in the only place in the world that deſerves it, which may ſeem an odd reaſon—but they ſay as how it's fulſome, and every body does it, (and, I ſuppoſe, every body ſays the ſame thing,) elſe I ſhould tell you a vaſt deal about the Coliſeum, and the Conclave, and the Capitol, and theſe matters. A-propos du Coliſée, if you don't know what it is, the Prince Borgheſe will be very capable of giving you ſome account of it, who told an Engliſhman that aſked what it was built for,—"They ſay 'twas for Chriſtians to fight tigers in."

We are juſt come from adoring a great piece of the true croſs, St. Longinus's ſpear, and St. Veronica's handkerchief; all which have been this evening expoſed to view in St. Peter's. In the ſame place, and on the ſame occaſion, laſt night, Walpole ſaw a poor creature, naked to the waiſt, diſcipline himſelf with a ſcourge filled with iron prickles, till he had made himſelf a raw doublet, that he took for red ſatin torn, and ſhowing the ſkin through. I ſhould tell you that he fainted away three times at the ſight, and I twice and a half at the repetition of it. All this performed by the light of a vaſt fiery croſs, compoſed of hundreds of little cryſtal lamps, which appear through the great altar under the grand tribuna, as if hanging by itſelf in the air.

All the confraternities of the city reſort thither in ſolemn proceſſion, habited in linen frocks, girt with a cord, and their heads covered with a cowl all over, that has only two holes before to ſee through. Some of theſe are all black, others parti-coloured and white; and with theſe maſqueraders that vaſt church is filled, who are ſeen thumping their breaſt, and kiſſing the pavement with extreme devotion. But methinks I am deſcribing—'tis an ill habit, but this, like every thing elſe, will wear off. We have ſent you our compliments by a friend of yours, and correſpondent in a corner, who ſeems a very agreeable man; one Mr. Williams: I am ſorry he ſtaid ſo little a while in Rome. I forget Porto Bello all this while; pray let us know where it is, and whether you or Aſheton had any hand in the taking of it. Duty to the Admiral.—Adieu! Ever yours,

T. Gray.

Letter XXXI.

MR. GRAY TO MR. WEST.

Tivoli, May 20, 1740.

THIS day being in the palace of his Highneſs the Duke of Modena, he laid his moſt ſerene commands upon me to write to Mr. Weſt, and ſaid he thought it for his glory, that I ſhould draw up an inventory of all his moſt ſerene poſſeſſions for the ſaid Weſt's peruſal.—Imprimis, a houſe, being in circumference a quarter of a mile, two feet and an inch; the ſaid houſe containing the following particulars, to wit, a great room. Item, another great room; item, a bigger room; item, another room; item, a vaſt room; item, a ſixth of the ſame; a ſeventh ditto; an eighth as before; a ninth as aboveſaid; a tenth (ſee No. 1.); item, ten more ſuch, beſides twenty beſides, which, not to be too particular, we ſhall paſs over. The ſaid rooms contain nine chairs, two tables, five ſtools and a cricket. From whence we ſhall proceed to the garden, containing two millions of ſuperfine laurel hedges, a clump of cypreſs trees, and half the river Teverone. Finis.—Dame Nature deſired me to put in a liſt of her little goods and chattels, and, as they were ſmall, to be very minute about them. She has built here three or four little mountains, and laid them out in an irregular ſemi-circle; from certain others behind, at a greater diſtance, ſhe has drawn a canal, into which ſhe has put a little river of hers, called Anio; ſhe has cut a huge cleft between the two innermoſt of her four hills, and there ſhe has left it to its own diſpoſal; which ſhe has no ſooner done, but, like a heedleſs chit, it tumbles headlong down a declivity fifty feet perpendicular, breaks itſelf all to ſhatters, and is converted into a ſhower of rain, where the ſun forms many a bow, red, green, blue, and yellow. To get out of our metaphors without any further trouble, it is the moſt noble ſight in the world. The weight of that quantity of waters, and the force they fall with, have worn the rocks they throw themſelves among into a thouſand irregular crags, and to a vaſt depth. In this channel it goes boiling along with a mighty noiſe till it comes to another ſteep, where you ſee it a ſecond time come roaring down (but firſt you muſt walk two miles farther) a greater height than before, but not with that quantity of waters; for by this time it has divided itſelf, being croſſed and oppoſed by the rocks, into four ſeveral ſtreams, each of which, in emulation of the great one, will tumble down too; and it does tumble down, but not from an equally elevated place; ſo that you have at one view all theſe caſcades intermixed with groves of olive and little woods, the mountains riſing behind them, and on the top of one (that which forms the extremity of one of the half-circle's horns) is ſeated the town itſelf. At the very extremity of that extremity, on the brink of the precipice, ſtands the Sibyl's temple, the remains of a little rotunda, ſurrounded with its portico, above half of whoſe beautiful Corinthian pillars are ſtill ſtanding and entire; all this on one hand. On the other, the open Campagna of Rome, here and there a little caſtle on a hillock, and the city itſelf on the very brink of the horizon, indiſtinctly ſeen (being 18 miles off) except the dome of St. Peter's; which, if you look out of your window, wherever you are, I ſuppoſe, you can ſee. I did not tell you that a little below the firſt fall, on the ſide of the rock, and hanging over that torrent, are little ruins which they ſhew you for Horace's houſe, a curious ſituation to obſerve the

> "Præceps Anio, & Tiburni lucus, & uda
> Mobilibus pomaria rivis."

Mæcenas did not care for ſuch a noiſe, it ſeems, and built him a houſe (which they alſo carry one to ſee) ſo ſituated that it ſees nothing at all of the matter, and for any thing he knew there might be no ſuch river in the world. Horace had another houſe on the other ſide of the Teverone, oppoſite to Mæcenas's; and they told us there was a bridge of communication, by which "andava il detto Signor per traſtullarſi coll iſteſſo Orazio." In coming hither we croſſed the Aquæ Albulæ, a vile little brook that ſtinks like a fury, and they ſay it has ſtunk ſo theſe thouſand years. I forgot the Piſcina of Quintilius

Varus, where he uſed to keep certain little fiſhes. This is very entire, and there is a piece of the aqueduct that ſupplied it too; in the garden below is old Rome, built in little, juſt as it was, they ſay. There are ſeven temples in it, and no houſes at all; They ſay there were none.

May 21.

We have had the pleaſure of going twelve miles out of our way to Paleſtrina. It has rained all day as if heaven and us were coming together. See my honeſty, I do not mention a ſyllable of the temple of Fortune, becauſe I really did not ſee it; which, I think, is pretty well for an old traveller. So we returned along the Via Præneſtina, ſaw the Lacus Gabinus and Regillus, where, you know, Caſtor and Pollux appeared upon a certain occaſion. And many a good old tomb we left on each hand, and many an aqueduct,

Dumb are whoſe fountains, and their channels dry.

There are, indeed, two whole modern ones, works of Popes, that run about thirty miles a-piece in length; one of them conveys ſtill the famous Aqua Virgo to Rome, and adds vaſt beauty to the proſpect. So we came to Rome again, where waited for us a ſplendidiſſimo regalo of letters; in one of which came You, with your huge characters and wide intervals, ſtaring. I would have you to know, I expect you ſhould take a handſome crow-quill when you write to me, and not leave room for a pin's point in four ſides of a ſheet of royal. Do you but find matter, I will find ſpectacles.

I have more time than I thought, and I will employ it in telling you about a ball that we were at the other evening. Figure to yourſelf a Roman villa; all its little apartments thrown open, and lighted up to the beſt advantage. At the upper end of the gallery, a fine concert, in which La Diamantina, a famous virtuoſa, played on the violin divinely, and ſung angelically; Giovannino and Paſqualini (great names in muſical ſtory) alſo performed miraculouſly. On each ſide were ranged all the ſecular grand monde of Rome, the Ambaſſadors, Princeſſes, and all that. Among the reſt Il Sereniſſimo Pretendente (as the Mantova gazette calls him) diſplayed his rueful length of perſon, with his two young ones, and all his miniſtry around him. "Poi nacque un grazioſo ballo," where the world danced, and I ſat in a corner regaling myſelf with iced fruits, and other pleaſant rinfreſcatives.

Letter XXXII.

MR. GRAY TO MR. WEST.

Rome, May, 1740.

MATER roſarum, cui teneræ vigent
Auræ Favonî, cui Venus it comes
Laſciva, Nympharum choreis
Et volucrum celebrata cantu!
Dic, non inertem fallere quâ diem
Amat ſub umbrâ, ſeu ſinit aureum
Dormire plectrum, ſeu retentat
Pierio Zephyrinus antro
Furore dulci plenus, et immemor
Reptantis inter frigora Tuſculi
Umbroſa, vel colles amici
Palladiæ ſuperantis Albæ.

Dilecta Fauno, et capripedum choris
Pineta, testor vos, Anio minax
Quæcunque per clivos volutus
Præcipiti tremefecit amne,
Illius altum Tibur, et Æsulæ
Audîsse sylvas nomen amabiles,
Illius et gratas Latinis
Naisin ingeminâsse rupes;
Nam me Latinæ Naides uvidâ
Vidêre ripâ, quâ niveas levi
Tam sæpe lavit rore plumas
Dulcè canens Venusinus ales;
Mirum! canenti conticuit nemus,
Sacrique fontes, et retinent adhuc
(Sic Musa jussit) saxa molles
Docta modos, veteresque lauri.
Mirare nec tu me citharæ rudem
Claudis laborantem numeris: loca
Amœna, jucundumque ver in-
compositum docuere carmen;

Hærent ſub omni nam folio nigri
Phœbea luci (credite) ſomnia,
Argutiuſque et lympha et auræ
Neſcio quid ſolito loquuntur.

I am to-day juſt returned from Alba, a good deal fatigued; for you know the Appian is ſomewhat tireſome. We dined at Pompey's; he indeed was gone for a few days to his Tuſculan, but, by the care of his Villicus, we made an admirable meal. We had the dugs of a pregnant ſow, a peacock, a diſh of thruſhes, a noble ſcarus juſt freſh from the Tyrrhene, and ſome conchylia of the Lake with garum ſauce: For my part I never eat better at Lucullus's table. We drank half-a-dozen cyathi a-piece of ancient Alban to Pholoë's health; and, after bathing, and playing an hour at ball, we mounted our eſſedum again, and proceeded up the mount to the temple. The prieſts there entertained us with an account of a wonderful ſhower of birds' eggs, that had fallen two days before, which had no ſooner touched the ground, but they were converted into gudgeons; as alſo that the night paſt, a dreadful voice had been heard out of the Adytum, which ſpoke Greek during a full half-hour, but nobody underſtood it. But quitting my Romanities, to your great joy and mine, let me tell you in plain Engliſh, that we come from Albano. The preſent town lies within the incloſure of Pompey's Villa in ruins. The Appian way runs through it, by the ſide of which, a little farther, is a large old tomb, with five pyramids upon it, which the learned ſuppoſe to be the burying-place of the family, becauſe they do not know whoſe it can be elſe. But the vulgar aſſure you it is the ſepulchre of the Curiatii, and by that name (ſuch is their power) it goes. One drives to Caſtel Gondolfo, a houſe of the Pope's, ſituated on the top of one of the Collinette, that forms a brim to the baſin, commonly called the Alban lake. It is ſeven miles round; and directly oppoſite to you, on the other ſide, riſes the Mons Albanus, much taller than the reſt, along whoſe ſide are ſtill diſcoverable (not to common eyes) certain little ruins of the old Alba Longa. They had need be very little, as having been nothing but ruins ever ſince the days of Tullus Hoſtilius. On its top is a houſe of the Conſtable Colonna's, where ſtood the temple of Jupiter Latialis. At the foot of the hill Gondolfo, are the famous outlets of the lake, built with hewn ſtone, a mile and a half under ground. Livy, you know, amply informs us of the fooliſh occaſion of this expence, and gives me this opportunity of diſplaying all my erudition, that I may appear conſiderable in your eyes. This is the proſpect from one window of the palace. From another you have the whole Campagna, the City, Antium, and the Tyrrhene ſea (twelve miles diſtant) ſo diſtinguiſhable, that you may ſee the veſſels ſailing upon it. All this is charming. Mr. Walpole ſays, our memory ſees more than our eyes in this country. Which is extremely true; ſince, for realities, Windſor, or Richmond Hill, is infinitely preferable to Albano or Freſcati. I am now at home, and going to the window to tell you it is the moſt beautiful of Italian nights, which, in truth, are but juſt begun (ſo backward has the ſpring been here, and every where elſe, they ſay). There is a moon! there are ſtars for you! Do not you hear the fountain? Do not you ſmell the orange flowers? That building yonder is the convent of S. Iſidore; and that eminence, with the cypreſs trees and pines upon it, the top of M. Quirinal. This is all true, and yet my proſpect is not two hundred yards in length. We ſend you ſome Roman inſcriptions to entertain you. The firſt two are modern, tranſcribed from the Vatican library by Mr. Walpole.

Pontifices olim quem fundavere priores,
  Præcipuâ Sixtus perficit arte tholum;[2]
Et Sixti tantum ſe gloria tollit in altum,
  Quantum ſe Sixti nobile tollit opus:
Magnus honos magni fundamina ponere templi,
  Sed finem cæptis ponere major honos.
Saxa agit Amphion, Thebana ut mænia condat:
  Sixtus & immenſæ pondera molis agit.[3]
Saxa trahunt ambo longè diverſa: ſed arte
  Hæc trahit Amphion; Sixtus & arte trahit.
At tantum exſuperat Dircæum Amphiona Sixtus,
  Quantum hic exſuperat cætera ſaxa lapis.

Mine is ancient, and I think not leſs curious. It is exactly tranſcribed from a ſepulchral marble at the villa Giuſtiniani. I put ſtops to it, when I underſtand it.

Dis Manibus
Claudiæ, Piſtes
Primus Conjugi
Optumae, Sanctae,
Et Piae, Benemeritate.

Non æquos, Parcae, ſtatuiſtis ſtamina vitæ.
Tam bene compoſitos potuiſtis ſede tenere.
Amiſſa eſt conjux. cur ego & ipſe moror?
Si · bella · eſſe · mî · iſte · mea · vivere · debuit ·
Triſtia contigerunt qui amiſsâ conjuge vivo.
Nil eſt tam miſerum, quam totam perdere vitam.
Nec vita enaſci dura peregiſtis crudelia penſa, ſorores,
Ruptaque deficiunt in primo munere fuſi.
O nimis injuſtæ ter denos dare munus in annos,
Deceptus · grautus · fatum · ſic · preſſit · egeſtas ·
Dum vitam tulero, Primus Piſtes lugea conjugium.

LETTER XXXIII.

MR. GRAY TO HIS MOTHER.

Naples, June 17, 1740.

OUR journey hither was through the moſt beautiful part of the fineſt country in the world; and every ſpot of it on ſome account or other, famous for theſe three thouſand years paſt. The ſeaſon has hitherto been juſt as warm as one would wiſh it; no unwholeſome airs, or violent heats, yet heard of: The people call it a backward year, and are in pain about their corn, wine, and oil; but we, who are neither corn, wine, nor oil, find it very agreeable. Our road was through Velletri, Ciſterna, Terracina, Capua, and Averſa, and ſo to Naples. The minute one leaves his Holineſs's dominions, the face of things begins to change from wide uncultivated plains to olive groves and well-tilled fields of corn, intermixed with ranks of elms, every one of which has its vine twining about it, and hanging in feſtoons between the rows from one tree to another. The great old fig-trees, the oranges in full bloom, and myrtles in every hedge, make one of the delightfulleſt ſcenes you can conceive; beſides that, the roads are wide, well-kept, and full of paſſengers, a ſight I have not beheld this long time. My wonder ſtill increaſed upon entering the city, which I think for number of people, outdoes both Paris and London. The ſtreets are one continued market, and thronged with populace ſo much that a coach can hardly paſs. The common ſort are a jolly lively kind of animals, more induſtrious than Italians uſually are; they work till evening; then take their lute or guitar (for they all play) and walk about the city, or upon the ſea-ſhore with it, to enjoy the freſco. One ſees their little brown children jumping about ſtark-naked, and the bigger ones dancing with caſtanets, while others play on the cymbal to them. Your maps will ſhow you the ſituation of Naples; it is on the moſt lovely bay in the world, and one of the calmeſt ſeas: It has many other beauties beſides thoſe of nature.

We have ſpent two days in viſiting the remarkable places in the country round it, ſuch as the bay of Baiæ, and its remains of antiquity; the lake Avernus, and the Solfatara, Charon's grotto, &c. We have been in the Sibyl's cave and many other ſtrange holes under ground (I only name them becauſe you may conſult Sandy's travels); but the ſtrangeſt hole I ever was in, has been to-day at a place called Portici, where his Sicilian Majeſty has a country-ſeat. About a year ago, as they were digging, they diſcovered ſome parts of ancient buildings above thirty feet deep in the ground: Curioſity led them on, and they have been digging ever ſince; the paſſage they have made, with all its turnings and windings, is now more than a mile long. As you walk you ſee parts of an amphitheatre, many houſes adorned with marble columns, and incruſted with the ſame; the front of a temple, ſeveral arched vaults of rooms painted in freſco. Some pieces of painting have been taken out from hence finer than any thing of the kind before diſcovered, and with theſe the king has adorned his palace; alſo a number of ſtatues, medals, and gems;

and more are dug out every day. This is known to be a Roman town, that in the emperor Titus's time was overwhelmed by a furious eruption of Mount Veſuvius, which is hard by. The wood and beams remain ſo perfect that you may ſee the grain! but burnt to a coal, and dropping into duſt upon the leaſt touch. We were to-day at the foot of that mountain, which at preſent ſmokes only a little, where we ſaw the materials that fed the ſtream of fire, which about four years ſince ran down its ſide. We have but a few days longer to ſtay here; too little in conſcience for ſuch a place. * * *

Letter XXXIV.

MR. GRAY TO HIS FATHER.

Florence, July 16, 1740.

AT my return to this city, the day before yesterday, I had the pleasure of finding yours dated June the 9th. The period of our voyages, at least towards the South, is come as you wish. We have been at Naples, spent nine or ten days there, and returned to Rome, where finding no likelihood of a Pope yet these three months, and quite wearied with the formal assemblies and little society of that great city, Mr. Walpole determined to return hither to spend the summer, where he imagines he shall pass his time more agreeably than in the tedious expectation of what, when it happens, will only be a great show. For my own part, I give up the thoughts of all that with but little regret; but the city itself I do not part with so easily, which alone has amuſements for whole years. However, I have paſſed through all that moſt people do, both ancient and modern; what that is you may ſee better than I can tell you, in a thouſand books. The Conclave we left in greater uncertainty than ever; the more than ordinary liberty they enjoy there, and the unuſual coolneſs of the ſeaſon, makes the confinement leſs diſagreeable to them than common, and conſequently maintains them in their irreſolution. There have been very high words, one or two (it is ſaid) have come even to blows; two more are dead within this laſt month, Cenci and Portia; the latter died diſtracted: and we left another (Altieri) at the extremity: Yet nobody dreams of an election till the latter end of September. All this gives great ſcandal to all good catholics, and every body talks very freely on the ſubject. The Pretender (whom you deſire an account of) I have had frequent opportunities of ſeeing at church, at the corſo, and other places; but more particularly, and that for a whole night, at a great ball given by Count Patrizii to the Prince and Princeſs Craon, (who were come to Rome at that time, that he might receive from the hands of the Emperor's miniſter there, the order of the golden fleece) at which he and his two ſons were preſent. They are good fine boys, eſpecially the younger, who has the more ſpirit of the two, and both danced inceſſantly all night long. For him, he is a thin ill-made man, extremely tall and awkward, of a moſt unpromiſing countenance, a good deal reſembling King James the Second, and has extremely the air and look of an idiot, particularly when he laughs or prays. The firſt he does not often, the latter continually. He lives private enough with his little court about him, conſiſting of Lord Dunbar, who manages every thing, and two or three of the Preſton Scotch Lords, who would be very glad to make their peace at home.

We happened to be at Naples on Corpus Chriſti Day, the greateſt feaſt in the year, ſo had an opportunity of ſeeing their Sicilian Majeſties to advantage. The King walked in the grand proceſſion, and the Queen (being big with child) ſat in a balcony. He followed the Hoſt to the Church of St. Clara, where high maſs was celebrated to a glorious concert of mufic. They are as ugly a little pair as one can fee: fhe a pale girl marked with the fmall-pox; and he a brown boy with a thin face, a huge nofe, and as ungain as poffible.

We are fettled here with Mr. Mann in a charming apartment; the river Arno runs under our windows, which we can fifh out of. The fky is fo ferene, and the air fo temperate, that one continues in the open air all night long in a flight nightgown without any danger; and the marble bridge is the refort of every body, where they hear mufic, eat iced fruits, and fup by moonlight; though as yet (the feafon being extremely backward every where) thefe amufements are not begun. You fee we are now coming northward again, though in no great hafte; the Venetian and Milanefe territories, and either Germany or the South of France, (according to the turn the war may take,) are all that remain for us, that we have not yet feen; as to Loretto, and that part of Italy, we have given over all thoughts of it.

Letter XXXV.

MR. GRAY TO MR. WEST.

Florence, July 16, 1740.

YOU do yourſelf and me juſtice, in imagining that you merit, and that I am capable of ſincerity. I have not a thought, or even a weakneſs, I deſire to conceal from you; and conſequently on my ſide deſerve to be treated with the ſame openneſs of heart. My vanity perhaps might make me more reſerved towards you, if you were one of the heroic race, ſuperior to all human failings; but as mutual wants are the ties of general ſociety, ſo are mutual weakneſſes of private friendſhips, ſuppoſing them mixt with ſome proportion of good qualities; for where one may not ſometimes blame, one does not much care ever to praiſe. All this has the air of an introduction deſigned to ſoften a very harſh reproof that is to follow; but it is no ſuch matter:

I only meant to aſk, Why did you change your lodging? Was the air bad, or the ſituation melancholy? If ſo, you are quite in the right. Only, is it not putting yourſelf a little out of the way of a people, with whom it ſeems neceſſary to keep up ſome ſort of intercourſe and converſation, though but little for your pleaſure or entertainment, (yet there are, I believe, ſuch among them as might give you both,) at leaſt for your information in that ſtudy, which, when I left you, you thought of applying to? for that there is a certain ſtudy neceſſary to be followed, if we mean to be of any uſe in the world, I take for granted; diſagreeable enough (as moſt neceſſities are) but, I am afraid, unavoidable. Into how many branches theſe ſtudies are divided in England, every body knows; and between that which you and I had pitched upon and the other two, it was impoſſible to balance long. Examples ſhew one that it is not abſolutely neceſſary to be a blockhead to ſucceed in this profeſſion. The labour is long, and the elements dry and unentertaining; nor was ever any body (eſpecially thoſe that afterwards made a figure in it) amuſed or even not diſguſted in the beginning; yet upon a further acquaintance, there is ſurely matter for curioſity and reflection. It is ſtrange if, among all that huge maſs of words, there be not ſomewhat intermixed for thought. Laws have been the reſult of long deliberation, and that not of dull men, but the contrary; and have ſo cloſe a connection with hiſtory, nay, with philoſophy itſelf, that they muſt partake a little of what they are related to ſo nearly. Beſides, tell me, have you ever made the attempt? Was not you frighted merely with the diſtant proſpect? Had the Gothic character and bulkineſs of thoſe volumes (a tenth part of which perhaps it will be no further neceſſary to conſult, than as one does a dictionary) no ill effect upon your eye? Are you ſure, if Coke had been printed by Elzevir, and bound in twenty neat pocket volumes, inſtead of one folio, you ſhould never have taken him for an hour, as you would a Tully, or drank your tea over him? I know how great an obſtacle ill ſpirits are to reſolution. Do you really think, if you rid ten miles every morning, in a week's time you ſhould not entertain much ſtronger hopes of the Chancellorſhip, and think it a much more probable thing than you do at preſent? The advantages you mention are not nothing; our inclinations are more than we imagine in our own power; reaſon and reſolution determine them, and ſupport under many difficulties. To me there hardly appears to be any medium between a public life and a private one; he who prefers the firſt, muſt put himſelf in a way of being ſerviceable to the reſt of mankind, if he has a mind to be of any conſequence among them: Nay, he muſt not refuſe being in a certain degree even dependent upon ſome men who are ſo already. If he has the good fortune to light on ſuch as will make no ill uſe of his humility, there is no ſhame in this: If not, his ambition ought to give place to a reaſonable pride, and he ſhould apply to the cultivation of his own mind thoſe abilities which he has not been permitted to uſe for others' ſervice. Such a private happineſs (ſuppoſing a ſmall competence of fortune) is almoſt always in every one's power, and the proper enjoyment of age, as the other is the employment of youth. You are yet young, have ſome advantages and opportunities, and an undoubted capacity, which you have never yet put to the trial. Set apart a few hours, ſee how the firſt year will agree with you, at the end of it you are ſtill the maſter; if you change your mind, you will only have got the knowledge of a little ſomewhat that can do no hurt, or give you cauſe of repentance. If your inclination be not fixed upon any thing elſe, it is a ſymptom that you are not abſolutely determined againſt this, and warns you not to miſtake mere indolence for inability. I am ſenſible there is nothing ſtronger againſt what I would perſuade you to, than my own practice; which may make you imagine I think not as I ſpeak. Alas! it is not ſo; but I do not act what I think, and I had rather be the object of your pity, than you ſhould be that of mine; and be aſſured, the advantage that I may receive from it, does not diminiſh my concern in hearing you want ſomebody to converſe with freely, whoſe advice might be of more weight, and always at hand. We have ſome time ſince come to the ſouthern period of our voyages; we ſpent about nine days at Naples. It is the largeſt and moſt populous city, as its environs are the moſt deliciouſly fertile country, of all Italy. We ſailed in the bay of Baiæ, ſweated in the Solfatara, and died in the grotto del Cane, as all ſtrangers do; ſaw the Corpus Chriſti proceſſion, and the King and the Queen, and the city underground, (which is a wonder I reſerve to tell you of another time,) and ſo returned to Rome for another fortnight; left it (left Rome!) and came hither for the ſummer. You have ſeen an Epiſtle to Mr. Aſhton,[4] that ſeems to me to be full of ſpirit and thought, and a good deal of poetic fire. I would know your opinion. Now I talk of verſes, Mr. Walpole and I have frequently wondered you ſhould never mention a certain imitation of Spenſer, publiſhed laſt year by a nameſake[5] of yours, with which we are all enraptured and enmarvailed.

Letter XXXVI.

MR. WALPOLE AND MR. GRAY TO MR. WEST.

Dear West, Florence, July 31, 1740, N. S.

I HAVE advifed with the moft noteable antiquarians of this city, on the meaning of *Thur gut Luetis;* I can get no fatisfactory interpretation. In my own opinion 'tis Welfh. I don't love offering conjectures on a language in which I have hitherto made little proficiency, but I will truft you with my explication. You know the famous Aglaughlan, mother of Cadwalladhor, was renowned for her conjugal virtues, and grief on the death of her royal fpoufe. I conclude this medal was ftruck in her regency, by her exprefs order, to the memory of her Lord, and that the infcription, *Thur gut Luetis*, means no more than her *dear Llewis*, or *Llewellin.*

In return for your coins I ſend you two or three of different kinds. The firſt is a money of one of the kings of Naples; the device a horſe; the motto, *Equitas regni.* This curious pun is on a coin in the Great Duke's collection, and by great chance I have met with a ſecond. Another is a ſatirical medal ſtruck on Lewis XIV.; 'tis a bomb, covered with flower-de-luces, burſting, the motto, *Se ipſiſſimo.* The laſt, and almoſt the only one I ever ſaw with a text well applied, is a German medal, with a rebellious town beſieged and blocked up; the inſcription, *This kind is not expelled but by faſting.*

Now I mention medals, have they yet ſtruck the intended one on the taking Porto Bello? Admiral Vernon will ſhine in our medallic hiſtory. We have juſt received the news of the bombarding Carthagena, and the taking Chagre. We are in great expectation of ſome important victory obtained by the ſquadron under Sir John Norris: we are told the Duke is to be of the expedition; is it true? All the letters too talk of France's ſuddenly declaring war; I hope they will defer it for a ſeaſon, or one ſhall be obliged to come through Germany. The Conclave ſtill ſubſiſts, and the diviſions ſtill increaſe; it was very near ſeparating laſt week, but by breaking into two Popes; they were on the dawn of a ſchiſm. Aldovrandi had thirty-three voices for three days, but could not procure the requiſite two more; the Camerlingo having engaged his faction to ſign a proteſtation againſt him, and each party were inclined to elect.

I don't know whether one ſhould wiſh for a ſchiſm or not; it might probably rekindle the zeal for the church in the powers of Europe, which has been ſo far decaying. On Wedneſday we expect a third ſhe-meteor. Thoſe learned luminaries the ladies P—— and W—— are to be joined by the lady M—— W—— M——. You have not been witneſs to the rhapſody of myſtic nonſenſe which theſe two fair ones debate inceſſantly, and conſequently cannot figure what muſt be the iſſue of this triple alliance; we have ſome idea of it. Only figure the coalition of prudery, debauchery, ſentiment, hiſtory, Greek, Latin, French, Italian, and metaphyſics; all except the ſecond underſtood by halves, by quarters, or not at all. You ſhall have the journals of this notable academy. Adieu, my dear Weſt. Yours ever,

HOR. WALPOLE.

THOUGH far unworthy to enter into ſo learned and political a correſpondence, I am employed pour barbouiller une page de ſept pouces et demie en hauteur, et cinq en largeur; and to inform you that we are at Florence, a city of Italy, and the capital of Tuſcany; the latitude I cannot juſtly tell, but it is governed by a Prince called Great Duke; an excellent place to employ all one's animal ſenſations in, but utterly contrary to one's rational powers. I have ſtruck a medal upon myſelf: the device is thus, O, and the motto *Nihiliſſimo*, which I take in the moſt conciſe manner to contain a full account of my perſon, ſentiments, occupations, and late glorious ſucceſſes. If you chooſe to be annihilated too, you cannot do better than undertake this journey. Here you ſhall get up at twelve o'clock, breakfaſt till three, dine till five, ſleep till ſix, drink cooling liquors till eight, go to the bridge till ten, ſup till two, and ſo ſleep till twelve again.

> Labore feſſi venimus ad larem noſtrum
> Deſideratoque acquieſcimus lecto:
> Hoc eſt, quod unum eſt, pro laboribus tantis.
> O quid ſolutis eſt beatius curis?

We ſhall never come home again; a univerſal war is juſt upon the point of breaking out; all out-lets will be ſhut up. I ſhall be ſecure in my nothingneſs, while you that will be ſo abſurd as to exiſt, will envy me. You don't tell me what proficiency you make in the noble ſcience of defence. Don't you ſtart ſtill at the ſound of a gun? Have you learned to ſay Ha! ha! and is your neck clothed with thunder? Are your whiſkers of a tolerable length? And have you got drunk yet with brandy and gunpowder? Adieu, noble Captain!

T. Gray.

Letter XXXVII.

MR. GRAY TO HIS MOTHER.

Florence, Aug. 21, N.S. 1740.

IT is ſome time ſince I have had the pleaſure of writing to you, having been upon a little excurſion croſs the mountains to Bologna. We ſet out from hence at ſun-ſet, paſſed the Appennines by moon-light, travelling inceſſantly till we came to Bologna at four in the afternoon next day. There we ſpent a week agreeably enough, and returned as we came. The day before yeſterday arrived the news of a Pope; and I have the mortification of being within four days journey of Rome, and not ſeeing his coronation, the heats being violent, and the infectious air now at its height. We had an inſtance, the other day, that it is not only fancy. Two country fellows, ſtrong men, and uſed to the country about Rome, having occaſion to come from thence hither, and travelling on foot, as common with them, one died ſuddenly on the road; the other got hither, but extremely weak, and in a manner ſtupid; he was carried to the hoſpital, but died in two days. So, between fear and lazineſs, we remain here, and muſt be ſatisfied with the accounts other people give us of the matter. The new Pope is called Benedict XIV. being created Cardinal by Benedict XIII. the laſt Pope but one. His name is Lambertini, a noble Bologneſe, and Archbiſhop of that city. When I was firſt there I remember to have ſeen him two or three times; he is a ſhort, fat man, about ſixty-five years of age, of a hearty, merry countenance, and likely to live ſome years. He bears a good character for generoſity, affability, and other virtues; and, they ſay, wants neither knowledge nor capacity. The worſt ſide of him is, that he has a nephew or two; beſides a certain young favourite, called Melára, who is ſaid to have had, for ſome time, the arbitrary diſpoſal of his purſe and family. He is reported to have made a little ſpeech to the Cardinals in the Conclave, while they were undetermined about an election, as follows: "Most eminent Lords, here are three Bolognese of different characters, but all equally proper for the Popedom. If it be your pleasures to pitch upon a Saint, there is Cardinal Gotti; if upon a Politician, there is Aldrovandi; if upon a Booby, here am I." The Italian is much more expressive, and, indeed, not to be translated; wherefore, if you meet with any body that understands it, you may show them what he said in the language he spoke it. "Eminssimi Sigri. Ci siamo tré, diversi sì, mà tutti idonei al Papato. Si vi piace un Santo, c' è l'Gotti; se volete una testa scaltra, e Politica, c' è l'Aldrovandi; se un Coglione, ecco mi!" Cardinal Coscia is restored to his liberty, and, it is said, will be to all his benefices. Corsini (the late Pope's nephew) as he has had no hand in this election, it is hoped, will be called to account for all his villanous practices. The Pretender, they say, has resigned all his pretensions to his eldest boy, and will accept of the Grand Chancellorship, which is thirty thousand crowns a-year; the pension he has at preſent is only twenty thouſand. I do not affirm the truth of this article; becauſe, if he does, it is neceſſary he ſhould take the eccleſiaſtical habit, and it will ſound mighty odd to be called his Majeſty the Chancellor. ——So ends my Gazette.

Letter XXXVIII.

MR. GRAY TO MR. WEST.

Florence, Sept. 25, N. S. 1740.

WHAT I ſend you now, as long as it is, is but a piece of a poem. It has the advantage of all fragments, to need neither introduction nor concluſion: Beſides, if you do not like it, it is but imagining that which went before, and came after, to be infinitely better. Look in Sandy's Travels for the hiſtory of Monte Barbaro, and Monte Nuovo.

" Weſt of Cicero's villa ſtands the eminent Gaurus, a " ſtony and deſolate mountain, in which there are diverſe " obſcure caverns, choked almoſt with earth, where many " have conſumed much fruitleſs induſtry in ſearching for " treaſure. The famous Lucrine Lake extended formerly " from Avernus to the aforeſaid Gaurus: But is now no

" other than a little ſedgy plaſh, choked up by the horrible " and aſtoniſhing eruption of the new mountain: whereof, " as oft as I think, I am eaſy to credit whatſoever is " wonderful. For who here knows not, or who elſewhere " will believe, that a mountain ſhould ariſe, (partly out of " a lake and partly out of the ſea,) in one day and a night, " unto ſuch a height as to contend in altitude with the " high mountains adjoining? In the year of our Lord " 1538, on the 29th of September, when for certain days " foregoing the country hereabout was ſo vexed with per- " petual earthquakes, as no one houſe was left ſo entire as " not to expect an immediate ruin; after that the ſea had " retired two hundred paces from the ſhore, (leaving " abundance of fiſh, and ſprings of freſh water riſing in " the bottom,) this mountain viſibly aſcended about the " ſecond hour of the night, with an hideous roaring, " horribly vomiting ſtones and ſuch ſtore of cinders as " overwhelmed all the building thereabout, and the ſalu- " brious baths of Tripergula, for ſo many ages celebrated; " conſumed the vines to aſhes, killing birds and beaſts: the

" fearful inhabitants of Puzzol flying through the dark " with their wives and children; naked, defiled, crying " out, and deteſting their calamities. Manifold miſchiefs " have they ſuffered by the barbarous, yet none like this " which Nature inflicted.——This new mountain, when " newly raiſed, had a number of iſſues; at ſome of them " ſmoking and ſometimes flaming; at others diſgorging " rivulets of hot waters; keeping within a terrible rum- " bling; and many miſerably periſhed that ventured to " deſcend into the hollowneſs above. But that hollow on " the top is at preſent an orchard, and the mountain " throughout is bereft of its terrors."—SANDY's *Travels*, book iv. pages 275, 277, and 278.

Nec procul infelix ſe tollit in æthera Gaurus,
Proſpiciens vitreum lugenti vertice pontum:
Triſtior ille diu, et veteri deſuetus olivâ
Gaurus, pampineæque, eheu! jam neſcius umbræ;
Horrendi tam ſæva premit vicinia montis,
Attonitumque urget latus, exuritque ferentem.

Nam ſama eſt olim, mediâ dum rura ſilebant
Nocte, Deo victa, et molli perfuſa quiete,
Infremuiſſe æquor ponti, auditamque per omnes
Latè tellurem ſurdùm immugire cavernas:
Quo ſonitu nemora alta tremunt: tremit excita tuto
Parthenopæa ſinu, flammantiſque ora Veſevi.
At ſubitò ſe aperire ſolum, vaſtoſque receſſus
Pandere ſub pedibus, nigrâque voragine fauces;
Tum piceas cinerum glomerare ſub æthere nubes
Vorticibus rapidis, ardentique imbre procellam.
Præcipites fugere feræ, perque avia longè
Sylvarum fugit paſtor, juga per deſerta,
Ah, miſer! increpitans ſæpe altâ voce per umbram
Nequicquam natos, creditque audire ſequentes.
Atque ille excelſo rupis de vertice ſolus
Reſpectans notaſque domos, et dulcia regna,
Nil uſquàm videt infelix præter mare triſti
Lumine percuſſum, et pallentes ſulphure campos
Fumumque, flammaſque, rotataque turbine ſaxa.
Quin ubi detonuit fragor, et lux reddita cœlo;

Mæſtos confluere agricolas, paſſuque videres
Tandem iterum timido deſerta requirere tecta:
Sperantes, ſi forte oculis, ſi forte darentur
Uxorum cineres, miſerorumve oſſa parentum
(Tenuia, ſed tanti ſaltem ſolatia luctûs)
Unà colligere et juſtâ componere in urnâ.
Uxorum nuſquam cineres, nuſquam oſſa parentum
(Spem miſeram!) aſſuetoſve Lares, aut rura videbunt.
Quippe ubi planities campi diffuſa jacebat;
Mons novus: ille ſupercilium, frontemque favillâ
Incanum oſtentans, ambuſtis cautibus, æquor
Subjectum, ſtragemque ſuam, mæſta arva, minaci
Deſpicit imperio, ſoloque in littore regnat.
  Hinc infame loci nomen, multoſque per annos
Immemor antiquæ laudis, neſcire labores
Vomeris, et nullo tellus revireſcere cultu.
Non avium colles, non carmine matutino
Paſtorum reſonare; adeò undique dirus habebat
Informes latè horror agros ſaltuſque vacantes.
Sæpius et longè detorquens navita proram

Monſtrabat digito littus, ſævæque revolvens
Funera narrabat noctis, veteremque ruinam.
  Montis adhuc facies manet hirta atque aſpera ſaxis:
Sed furor extinctus jamdudum, et flamma quievit,
Quæ naſcenti aderat; ſeu fortè bituminis atri
Defluxere olim rivi, atque effœta lacuna
Pabula ſufficere ardori, vireſque recuſat;
Sive in viſceribus meditans incendia jam nunc
(Horrendùm) arcanis glomerat genti eſſe futuræ
Exitio, ſparſos tacituſque recolligit ignes.
  Raro per clivos haud ſecius ordine vidi
Caneſcentem oleam: longum poſt tempus amicti
Vite virent tumuli; patriamque reviſere gaudens
Bacchus in aſſuetis tenerum caput exerit arvis
Vix tandem, infidoque audet ſe credere cœlo.

There was a certain little ode ſet out from Rome in a letter of recommendation to you, but poſſibly fell into the enemies' hands, for I never heard of its arrival. It is a little impertinent to enquire after its welfare; but you, that are a father, will excuse a parent's foolish fondness. Last post I received a very diminutive letter: It made excuses for its unentertainingness, very little to the purpose; since it assured me, very strongly, of your esteem, which is to me the thing; all the rest appear but as the petits agrémens, the garnishing of the dish. P. Bougeant, in his Langage des Bêtes, fancies that your birds, who continually repeat the same note, say only in plain terms, "Je vous aime, ma chère; ma chère, je vous aime;" and that those of greater genius indeed, with various trills, run divisions upon the subject; but that the *fond*, from whence it all proceeds, is "toujours je vous aime." Now you may, as you find yourself dull or in humour, either take me for a chaffinch or nightingale; sing your plain song, or show your skill in music, but in the bottom let there be, toujours de l'amitié.

As to what you call my serious letter; be assured, that your future state is to me entirely indifferent. Do not be angry, but hear me; I mean with respect to myself. For whether you be at the top of Fame, or entirely unknown to mankind; at the Council-table, or at Dick's coffee-houſe; ſick and ſimple, or well and wiſe; whatever alteration mere accident works in you, (ſuppoſing it utterly impoſſible for it to make any change in your ſincerity and honeſty, ſince theſe are conditions ſine quâ non) I do not ſee any likelihood of my not being yours ever.

Letter XXXIX.

MR. GRAY TO HIS FATHER.

Florence, Oct. 9, 1740.

THE beginning of next ſpring is the time determined for our return at furtheſt; poſſibly it may be before that time. How the interim will be employed, or what route we ſhall take is not ſo certain. If we remain friends with France, upon leaving this country we ſhall croſs over to Venice, and ſo return through the cities north of the Po to Genoa; from thence take a felucca to Marſeilles, and come back through Paris. If the contrary fall out, which ſeems not unlikely, we muſt take the Milaneſe, and thoſe parts of Italy, in our way to Venice; from thence paſs through the Tirol into Germany, and come home by the Low-Countries. As for Florence, it has been gayer than ordinary for this laſt month, being one round of balls and entertainments, occaſioned by the arrival of a great Milaneſe Lady; for the only thing the Italians ſhine in, is their reception of ſtrangers. At ſuch times every thing is magnificence: The more remarkable, as in their ordinary courſe of life they are parſimonious, even to a degree of naſtineſs. I ſaw in one of the vaſteſt palaces in Rome (that of Prince Pamfilio) the apartment which he himſelf inhabited, a bed that moſt ſervants in England would diſdain to lie in, and furniture much like that of a ſoph at Cambridge, for convenience and neatneſs. This man is worth 30,000*l.* ſterling a year. As for eating, there are not two Cardinals in Rome that allow more than ſix paoli, which is three ſhillings a day, for the expence of their table: and you may imagine they are ſtill leſs extravagant here than there. But when they receive a viſit from any friend, their houſes and perſons are ſet out to the greateſt advantage, and appear in all their ſplendour; it is, indeed, from a motive of vanity, and with the hopes of having it repaid them with intereſt, whenever they have occaſion to return the viſit. I call viſits going from one city of Italy to another; for it is not ſo among acquaintance of the ſame place on common occaſions. The new Pope has retrenched the charges of his own table to a ſequin (ten ſhillings) a meal. The applauſe which all he ſays and does meets with, is enough to encourage him really to deſerve fame. They ſay he is an able and honeſt man; he is reckoned a wit too. The other day, when the Senator of Rome came to wait upon him, at the firſt compliments he made him, the Pope pulled off his cap: His Maſter of the Ceremonies, who ſtood by his ſide, touched him ſoftly, as to warn him that ſuch a condeſcenſion was too great in him, and out of all manner of rule: Upon which he turned to him and ſaid, "Oh! I cry you mercy, good Maſter, it is true, I am but a Novice of a Pope; I have not yet ſo much as learned ill manners." * * *

Letter XL.

MR. GRAY TO HIS FATHER.

Florence, Jan. 12, 1741.

WE ſtill continue conſtant at Florence, at preſent one of the dulleſt cities in Italy. Though it is the middle of the Carnival there are no public diverſions; nor is maſquerading permitted as yet. The Emperor's obſequies are to be celebrated publicly the 16th of this month; and after that, it is imagined every thing will go on in its uſual courſe. In the mean time, to employ the minds of the populace, the Government has thought fit to bring into the city in a ſolemn manner, and at a great expence, a famous ſtatue of the Virgin called the Madonna dell' Impruneta, from the place of her reſidence, which is upon a mountain ſeven miles off. It never has been practiſed but at times of public calamity; and was done at preſent to avert the ill effects of a late great inundation, which it was feared might cause some epidemical distemper. It was introduced a fortnight ago in procession, attended by the Council of Regency, the Senate, the Nobility, and all the Religious Orders, on foot and bare-headed, and so carried to the great church, where it was frequented by an infinite concourse of people from all the country round. Among the rest I paid my devotions almost every day, and saw numbers of people possessed with the devil who were brought to be exorcised. It was indeed in the evening, and the church-doors were always shut before the ceremonies were finished, so that I could not be eye-witness of the event; but that they were all cured is certain, for one never heard any more of them the next morning. I am to-night just returned from seeing our Lady make her exit with the same solemnities she entered. The show had a finer effect than before; for it was dark; and every body (even those of the mob that could afford it) bore a white wax flambeau. I believe there were at least five thousand of them, and the march was near three hours in passing before the window.

The ſubject of all this devotion is ſuppoſed to be a large Tile with a rude figure in bas-relief upon it. I ſay ſuppoſed, becauſe ſince the time it was found (for it was found in the earth in ploughing) only two people have ſeen it; the one was, by good luck, a ſaint; the other was ſtruck blind for his preſumption. Ever ſince ſhe has been covered with ſeven veils; nevertheleſs, thoſe who approach her tabernacle caſt their eyes down, for fear they ſhould ſpy her through all her veils. Such is the hiſtory, as I had it from the Lady of the houſe where I ſtood to ſee her paſs; with many other circumſtances; all which ſhe firmly believes, and ten thouſand beſides.

We ſhall go to Venice in about ſix weeks, or ſooner. A number of German troops are upon their march into this State, in caſe the King of Naples thinks proper to attack it. It is certain he has aſked the Pope's leave for his troops to paſs through his country. The Tuſcans in general are much diſcontented, and fooliſh enough to wiſh for a Spaniſh government, or any rather than this. * * *

Letter XLI.

MR. GRAY TO MR. WEST.

Florence, April 21, 1741.

I KNOW not what degree of ſatisfaction it will give you to be told that we ſhall ſet out from hence the 24th of this month, and not ſtop above a fortnight at any place in our way. This I feel, that you are the principal pleaſure I have to hope for in my own country. Try at leaſt to make me imagine myſelf not indifferent to you; for I muſt own I have the vanity of deſiring to be eſteemed by ſomebody, and would chooſe that ſomebody ſhould be one whom I eſteem as much as I do you. As I am recommending myſelf to your love, methinks I ought to ſend you my picture (for I am no more what I was, ſome circumſtances excepted, which I hope I need not particularize to you); you muſt add then, to your former idea, two years of age, a reaſonable quantity of dullneſs, a great deal of ſilence, and ſomething that rather reſembles, than is, thinking; a confuſed notion of many ſtrange and fine things that have ſwum before my eyes for ſome time, a want of love for general ſociety, indeed an inability to it. On the good ſide you may add a ſenſibility for what others feel, and indulgence for their faults and weakneſſes, a love of truth, and deteſtation of every thing elſe. Then you are to deduct a little impertinence, a little laughter, a great deal of pride, and ſome ſpirits. Theſe are all the alterations I know of, you perhaps may find more. Think not that I have been obliged for this reformation of manners to reaſon or reflection, but to a ſeverer ſchool-miſtreſs, Experience. One has little merit in learning her leſſons, for one cannot well help it; but they are more uſeful than others, and imprint themſelves in the very heart. I find I have been haranguing in the ſtyle of the Son of Sirach, ſo ſhall finiſh here, and tell you that our route is ſettled as follows: Firſt to Bologna for a few days, to hear the Viſcontina ſing; next to Reggio, where is a Fair. Now, you muſt know, a Fair here is not a place where one eats gingerbread or rides upon hobby-horſes; here are no muſical clocks, nor tall Leiceſterſhire women; one has nothing but maſquing, gaming, and ſinging. If you love operas, there will be the moſt ſplendid in Italy, four tip-top voices, a new theatre, the Duke and Ducheſs in all their pomps and vanities. Does not this ſound magnificent? Yet is the city of Reggio but one ſtep above Old Brentford. Well; next to Venice by the 11th of May, there to ſee the old Doge wed the Adriatic Whore. Then to Verona, ſo to Milan, ſo to Marſeilles, ſo to Lyons, ſo to Paris, ſo to Weſt, &c. in ſæcula ſæculorum. Amen.

Eleven months, at different times, have I paſſed at Florence; and yet (God help me) know not either people or language. Yet the place and the charming proſpects demand a poetical farewell, and here it is.

* * Oh Fæſulæ amœna
Frigoribus juga, nec nimiùm ſpirantibus auris!
Alma quibus Tuſci Pallas decus Apennini

Esse dedit, glaucâque suâ canescere sylvâ!
Non ego vos posthàc Arni de valle videbo
Porticibus circum, et candenti cincta coronâ
Villarum longè nitido consurgere dorso,
Antiquamve Ædem, et veteres præferre Cupressus
Mirabor, tectisque super pendentia tecta.

I will send you, too, a pretty little Sonnet of a Sig^r Abbate Buondelmonte, with my imitation of it.

Spesso Amor sotto la forma
D'amistà ride, e s'asconde:
Poi si mischia, e si confonde
Con lo sdegno, e col rancor.
In Pietade ei si trasforma;
Par trastullo, e par dispetto;
Mà nel suo diverso aspetto
Sempr' egli, è l' istesso Amor.

Lusit amicitiæ interdum velatus amictu,
Et bene compositâ veste fefellit Amor.

Mox iræ aſſumpſit cultus, faciemque minantem,
   Inque odium verſus, verſus et in lacrymas:
Ludentem fuge, nec lacrymanti, aut crede furenti;
   Idem eſt diſſimili ſemper in ore Deus.

Here comes a letter from you.—I muſt defer giving my opinion of Pauſanias till I can ſee the whole, and only have ſaid what I did in obedience to your commands. I have ſpoken with ſuch freedom on this head, that it ſeems but juſt you ſhould have your revenge; and therefore I ſend you the beginning not of an Epic Poem, but of a Metaphyſic one. Poems and Metaphyſics (ſay you, with your ſpectacles on) are inconſiſtent things. A metaphyſical poem is a contradiction in terms. It is true, but I will go on. It is Latin too to increaſe the abſurdity. It will, I ſuppoſe, put you in mind of the man who wrote a treatiſe of Canon Law in Hexameters. Pray help me to the deſcription of a mixt mode, and a little Epiſode about Space.

Letter XLII.

MR. GRAY TO MR. WEST.

I TRUST to the country, and that eaſy indolence you ſay you enjoy there, to reſtore you your health and ſpirits; and doubt not but, when the ſun grows warm enough to tempt you from your fireſide, you will (like all other things) be the better for his influence. He is my old friend, and an excellent nurſe, I aſſure you. Had it not been for him, life had often been to me intolerable. Pray do not imagine that Tacitus, of all authors in the world, can be tedious. An annaliſt, you know, is by no means maſter of his ſubject; and I think one may venture to ſay, that if thoſe Pannonian affairs are tedious in his hands, in another's they would have been inſupportable. However, fear not, they will ſoon be over, and he will make ample amends. A man, who could join the *brilliant* of wit and concise sententiousness peculiar to that age, with the truth and gravity of better times, and the deep reflection and good sense of the best moderns, cannot choose but have something to strike you. Yet what I admire in him above all this, is his detestation of tyranny, and the high spirit of liberty that every now and then breaks out, as it were, whether he would or no. I remember a sentence in his Agricola that (concise as it is) I always admired for saying much in a little compass. He speaks of Domitian, who upon seeing the last will of that General, where he had made him Coheir with his Wife and Daughter, "Satis constabat lætatum eum, velut honore, judicioque: tam cæca & corrupta mens assiduis adulationibus erat, ut nesciret a bono patre non scribi hæredem, nisi malum principem."

As to the Dunciad, it is greatly admired: the Genii of Operas and Schools, with their attendants, the pleas of the Virtuosos and Florists, and the yawn of dulness in the end, are as fine as any thing he has written. The Metaphysicians' part is to me the worst; and here and there a few ill-expressed lines, and some hardly intelligible.

I take the liberty of ſending you a long ſpeech of Agrippina; much too long, but I could be glad you would retrench it. Aceronia, you may remember, had been giving quiet counſels. I fancy, if it ever be finiſhed, it will be in the nature of Nat. Lee's Bedlam Tragedy, which had twenty-five acts and ſome odd ſcenes.

ACT I. SCENE I.

AGRIPPINA. ACERONIA.

AGRIPPINA.

'TIS well, begone! your errand is perform'd,
[*Speaks as to* ANICETUS *entering*.
The meſſage needs no comment. Tell your maſter,
His mother ſhall obey him. Say you ſaw her
Yielding due reverence to his high command:
Alone, unguarded and without a lictor,
As fits the daughter of Germanicus.
Say, ſhe retired to Antium; there to tend

Her houſeſhold cares, a woman's beſt employment.
What if you add, how ſhe turn'd pale and trembled:
You think, you ſpied a tear ſtand in her eye,
And would have dropp'd, but that her pride reſtrain'd it?
(Go! you can paint it well) 'twill profit you,
And pleaſe the ſtripling. Yet 'twould daſh his joy
To hear the ſpirit of Britannicus
Yet walks on earth: at leaſt there are who know
Without a ſpell to raiſe, and bid it fire
A thouſand haughty hearts, unuſed to ſhake
When a boy frowns, nor to be lured with ſmiles
To taſte of hollow kindneſs, or partake
His hoſpitable board: they are aware
Of th' unpledged bowl, they love not aconite.

ACERONIA.

He's gone: and much I hope theſe walls alone
And the mute air are privy to your paſſion.
Forgive your ſervant's fears, who ſees the danger
Which fierce reſentment cannot fail to raiſe
In haughty youth, and irritated power.

AGRIPPINA.

And doſt thou talk to me, to me of danger,
Of haughty youth and irritated power,
To her that gave it being, her that arm'd
This painted Jove, and taught his novice hand
To aim the forked bolt; while he ſtood trembling,
Scared at the ſound, and dazzled with its brightneſs?
'Tis like thou haſt forgot, when yet a ſtranger
To adoration, to the grateful ſteam
Of flatt'ry's incenſe, and obſequious vows
From voluntary realms, a puny boy,
Deck'd with no other luſtre, than the blood
Of Agrippina's race, he lived unknown
To fame or fortune; haply eyed at diſtance
Some edileſhip, ambitious of the power
To judge of weights and meaſures; ſcarcely dared
On expectation's ſtrongeſt wing to ſoar
High as the conſulate, that empty ſhade
Of long-forgotten liberty: when I
Oped his young eye to bear the blaze of greatneſs;

Show'd him where empire tower'd, and bade him ſtrike
The noble quarry. Gods! then was the time
To ſhrink from danger; fear might then have worn
The maſk of prudence; but a heart like mine,
A heart that glows with the pure Julian fire,
If bright ambition from her craggy ſeat
Diſplay the radiant prize, will mount undaunted,
Gain the rough heights, and graſp the dangerous honour.

ACERONIA.

Through various life I have purſued your ſteps,
Have ſeen your ſoul, and wonder'd at its daring:
Hence riſe my fears. Nor am I yet to learn
How vaſt the debt of gratitude which Nero
To ſuch a mother owes; the world, you gave him,
Suffices not to pay the obligation.
I well remember too (for I was preſent)
When in a ſecret and dead hour of night,
Due ſacrifice perform'd with barb'rous rites
Of mutter'd charms, and ſolemn invocation,
You made the Magi call the dreadful powers,

That read futurity, to know the fate
Impending o'er your ſon: their anſwer was,
If the ſon reign, the mother periſhes.
Periſh (you cried) the mother! reign the ſon!
He reigns, the reſt is heav'n's; who oft has bade,
Ev'n when its will ſeem'd wrote in lines of blood,
Th' unthought event diſcloſe a whiter meaning.
Think too how oft in weak and ſickly minds
The ſweets of kindneſs laviſhly indulged
Rankle to gall; and benefits too great
To be repaid, ſit heavy on the ſoul
As unrequited wrongs. The willing homage
Of proſtrate Rome, the ſenate's joint applauſe,
The riches of the earth, the train of pleaſures
That wait on youth, and arbitrary ſway:
Theſe were your gift, and with them you beſtow'd
The very power he has to be ungrateful.

AGRIPPINA.

[6] Thus ever grave and undiſturb'd reflection
Pours its cool dictates in the madding ear

Of rage, and thinks to quench the fire it feels not.
Say'ſt thou I muſt be cautious, muſt be ſilent,
And tremble at the phantom I have raiſed?
Carry to him thy timid counſels. He
Perchance may heed 'em: tell him too, that one
Who had ſuch liberal power to give, may ſtill
With equal power reſume that gift, and raiſe
A tempeſt that ſhall ſhake her own creation
To its original atoms—tell me! ſay
This mighty emperor, this dreaded hero,
Has he beheld the glittering front of war?
Knows his ſoft ear the trumpet's thrilling voice,
And outcry of the battle? Have his limbs
Sweat under iron harneſs? Is he not
The ſilken ſon of dalliance, nurſed in eaſe
And pleaſure's flow'ry lap?—Rubellius lives,
And Sylla has his friends, though ſchool'd by fear
To bow the ſupple knee, and court the times
With ſhows of fair obeiſance; and a call
Like mine, might ſerve belike to wake pretenſions

Drowſier than theirs, who boaſt the genuine blood
Of our imperial houſe.

ACERONIA.

Did I not wiſh to check this dangerous paſſion,
I might remind my miſtreſs that her nod
Can rouſe eight hardy legions, wont to ſtem
With ſtubborn nerves the tide, and face the rigour
Of bleak Germania's ſnows. Four, not leſs brave,
That in Armenia quell the Parthian force
Under the warlike Corbulo, by you
Mark'd for their leader: theſe, by ties confirm'd,
Of old reſpect and gratitude, are yours.
Surely the Maſians too, and thoſe of Egypt,
Have not forgot your ſire: the eye of Rome,
And the Prætorian camp, have long revered
With cuſtom'd awe, the daughter, ſiſter, wife,
And mother of their Cæſars.

AGRIPPINA.

Ha! by Juno,
It bears a noble ſemblance. On this baſe

My great revenge ſhall riſe; or ſay we ſound
The trump of liberty; there will not want,
Even in the ſervile ſenate, ears to own
Her ſpirit-ſtirring voice; Soranus there,
And Caſſius; Vetus too, and Thraſea,
Minds of the antique caſt, rough, ſtubborn ſouls,
That ſtruggle with the yoke. How ſhall the ſpark
Unquenchable, that glows within their breaſts,
Blaze into freedom, when the idle herd
(Slaves from the womb, created but to ſtare,
And bellow in the Circus) yet will ſtart,
And ſhake 'em at the name of liberty,
Stung by a ſenſeleſs word, a vain tradition,
As there were magic in it? Wrinkled beldams
Teach it their grandchildren, as ſomewhat rare
That anciently appear'd, but when, extends
Beyond their chronicle—oh! 'tis a cauſe
To arm the hand of childhood, and rebrace
The ſlacken'd ſinews of time-wearied age.
Yes, we may meet, ungrateful boy, we may!

Again the buried Genius of old Rome
Shall from the duſt uprear his reverend head,
Rouſed by the ſhout of millions: there before
His high tribunal thou and I appear.
Let majeſty ſit on thy awful brow,
And lighten from thy eye: around thee call
The gilded ſwarm that wantons in the ſunſhine
Of thy full favour; Seneca be there
In gorgeous phraſe of labour'd eloquence
To dreſs thy plea, and Burrhus ſtrengthen it
With his plain ſoldier's oath, and honeſt ſeeming.
Againſt thee, liberty and Agrippina:
The world, the prize; and fair befall the victors.
But ſoft! why do I waſte the fruitleſs hours
In threats unexecuted? Haſte thee, fly
Theſe hated walls that ſeem to mock my ſhame,
And caſt me forth in duty to their lord.

ACERONIA.

'Tis time to go, the ſun is high advanced,
And, ere mid-day, Nero will come to Baiæ.

AGRIPPINA.

My thought aches at him; not the bafilifk
More deadly to the fight, than is to me
The cool injurious eye of frozen kindnefs.
I will not meet its poifon. Let him feel
Before he fees me.

ACERONIA.

Why then ftays my fovereign,
Where he fo foon may—

AGRIPPINA.

Yes, I will be gone,
But not to Antium—all fhall be confefs'd,
Whate'er the frivolous tongue of giddy fame
Has fpread among the crowd; things, that but whifper'd
Have arch'd the hearer's brow, and riveted
His eyes in fearful extafy: no matter
What; fo't be ftrange and dreadful.—Sorceries,
Affaffinations, poifonings—the deeper
My guilt, the blacker his ingratitude.

And you, ye manes of ambition's victims,

Enſhrined Claudius, with the pitied ghoſts
Of the Syllani, doom'd to early death,
(Ye unavailing horrors, fruitleſs crimes!)
If from the realms of night my voice ye hear,
In lieu of penitence, and vain remorſe,
Accept my vengeance. Though by me ye bled,
He was the cauſe. My love, my fears for him,
Dried the ſoft ſprings of pity in my heart,
And froze them up with deadly cruelty.
Yet if your injured ſhades demand my fate,
If murder cries for murder, blood for blood,
Let me not fall alone; but cruſh his pride,
And ſink the traitor in his mother's ruin.

[*Exeunt.*

SCENE II. OTHO, POPPÆA.

OTHO.

THUS far we're ſafe. Thanks to the roſy queen
Of amorous thefts: and had her wanton ſon

Lent us his wings, we could not have beguiled
With more eluſive ſpeed the dazzled ſight
Of wakeful jealouſy. Be gay ſecurely;
Diſpel, my fair, with ſmiles, the tim'rous cloud
That hangs on thy clear brow. So Helen look'd,
So her white neck reclined, ſo was ſhe borne
By the young Trojan to his gilded bark
With fond reluctance, yielding modeſty,
And oft reverted eye, as if ſhe knew not
Whether ſhe fear'd, or wiſh'd to be purſued.

* * * * *

Letter XLIII.

MR. GRAY TO MR. WEST.

London, April, Thurſday.

YOU are the firſt who ever made a Muſe of a Cough; to me it ſeems a much more eaſy taſk to verſify in one's ſleep, (that indeed you were of old famous for,) than for want of it. Not the wakeful nightingale (when ſhe had a cough) ever ſung ſo ſweetly. I give you thanks for your warble, and wiſh you could ſing yourſelf to reſt. Theſe wicked remains of your illneſs will ſure give way to warm weather and gentle exerciſe; which I hope you will not omit as the ſeaſon advances. Whatever low ſpirits and indolence, the effect of them, may adviſe to the contrary, I pray you add five ſteps to your walk daily for my ſake; by the help of which, in a month's time, I propoſe to ſet you on horſeback.

I talked of the Dunciad as concluding you had ſeen it;

if you have not, do you choofe I fhould get and fend it you? I have myfelf, upon your recommendation, been reading Jofeph Andrews. The incidents are ill laid and without invention; but the characters have a great deal of nature, which always pleafes even in her loweft fhapes. Parfon Adams is perfectly well; fo is Mrs. Slipflop, and the ftory of Wilfon; and throughout he fhows himfelf well read in Stage-Coaches, Country Squires, Inns, and Inns of Court. His reflections upon high people and low people, and miffes and mafters, are very good. However the exaltednefs of fome minds (or rather as I fhrewdly fufpect their infipidity and want of feeling or obfervation) may make them infenfible to thefe light things, (I mean fuch as characterize and paint nature,) yet furely they are as weighty and much more ufeful than your grave difcourfes upon the mind, the paffions, and what not. Now as the paradifaical pleafures of the Mahometans confift in playing upon the flute and lying with Houris, be mine to read eternal new romances of Marivaux and Crebillon.

You are very good in giving yourfelf the trouble to read

and find fault with my long harangues. Your freedom (as you call it) has ſo little need of apologies, that I ſhould ſcarce excuſe your treating me any otherwiſe; which, whatever compliment it might be to my vanity, would be making a very ill one to my underſtanding. As to matter of ſtyle, I have this to ſay: The language of the age is never the language of poetry; except among the French, whoſe verſe, where the thought or image does not ſupport it, differs in nothing from proſe. Our poetry, on the contrary, has a language peculiar to itſelf; to which almoſt every one, that has written, has added ſomething by enriching it with foreign idioms and derivatives: Nay ſometimes words of their own compoſition or invention. Shakeſpear and Milton have been great creators this way; and no one more licentious than Pope or Dryden, who perpetually borrow expreſſions from the former. Let me give you ſome inſtances from Dryden, whom every body reckons a great maſter of our poetical tongue.——Full of *muſeful mopeings*—unlike the *trim* of love—a pleaſant *beverage*—a *roundelay* of love—ſtood ſilent in his *mood*—with knots and *knares* deformed—his *ireful mood*—in proud *array*—his *boon* was granted—and *disarray* and shameful rout—*wayward* but wise—*furbished* for the field—the *foiled dodderd* oaks—*disherited*—*smouldering* flames—*retchless* of laws—*crones* old and ugly—the *beldam* at his side—the *grandam-hag*—*villanize* his Father's fame.——But they are infinite: And our language not being a settled thing (like the French) has an undoubted right to words of an hundred years old, provided antiquity have not rendered them unintelligible. In truth, Shakespear's language is one of his principal beauties; and he has no less advantage over your Addisons and Rowes in this, than in those other great excellences you mention. Every word in him is a picture. Pray put me the following lines into the tongue of our modern Dramatics:

But I, that am not shaped for sportive tricks,
Nor made to court an amorous looking-glass:
I, that am rudely stampt, and want love's majesty
To strut before a wanton ambling nymph:
I, that am curtail'd of this fair proportion,
Cheated of feature by dissembling nature,

Deform'd, unfiniſh'd, ſent before my time
Into this breathing world, ſcarce half made up—

And what follows. To me they appear untranſlatable; and if this be the caſe, our language is greatly degenerated. However, the affectation of imitating Shakeſpear may doubtleſs be carried too far; and is no ſort of excuſe for ſentiments ill-ſuited, or ſpeeches ill-timed, which I believe is a little the caſe with me. I gueſs the moſt faulty expreſſions may be theſe—*ſilken* ſon of *dalliance*—*drowſier* pretenſions—wrinkled *beldams*—*arched* the hearer's brow and *riveted* his eyes in *fearful extaſie*. Theſe are eaſily altered or omitted: and indeed if the thoughts be wrong or ſuperfluous, there is nothing eaſier than to leave out the whole. The firſt ten or twelve lines are, I believe, the beſt; and as for the reſt, I was betrayed into a good deal of it by Tacitus; only what he has ſaid in five words, I imagine I have ſaid in fifty lines. Such is the misfortune of imitating the inimitable. Now, if you are of my opinion, una litura may do the buſineſs better than a dozen; and you need not fear unravelling my web. I am a ſort of ſpider; and have little elſe to do but ſpin it over again, or creep to ſome other place and ſpin there. Alas! for one who has nothing to do but amuſe himſelf, I believe my amuſements are as little amuſing as moſt folks'. But no matter; it makes the hours paſs; and is better than ἐν ἀμαθίᾳ καὶ ἀμουσίᾳ καταβιῶναι. Adieu.

Letter XLIV.

MR. GRAY TO MR. WEST.

London, April, 1742.

I SHOULD not have failed to anſwer your letter immediately, but I went out of town for a little while, which hindered me. Its length (beſides the pleaſure naturally accompanying a long letter from you) affords me a new one, when I think it is a ſymptom of the recovery of your health, and flatter myſelf that your bodily ſtrength returns in proportion. Pray do not forget to mention the progreſs you make continually. As to Agrippina, I begin to be of your opinion; and find myſelf (as women are of their children) leſs enamoured of my productions the older they grow. She is laid up to ſleep till next ſummer; ſo bid her good night. I think you have tranſlated Tacitus very juſtly, that is, freely; and accommodated his thoughts to the turn and genius of our language; which, though I commend your judgment, is no commendation of the Engliſh tongue, which is too diffuſe, and daily grows more and more enervate. One ſhall never be more ſenſible of this, than in turning an Author like Tacitus. I have been trying it in ſome parts of Thucydides (who has a little

---

QUOD mihi ſi tantum, Mæcenas, fata dediſſent,
Ut poſſem heroas ducere in arma manus:
Non ego Titanas canerem, non Oſſan Olympo
Impoſitum, ut cœlo Pelion eſſet iter:
Non veteres Thebas, nec Pergama nomen Homeri,
Xerxis et imperio bina coiſſe vada:
Regnave prima Remi, aut animos Carthaginis altæ,
Cimbrorumque minas, et benefacta Marî.
Bellaque reſque tui memorarem Cæſaris; et tu
Cæſare ſub magno cura ſecunda fores.

reſemblance of him in his conciſeneſs) and endeavoured to do it cloſely, but found it produced mere nonſenſe. If you have any inclination to ſee what figure Tacitus makes in Italian, I have a Tuſcan tranſlation of Davanzati, much eſteemed in Italy; and will ſend you the ſame ſpeech you ſent me; that is, if you care for it. In the mean time accept of Propertius.

YET would the tyrant Love permit me raiſe
My feeble voice, to ſound the victor's praiſe,
To paint the hero's toil, the ranks of war,
The laurell'd triumph, and the ſculptured car;
No giant race, no tumult of the ſkies,
No mountain-ſtructures in my verſe ſhould riſe,
Nor tale of Thebes, nor Ilium there ſhould be,
Nor how the Perſian trod the indignant ſea;
Not Marius' Cimbrian wreaths would I relate,
Nor lofty Carthage ſtruggling with her fate.
Here ſhould Auguſtus great in arms appear,
And thou, Mæcenas, be my ſecond care;

Nam quoties Mutinam, aut civilia bufta Philippos,
  Aut canerem Siculæ claſſica bella fugæ:
Everſoſque focos antiquæ gentis Etruſcæ,
  Et Ptolemææe litora capta Phari:
Aut canerem Ægyptum, et Nilum, cum tractus in urbem
  Septem captivis debilis ibat aquis:
Aut regum auratis circumdata colla catenis,
  Actiaque in ſacrâ currere roſtra viâ:
Te mea Muſa illis ſemper contexeret armis,
  Et ſumtâ, et poſitâ pace fidele caput.
Theſeus infernis, ſuperis teſtatur Achilles,
  Hic Ixioniden, ille Menœtiaden.
Sed neque Phlegræos Jovis, Enceladique tumultus
  Intonet anguſto pectore Callimachus:
Nec mea conveniunt duro præcordia verſu
  Cæſaris in Phrygios condere nomen avos.
Navita de ventis, de tauris narrat arator,
  Enumerat miles vulnera, paſtor oves.
Nos contrà anguſto verſamus prœlia lecto.
  Quâ pote quiſque, in eâ conterat arte diem.

Here Mutina from flames and famine free,
And there the enſanguined wave of Sicily,
And ſcepter'd Alexandria's captive ſhore,
And ſad Philippi, red with Roman gore:
Then, while the vaulted ſkies loud Ios rend,
In golden chains ſhould loaded monarchs bend,
And hoary Nile with penſive aſpect ſeem
To mourn the glories of his ſevenfold ſtream,
While prows, that late in fierce encounter met,
Move through the ſacred way and vainly threat,
Thee too the Muſe ſhould conſecrate to fame,
And with her garlands weave thy ever-faithful name.
  But nor Callimachus' enervate ſtrain
May tell of Jove, and Phlegra's blaſted plain;
Nor I with unaccuſtom'd vigour trace
Back to its ſource divine the Julian race.
Sailors to tell of winds and ſeas delight,
The ſhepherd of his flocks, the ſoldier of the fight.
A milder warfare I in verſe diſplay;
Each in his proper art ſhould waſte the day:

Laus in amore mori: laus altera, ſi datur uno
    Poſſe frui, fruar O ſolus amore meo.
His ſaltem ut tenear jam finibus; aut, mihi ſi quis
    Venerit alter amor, acriùs ut moriar.
Si memini, ſolet illa leves culpare puellas,
    Et totam ex Helenâ non probat Iliada.
Seu mihi ſint tangenda novercæ pocula Phædræ,
    Pocula privigno non nocitura ſuo:
Seu mihi Circæo pereundum gramine, ſive
    Colchis Iolciacis urat ahena focis;
Una meos quoniam prædata eſt fœmina ſenſus,
    Ex hac ducentur funera noſtra domo.
Omnes humanos ſanat medicina dolores,
    Solus amor morbi non amat artificem.
Tarda Philoctetæ ſanavit crura Machaon,
    Phœnicis Chiron lumina Phillyrides.

Nor thou my gentle calling diſapprove,
To die is glorious in the bed of Love.
  Happy the youth, and not unknown to fame,
Whoſe heart has never felt a ſecond flame.
Oh, might that envied happineſs be mine!
To Cynthia all my wiſhes I confine;
Or if, alas! it be my fate to try
Another love, the quicker let me die:
But ſhe, the miſtreſs of my faithful breaſt,
Has oft the charms of conſtancy confeſt,
Condemns her fickle ſex's fond miſtake,
And hates the tale of Troy for Helen's ſake.
Me from myſelf the ſoft enchantreſs ſtole;
Ah! let her ever my deſires control,
Or if I fall the victim of her ſcorn,
From her loved door may my pale corſe be borne.
The power of herbs can other harms remove,
And find a cure for every ill, but love.
The Lemnian's hurt Machaon could repair,
Heal the ſlow chief, and ſend again to war;

Et deus exſtinctum Creſſis Epidaurius herbis
Reſtituit patriis Androgeona focis.
Myſus et Æmoniâ juvenis quâ cuſpide vulnus
Senſerat, hac ipſâ cuſpide ſenſit opem.
Hoc ſi quis vitium poterit mihi demere, ſolus
Tantaleæ poterit tradere poma manu.
Dolia virgineis idem ille repleverit urnis,
Ne tenera aſſiduâ colla graventur aquâ.
Idem Caucaſiâ ſolvet de rupe Promethei
Brachia, et a medio pectore pellet avem.
Non hîc herba valet: non hîc nocturna Cytæis:
Non Perimedeâ gramina cocta manu.
Quippe ubi nec cauſas, nec apertos cernimus ictus,
Unde tamen veniant tot mala, cæca via eſt.
Non eget hic medicis, non lectis mollibus æger:
Huic nullum cœli tempus, et aura nocet.
Ambulat, et ſubitò mirantur funus amici.
Sic eſt incautum quicquid habetur amor.
Quandocunque igitur vitam mea fata repoſcent,
Et breve in exiguo marmore nomen ero:

To Chiron Phœnix owed his long-loſt ſight,
And Phœbus' ſon recall'd Androgeon to the light.
Here arts are vain, e'en magic here muſt fail,
The powerful mixture and the midnight ſpell;
The hand that can my captive heart releaſe,
And to this boſom give its wonted peace,
May the long thirſt of Tantalus allay,
Or drive the infernal vulture from his prey.
For ills unſeen what remedy is found?
Or who can probe the undiſcover'd wound?
The bed avails not, nor the leech's care,
Nor changing ſkies can hurt, nor ſultry air.
'Tis hard th' eluſive ſymptoms to explore:
To-day the lover walks, to-morrow is no more;
A train of mourning friends attend his pall,
And wonder at the ſudden funeral.
  When then the fates that breath they gave ſhall claim,
And the ſhort marble but preſerve a name,
A little verſe my all that ſhall remain;
Thy paſſing courſer's ſlacken'd ſpeed reſtrain;

Mæcenas noſtræ ſpes invidioſa juventæ,
Et vitæ, et morti gloria juſta meæ ;
Si te forte meo ducet via proxima buſto,
Eſſeda cælatis ſiſte Britanna jugis,
Taliaque inlacrymans mutæ jace verba favillæ :
Huic miſero fatum dura puella fuit.

(Thou envied honour of thy poet's days,
Of all our youth the ambition and the praiſe !)
Then to my quiet urn awhile draw near,
And ſay, while o'er that place you drop the tear,
Love and the fair were of his youth the pride ;
He lived, while ſhe was kind ; and when ſhe frown'd, he
 died.

Letter XLV.

MR. GRAY TO MR. WEST.

London, May 27, 1742.

MINE, you are to know, is a white Melancholy, or rather Leucocholy for the moſt part; which, though it ſeldom laughs or dances, nor ever amounts to what one calls Joy or Pleaſure, yet is a good eaſy ſort of a ſtate, and ça ne laiſſe que de s'amuſer. The only fault of it is inſipidity; which is apt now and then to give a ſort of Ennui, which makes one form certain little wiſhes that ſignify nothing. But there is another ſort, black indeed, which I have now and then felt, that has ſomewhat in it like Tertullian's rule of faith, Credo quia impoſſibile eſt; for it believes, nay, is ſure of every thing that is unlikely, ſo it be but frightful; and on the other hand excludes and ſhuts its eyes to the moſt poſſible hopes, and every thing that is pleaſurable;

from this the Lord deliver us! for none but he and ſunſhiny weather can do it. In hopes of enjoying this kind of weather, I am going into the country for a few weeks, but ſhall be never the nearer any ſociety; ſo, if you have any charity, you will continue to write. My life is like Harry the Fourth's ſupper of Hens,[7] "Poulets à la broche, Poulets en Ragoût, Poulets en Hâchis, Poulets en Fricaſées." Reading here, Reading there; nothing but books with different ſauces. Do not let me loſe my deſert then; for though that be Reading too, yet it has a very different flavour. The May ſeems to be come ſince your invitation; and I propoſe to baſk in her beams and dreſs me in her roſes.

Et Caput in vernâ ſemper habere rosâ.[8]

I ſhall ſee Mr. * * and his Wife, nay, and his Child too, for he has got a Boy. Is it not odd to conſider one's Cotemporaries in the grave light of Huſband and Father? There is my Lords * * and * * *, they are Stateſmen: Do not you remember them dirty boys playing at cricket? As for me, I am never a bit the older, nor the bigger, nor the wiſer than I was then : No, not for having been beyond ſea. Pray how are you?

I ſend you an inſcription for a wood joining to a park of mine; (it is on the confines of Mount Cithœron, on the left hand as you go to Thebes,) you know I am no friend to hunters, and hate to be diſturbed by their noiſe.

Ἀζόμενος πολύθηρον ἑκηβόλου ἄλσος ἀνάσσας,
    Τᾶς δεινᾶς τεμένη λεῖπε, κυναγὲ, θεᾶς,
Μοῦνοι ἄρ᾽ ἔνθα κύνων ζαθέων κλαγγεῦσιν ὕλαγμοι,
    Ἀνταχεῖς Νυμφᾶν ἀγροτερᾶν κελάδῳ.

Here follows alſo the beginning of an Heroic Epiſtle; but you muſt give me leave to tell my own ſtory firſt, becauſe Hiſtorians. differ. Maſſiniſſa was the ſon of Gala King of the Maſſyli; and, when very young, at the head of his father's army, gave a moſt ſignal overthrow to Syphax, King of the Maſæſylians, then an ally of the Romans. Soon after Aſdrubal, ſon of Giſgo the Carthaginian General, gave the beautiful Sophoniſba, his daughter, in marriage to the young prince. But this marriage was not consummated on account of Massinissa's being obliged to hasten into Spain, there to command his father's troops, who were auxiliaries of the Carthaginians. Their affairs at this time began to be in a bad condition; and they thought it might be greatly for their interest, if they could bring over Syphax to themselves. This in time they actually effected; and to strengthen their new alliance, commanded Asdrubal to give his daughter to Syphax. (It is probable their ingratitude to Massinissa arose from the great change of affairs, which had happened among the Massylians during his absence; for his father and uncle were dead, and a distant relation of the royal family had usurped the throne.) Sophonisba was accordingly married to Syphax; and Massinissa, enraged at the affront, became a friend to the Romans. They drove the Carthaginians before them out of Spain, and carried the war into Africa, defeated Syphax, and took him prisoner; upon which Cirtha (his capital) opened her gates to Lælius and Massinissa. The rest of the affair, the marriage, and the sending of poison, every body knows. This is partly taken from Livy, and partly from Appian.

EGREGIUM accipio promissi Munus amoris,
　Inque manu mortem, jam fruitura, fero:
Atque utinam citius mandasses, luce vel unâ;
　Transieram Stygios non inhonesta lacus.
Victoris nec passa toros, nova nupta, mariti,
　Nec fueram fastus, Roma superba, tuos.
Scilicet hæc partem tibi, Masinissa, triumphi
　Detractam, hæc pompæ jura minora suæ
Imputat, atque uxor quòd non tua pressa catenis,
　Objecta et sævæ plausibus orbis eo:
Quin tu pro tantis cepisti præmia factis,
　Magnum Romanæ pignus amicitiæ!
Scipiadæ excuses, oro, si, tardius utar
　Munere. Non nimiùm vivere, crede, velim.
Parva mora est, breve sed tempus mea fama requirit:
　Detinet hæc animam cura suprema meam.
Quæ patriæ prodesse meæ Regina ferebar,

Inter Elifæas gloria prima nurus,
Ne videar flammæ nimis indulfiffe fecundæ,
Vel nimis hoftiles extimuiffe manus.
Fortunam atque annos liceat revocare priores,
Gaudiaque heu! quantis noftra repenfa, malis!
Primitiafne tuas meminifti atque arma Syphacis
Fufa, et per Tyrias ducta trophæa vias?
(Laudis at antiquæ forfan meminiffe pigebit,
Quodque decus quondam caufa ruboris erit.)
Tempus ego certe memini, felicia Pœnis
Quo te non puduit folvere vota deis;
Mœniaque intrantem vidi: longo agmine duxit
Turba falutantum, purpureique patres.
Fœminea ante omnes longe admiratur euntem
Hæret et afpectu tota caterva tuo.
Jam flexi, regale decus, per colla capilli,
Jam decet ardenti fufcus in ore color!
Commendat frontis generofa modeftia formam,
Seque cupit laudi furripuiffe fuæ.
Prima genas tenui fignat vix flore juventas,

Et dextræ ſoli credimus eſſe virum.
Dum faciles gradiens oculos per ſingula jactas,
(Seu rexit caſus lumina, ſive Venus)
In me (vel certè viſum eſt) converſa morari
Senſi; virgineus perculit ora pudor.
Neſcio quid vultum molle ſpirare tuendo,
Credideramque tuos lentius ire pedes.
Quærebam, juxta æqualis ſi dignior eſſet,
Quæ poterat viſus detinuiſſe tuos:
Nulla fuit circum æqualis quæ dignior eſſet,
Aſſeruitque decus conſcia forma ſuum.
Pompæ finis erat. Totâ vix nocte quievi,
Sin premat invitæ lumina victa ſopor,
Somnus habet pompas, eademque recurſat imago;
Atque iterum heſterno munere victor ades.

* * * * *

NOTES TO THE LETTERS.

NOTES.

Page 215, note 1.

AT Burnham, in Buckinghamſhire.

P. 218, note 2.—At this time with his father at Houghton. Mr. Gray writes from the ſame place he did before, from his Uncle's houſe in Buckinghamſhire.—*Maſon.*

P. 219, note 3.—A lanthorn for eighteen candles, of copper-gilt, hung in the hall at Houghton. It became a favourite object of Tory ſatire at the time; ſee the *Craftſman.* This lanthorn was afterwards ſold to the Earl of Cheſterfield. See *Walpole's Works*, vol. ii. p. 263; and *Letters to H. Mann*, vol. ii. p. 368.

P. 221, note 4.—Of Poſidippus. *Vide Anthologia, H. Stephan.* p. 220. Mr. Gray, in his MS. notes to this edition of the Anthologia, inſerts this tranſlation, and adds "Deſcriptio pulcherrima & quæ tenuem illum græcorum ſpiritum mirificè ſapit;" and in concluſion, "Poſidippus inter principes Anthologiæ poetas emicat, Ptolemæi Philadelphi ſeculo vixit."—*Maſon.*

P. 224, note 5.—*Hom. Il.* Δ. v. 191.

P. 230, note 6.—Mr. Walpole was juſt named to that poſt, which he exchanged ſoon after for that of Uſher of the Exchequer.—*Maſon.*

P. 230, note 7.—*Ovidii Met.* II. v. 846-7.

P. 230, note 8.—Dr. Long, the Maſter of Pembroke Hall, at this time read lectures in experimental philoſophy.—*Maſon.*

P. 232, note 9.—Orator Henley.

P. 241, note 1.—The French opera has only three acts, but often a prologue on a different ſubject, which (as Mr. Walpole informs me, who ſaw it at the ſame time) was the caſe in this very repreſentation.—*Maſon.*

P. 247, note 2.—The Comte de Cambis was lately returned from his embaſſy in England.—*Maſon.*

P. 257, note 3.—See *Walpole's Memoirs*, pp. 414-18. From Pitt's Speech, comparing Fox and the Duke of Newcaſtle to the Rhône and Saône.

P. 261, note 4.—*Not pine trees*, but beech and firs.

P. 275, note 5.—See *Livii Hiſt.* lib. xxi. cap. xxxii.

P. 276, note 6.—See *Livii Hiſt.* lib. xxi. cap. xxxvii.

P. 279, note 7.—The famous Andrea Doria.

P. 285, note 8.—Now Sir Horace Mann, and Envoy Extraordinary at the ſame court.—*Maſon.*

P. 286, note 9.—See *Walpole's Letters to H. Mann*, vol. ii. p. 283, l. cxcviii.

P. 300, note 1.—Clement the Twelfth.

P. 329, note 2.—Sixtus V. built the dome of St. Peter's.—*Maſon.* St. Peter's was begun by Nicholas V. in 1450; the Cupola was completed in 1590; in 1612-14, the Church and Veſtibule were finiſhed: in 1667 the Colonnade. Up to 1694 it is computed that forty-ſeven millions of Scudi, upwards of ten million and a half ſterling, have been expended upon it.

P. 329, note 3.—He raiſed the obeliſk in the great area.

P. 344, note 4.—The reader will find this in Dodſley's Miſcellany, and alſo amongſt Mr. Walpole's Fugitive Pieces.—*Maſon.*

P. 344, note 5.—Gilbert Weſt, Eſq. This poem, "On the abuſe of Travelling," is alſo in Dodſley's Miſcellany.—*Maſon.*

P. 379, note 6.—In Gray's MS. Agrippina's was one continued ſpeech from this line to the end of the ſcene. Mr. Maſon informs us, that he has altered it to the ſtate in which it now ſtands.

P. 405, note 7.—Francis the Firſt's Supper of Hens, *v.* Boccaccio.—*Rogers.*

P. 405, note 8.—Propert. III. iii. 44.

FINIS.

CPSIA information can be obtained
at www.ICGtesting.com
Printed in the USA
LVHW110804120522
718525LV00003B/31

9 783375 001513